A Rich Decay

A Rich Decay

T. L. Butt

Terry Butt

First Printing, 2021

One

The wind was harsh today — especially for how cold it was out on the water. It was an August afternoon on the North Carolina coast. Rich Harris drove his patrol boat up the Intracoastal Waterway, near Everett Bay, just outside of Holly Ridge. As an officer of the North Carolina Wildlife Resource Commission, or NCWRC, his typical day consisted of cruising the waterways in search of boating and fishing violations, or any unsafe activities in his area. He would enforce boater safety and ensure that anyone who was fishing had the proper licenses, their boats were registered and current, people obeyed the laws, like not driving a boat while intoxicated — that sort of thing. It wasn't exactly a glamorous job, but at least he got to spend his days on the water, and the best part was he got to be a law enforcement officer, which had been a dream of his since he was a kid.

Today, as usual, Rich was on the lookout for trouble. Of course, he didn't actually want to find trouble. No law enforcement officer should really *want* to find trouble, but this was different. Rich would come to the point of noxiousness at the thought of finding someone doing something wrong. Not because of the potential harm they could cause themselves or others around them, but because if he sees wrongdoing, he would have to confront it. Confrontation was Rich's biggest fear.

Rich didn't always want to be a wildlife officer exactly; this was sort of his fall back career. Ever since he was a kid, he dreamed of being in law enforcement and even fantasized about maybe one day becoming a police detective. But there was one big problem — confrontation.

Growing up, Rich got into a few scuffles here and there with other kids over this or that. And as the years passed by and he lost more and more of those scuffles to bigger, stronger kids, or fell victim to the bullies that all schools inevitably have, Rich began developing a fear of confrontation. The constant humiliation of being picked on just built upon his fear until it became a part of who he was.

Rich eventually learned, after much research, watching videos on the Internet, and reading books about police officers, that there was far too much confrontation in a job like that. He became quite timid, avoiding conflict whenever possible, and this wasn't exactly the typical trait of a law enforcement officer. He couldn't handle the day to day stresses a typical police officer faced, and he quickly realized this wasn't the career for him.

One day though, during a ferry trip to Bear Island- a tiny island just outside of Swansboro, NC that tourists and locals frequent in the summer- he picked the brain of one of the wildlife officers working on the ferry. After learning the extremely vague details of the job, and more importantly, the fact that it's not nearly as dangerous as the day-to-day job of a police officer, he decided that this was a fantastic way to get into law enforcement. He didn't know that a wildlife officer also had many stressful duties, and that they had frequent altercations with citizens violating the law. Rich was blinded by nativity, and he decided to join the North Carolina Wildlife Resource Commission, and has worked there for a little under two years.

On this particular morning, the waters were a little rougher than usual due to the wind, so the boat ride was far more turbulent, but that didn't bother Rich. He was daydreaming again about nothing in particular, but his thoughts drifted, as they always did, to his eventual ascent to something more. He didn't know exactly what, but he knew it was some form of wealth and power.

Rich came from a lower-class family, but coming from nothing wasn't hard for him, he just didn't want to stay that way forever. There was a problem with one day becoming wealthy and powerful, and that was that he didn't have any talents or ideas on how to achieve success. This would be a significant roadblock, but it would never stop Rich from daydreaming. He would think about what he would do if he had ever won the lottery, or if he had ever inherited a bunch of money from a rich uncle he had never known, but the thoughts were just pipe dreams. Rich was working in a job that would not make him wealthy, but dreaming was fun anyway.

Up ahead there was a small skiff trolling around for fish. Its three passengers seemed to be having a good time on the water, but Rich had to stop them. Not that they had necessarily done anything wrong, but Rich had a quota to reach. He doesn't have a ticket quota, but a contact quota. Rich's captain recognized his difficulty with confrontation, so he forced Rich, by way of quota, to make a certain amount of contact each day. He would keep a log of each transaction, proving this contact. This was, of course, humiliating to Rich, but he would never say anything about it to anyone. The captain's train of thought in assigning the contact quota was that once the ice was broken between Rich and the citizen he contacted it should be smooth transactions, but that wasn't always the case.

This particular skiff was the 10th boat that Rich had come across, thus rendering it the next to be randomly inspected. It also helped that he had noticed that the boat's numbers, the registration numbers found on the side of the hull, were falling off. As Rich approached the small skiff, a couple of the men started poking fun at the driver and said, "You did it now, man. You're getting busted. The Po Po's coming to get you." They'd each laugh, completely minimizing Rich's authority as a law enforcement officer, but this sort of thing wasn't uncommon on the waters. No one really thought of Wildlife officers as actual law enforcement. People figured that the Coast Guard handled law enforcement on the water. This wasn't true though, the Wildlife Commission was very much a law enforcement organization, and not just on the water, but it was a common misconception, especially among drunken boaters.

Rich would check a boater's credentials, check the safety equipment on board and, nine times out of ten, find nothing.

"Good afternoon, gentlemen," Rich said, "my name is Officer Harris, and I'm performing random inspections to ensure compliance with North Carolina boating and fishing laws as well as general safety regulations. This will only take a couple of minutes. Which of you is the owner of this boat?" His well-rehearsed speech came out of his mouth with a profound lack of conviction, but he found that it helped get the ball rolling whenever he had to stop anyone, so he would keep saying it.

The shortest of the three spoke up, "It's my boat. Did we do somethin' wrong?" His thick southern accent carried a hint of alcohol, but Rich wasn't sure he was drunk, so he wouldn't press the issue.

"Your numbers seem to be falling off, that's why I stopped you," Rich said, "I need to see your paperwork just to make sure it's current." The boat's owner took on a very puzzled expression and looked over the side to see if this allegation was true. He acted as if the numbers were right a few minutes ago, but that somehow now they were all-of-a-sudden falling off. They had clearing been dissolving for quite some time.

The man took on a completely puzzled expression and said, "Jeeze, I didn't even know they was fallin' off, sir. I'll git it fixed soon's I git back to the house."

Rich knew the man was placating him. He also knew that if he didn't write a ticket and another patrol boat noticed the numbers, his fellow officers would hassle him for not citing the boat's owner. Even still, this was such a small infraction that Rich just wanted to be on his way and let the boat owner and his passengers be on theirs. He didn't want to cause a ruckus over this, and he sensed that the boat's owner was teetering on the edge of belligerence. He didn't want anything to get heated, so he figured he would just let it go. This was the sort of internal struggle that had become all too familiar to Rich. He so hated confrontation that it affected his ability to carry out his duties.

"I'm going to need you to get the boat out of the water as soon as possible, then. This will be a warning, but it really needs to get fixed immediately," Rich said, "The next officer to stop you won't give the same warning." He hoped they would respect him, be glad they didn't get a ticket, and comply with his orders. These were high hopes.

The men looked relieved to be getting let off with a warning and were a little overly polite. "Thanks so much, sir. I will, I'll git right back to the ramp here in a sec and git it took care of." The owner did the talking while the other passengers smirked at the entire conversation as if they were going to erupt with laughter at any minute.

Rich grabbed his contact log and began filling out information about the stop. He figured that doing this in the presence of the skiff and its passengers would give them the impression that he was logging the warning just in case they didn't feel like complying. It seemed to have worked because the smirks had vanished from the passengers' faces as they all began stowing their rods in order to head back home. As Rich pulled away, he felt a bit more authoritative than usual- like he had actually made a difference.

He continued cruising north on his way back to the station as the sun was setting and the end of his 8-hour shift neared. Within a few minutes he reached the New River Inlet where the ocean met the inland waters surrounded by the military base, Camp Lejeune. Navigating across the inlet and continuing up the Intracoastal required a bit of attention as there are several small islands and sandbars sprinkled throughout the area.

Rich drove up and around the inlet, passing a couple of popular sandbars where boaters would beach their boats and enjoy fun in the sun on the beach. This was a good area to look for inebriated boaters, though Rich wasn't very comfortable with that, so he avoided the sandbars whenever possible. He kept on up the Intracoastal, thankfully not noticing any violations of the law. Back to daydreaming, he thought of the boat he would eventually own once he figured out how to make his fortune- the Leopard 44; A 42 ft. catamaran with 4 staterooms. It had become his dreamboat ever since he saw one at a boat show about 5 years ago. The one at the show cost about $400,000 — far too much for Rich to afford, but that wouldn't stop him from dreaming. He didn't even know how to sail, but he had been on a sailboat once as a kid and he had absolutely loved it.

By the time he had conjured up the complete interior design of the ship in his mind, he was reawakened by a sputter of his actual boat's engine. The engine was making a very loud clanking sound, like parts were rattling around inside. Rich looked around to get his bearing and realized that he was just outside of Bear Island. He normally worked his way toward the island every time he was returning to the docks, so it wasn't strange that he was no longer on the path of the Intracoastal 'straight-shotting' it to the dock. He had taken a series of familiar turns, while daydreaming, to get to the island's south side. Bear Island was a popular tourist spot, but they generally stayed at the north and central areas, as these were where the campsites and activities were. Except for the occasional fisherman, this area was pretty vacant. Even now there wouldn't be anyone on the island except for campers at the north end.

Rich pulled the boat up to a beach in order to take a look at the engine without worrying about running in to anything. He quickly grabbed his radio and called in to dispatch to let them know he was having engine trouble. "Dispatch, this is Officer Harris. I'm having engine issues on return," He said, "I'm going to check it out and let you know if I need assistance." He waited for a reply while he removed the cover of the 225 hp Mercury. After about a minute of looking around, he noticed he had not received a reply from dispatch, so he picked up the radio and tried again, "dispatch, this is Officer Harris. Do you copy?" He waited a second and gave up, unconcerned. This wasn't a big deal; he'd just call them with his cell phone if he needed help. He returned to the engine, but had to grab a flashlight now as dusk approached. It always seemed darker on the water and the surrounding islands than it did back home, but that was because of the lack of city lights. That's why you can see the stars better when you're out to sea.

Rich knew nothing about engines, but he hoped that something obvious would be disconnected or something. He fiddled around here and there, knocking on lines and parts as if to knock away some debris, but nothing was working. He had no idea what the problem was, and now the engine wouldn't start. Realizing that his boat would need a tow back to the dock, he reached into his pocket and pulled out his cell phone, his dead cell phone. *"How could this be?"* he thought, *"It was at 95% when*

I left today and I haven't used it." But it was dead anyway, despite his completely logical internal argument. He hopped off the boat and tied it up to a tree. He grabbed the key and decided to head inland. He would find a camper with a cell phone and make the embarrassing call to dispatch and get towed home.

As Rich made his way up the island, he realized that he never been on this side of it before. As a matter of fact, he had only been to the populated areas, never straying or hiking around and venturing out. The brush grew thicker after a few minutes of walking, and it had just occurred to him that he should have just walked around toward the ocean side of the island and up the beach. This was a terrible idea, and it would take forever to get across the island.

Just as he stopped to ponder his recent decision and weigh the pros and cons of making his way to the beach, he saw something move a couple feet in front of him. Rich walked forward slowly, trying to see what it could have been. He flashed his light through the bushes and continued a slow creeping walk forward. He almost put a hand on his sidearm, but decided that may be a little dramatic for this point in his pursuit of nothing in particular. Just then the sand and dirt swept forward as if blown by wind, but there was none. It looked like someone had taken a broom and slowly swept a path, but the sweeping was slow and the sand moved all at once instead of starting in one place and being moved to another. Rich was intrigued, and for some reason, not scared out of his mind. He followed the path forward through the brush and more dirt and sand was moved. *"What in the hell is happening to the ground?"* he thought. *"And why am I following it?"* But right when he decided how stupid the idea of following strangely possessed dirt was, he felt a difference in the ground where he stood. It felt like he had walked onto a bridge or something. The ground was not as sturdy as it had been 3 feet back. He kicked the sand around under his feet to see if the ground looked any different and before he could react he felt the branches and dirt under him shift. The branches cracked and gave out under him, and he fell. What should have been a descent of a foot or two turned into about 15 feet, but seemed like forever. He landed hard on top of the wood that fell under him. He couldn't support the weight of his falling body on his legs alone, so he fell to his side so hard he made a loud grunt from the impact. Lying on his side in this dark hole, he wondered how his day had suddenly gone so horribly wrong.

Two

Rich quickly worked his way back to his feet. His mind and heart wear racing now. He looked around frantically, seeing nothing. He had dropped his flashlight. The only thing he could make out was the light from his dropped flashlight, partially hidden under some fallen debris. He made his way slowly to the light and cautiously clutched it. Turning on the flashlight, he looked around this hole he had fallen in. He noticed sticks lying around the ground and leaned against the walls of what now resembled more of a cave. It appeared to be about 10 feet by 15, though there wasn't really any way to tell for sure. Then Rich discovered something else. He saw what appeared to be human remains lying on the ground right next to him, and he jumped. Now terrified, he flashed the light around the cave to find at least 4 more skeletons. This was a tomb! It had to be.

Rich's breathing was quick and heavy as he assessed the situation. The bodies were completely decayed, so it wasn't as bad as seeing a real dead body. He remembered being called to an accident on the water a few months ago where there had been a dead body. This site was scary, but not as scary as the body he had seen on that day. That one in the accident was freshly deceased. It was a middle-aged man who had fallen off of his boat and drowned. The body wasn't bloated yet because it was reported almost immediately after the man had fallen off the boat. He looked like he could have just been sleeping, except there was definitely something missing. It was as if the soul was visibly absent from the body. Rich would never forget the look on the dead man's face. It was a look of surprise, as if the man was shocked that it was his time to go. His eyes were slightly opened. That image was terrifying.

These remains didn't feel liked they'd ever really been people. These seemed more like haunted house props. They were dressed in rags that had decayed along with their owners' flesh over at least a century. Rich walked toward one of the skeletons, the closest one, and shined the light directly on its face. Still shaken from the fall, and scared from the sheer weight of the entire situation, he was still curious. He thought this skeleton was a man because of the clothing, but noticed a large earring by the left side of the skull on the ground. The skull looked menacing and fierce. But then, don't they all look that way? Rich made his way around the cave and examined the remains, one skeleton, or body, at a time. One of them appeared to have been a woman as her clothing resembled a skirt or dress of some kind. Rich wondered why she had been buried down here with men. Were they buried? Entombed together because they were family, or because they had committed some crime and were being punished? Nothing seemed logical. Why here? Why Bear Island? Even back in the 1700s and 1800s, there were no people that dwelled here. But Rich began to see a common element amongst the dead. He noticed a similarity in their clothing and in their jewelry. As he began to formulate a theory in his head of their origin, he noticed that one of the bodies was sprawled across a crate. The skeleton seemed to have laid backwards across it or had fallen back on it when he died. More snooping around had lead Rich to find rings on the ground below the skeleton's hands. These were expensive! These were real!

Rich began to get excited that he had found all of this jewelry, but then he thought of the situation in which he had found himself. How could he keep this jewelry? Wouldn't he have to report all of this? There were bodies down here. This had to be reported. But no one had to know that the bodies had jewelry. Rich picked up all the rings he could find, along with necklaces and anything else of value that he could find. These people must have been rich to have had all of these expensive items. Two of the skeletons had daggers: one still held a dagger, and the other had a dagger lying on the ground near his hand.

Now Rich wondered what was in the box that one of the bodies laid across. His imagination ran wild with excitement. He used a cloth he found on the ground to move the skeleton to the side gently. He was surprised at how easily the bones had shifted out of the way. It occurred to Rich that he was the first person to see these people since they had died.

There was a lock on the latch of the crate, but it was as old as the dead bodies surrounding it, so it should be easy to break. *"This is crazy,"* Rich thought, *"I can't just break into this thing. It's not mine. Someone buried it here."* But that seemed illogical, too. No one knows this is here. Rich would have read about this or learned about it in one of the nearby museums. He was knowledgeable about the history of this area, and he does not remember hearing about any tombs. Just as he thought about the history of the area, a startling realization made its way into Rich's mind. These are pirates. They dressed like the pirates Rich had seen in the museums and even in the movies. Two of them had daggers on their sides, a discovery Rich had only just made during this realization. The one Rich had just moved off of the crate had a sword by his side. Then this isn't a crate. It's a chest — a treasure chest!

Rich frantically searched the cave for a rock or something heavy to use to break the lock. He found a large stick lying by one of the bodies, under the hole where he had fallen in. He struggled to lift the stick as he swung hard at the latch, making a loud bang, but not breaking the lock. He gave it another hard swing and smashed the lock hard, this time breaking it off and the entire latch with it. Rich quickly lifted the top of the chest and peered in at its contents. Treasure. This really is a treasure. He saw hundreds of gold and silver coins, some necklaces, bracelets, a golden wine chalice, some rings. There was so much to look at he could hardly contain himself. Rich had never seen this much money or valuable jewelry before in his life. It was amazing. It was beautiful. It was his.

After a few minutes of sifting through the chest, examining pieces more closely, Rich remembered that he was at the bottom of a cave with no way out. He looked at his surroundings again, but this time he looked for solutions to his problem. Over by the spot where he had fallen, he noticed two large boards leaning against the cave wall and up to the hole. It looked as if the people had set this up before they were closed in. They must have come here to hide the treasure. Then how did they die? Why didn't they leave? Rich only thought about this for a minute or two and quickly wondered how he'd get himself and the treasure out and back home. That wasn't as important as the realization that he was now very wealthy.

He walked toward the hole he had fallen through in search of a way out of the cave. The beams of wood were sturdy enough to support his weight, so he lined them up and tried working his way up toward the hole. He sat facing backwards and scooted back little by little up the beams until he was at the top, just under the hole. As he looked up through the hole, he noticed the stars shining brighter than usual. This was probably because he had been in the dark for so long and his eyes adjusted accordingly. Still, the stars shined brightly in the absence of city lights. He slid back down the beams now, confident that he'd be able to come and go as he needed in case he couldn't get the whole treasure out tonight. Even if he got the treasure to the boat, there was the small matter of the non-working engine he had yet to attend to.

After pondering his options for a bit, Rich decided that he would hide the treasure until tomorrow when he could come back better prepared. Besides, he at least had the few items he had picked up when he first discovered the skeletons. These would be enough to entertain him until he retrieved the rest. He only had to work for a couple of hours tomorrow, mostly filing paperwork. He worked his way up the beams slowly, looking down on his wonderful discovery. This incredible scene that would surely make its way into the newspapers had he not already decided against telling anyone about it.

Once he reached the top of the cave and made his way out of the hole, Rich quickly covered it back up with small branches and dirt until it was completely hidden. He worried that it would be more easily spotted in the light of day, but this side of the island was rarely visited if ever, so that was a very small concern. The next concern would be his recollection of the cave's location tomorrow. Would he be able to find his way back? The sound of the ocean gave Rich his bearings, so he was able to assume the direction in which his boat was beached. Then he thought of pirates. How did pirates do it? How did they hide their treasures? Surely they did so during the light of day, and not on their own. They probably had something to write on; a map. Rich decided that he would count his paces back to the boat, but since that was still a long shot, and the terrain all looked the same, he would leave an article of clothing. After all, even if someone did happen to come to this side of the island and see the clothing, they'd never recognize where the hole was. Rich would recognize it though, he could see it clearly enough with the light of his flashlight. He studied the covered hole until he was confident he could find it again. Then he removed his uniform shirt and took off the white t-shirt he was wearing underneath. He placed the t-shirt on the ground where he'd be able to see it if he came within 20 feet of it, then he put his uniform shirt back on and headed toward his boat. He counted his paces and took very calculated steps, ensuring they were full strides. Tripping occasionally and stumbling around bushes, he made his way back across the island, keeping his pace count the entire way.

Rich finally reached the small boat, and he quickly found a notebook onboard where he wrote down his pace count and a rough location of the shirt and treasure. He was careful not to write anything that would be suspicious if read by anyone else. After all, this was his treasure, and he didn't want to risk anyone else finding it. He tried the radio again and to his amazement this time it worked like a charm. That was strange. It didn't work at all before, and now it was as if it was brand new. "Dispatch, this is Officer Harris, do you copy?" He said.

An officer from dispatch responded frantically, "HARRIS! Where have you been?" they yelled, "Are you ok?", they asked, worried after having sent two search boats out, but relieved to hear that he was ok.

"I'm fine. My engine is out. I'm beached on Bear," he said. "I tried radioing, but it was down until now, and my cell is dead. Can you send a boat?" As he spoke, he decided to try the engine again for no particular reason, as he knew it wouldn't start. As he turned the key, the engine turned over in one try. Just like the radio, it worked like new, as if it had not had issues at all. "Wait," he said, confused by the situation, "it's working now."

"Which is it, Harris? Do you need a tow or not?"

"No, I think I'm good. I'm heading back now, I'll call if I need assistance. I should be there in 20 minutes or so." Rich jumped down to untie the boat from the tree. He threw the lines in the boat and got behind the wheel. As he backed away from the shore, he reached a hand down and felt the outside of his pocket. The lumps he felt of his newly claimed treasure reminded him that this wasn't a dream. He really did see what he saw. He really did find what he found. Now his mind was racing as he slowly made his way back to the docks. The slow boat ride back gave him plenty of time to ponder all the things he could do with his newfound wealth.

Back at the docks, Officer Stengele, one of the officers working the night shift, greeted Rich. "Damn, Harris, you get lost?" Stengele said with a chuckle, "you'd think you were a rookie out there gittin' stranded on Bear." His condescending tone was all too familiar to Rich.

"Yeah, my engine was rattling really loud and finally quit on me," Rich explained, "my radio, cell, nothing worked. I finally got her started back up, but JT's gonna need to take a look at it in the morning". JT was the local mechanic in charge of maintenance for the entire local fleet of NCWRC boats. He was a good old boy, born and raised in Swansboro, who knew all there was to know about engines.

Uninterested in Rich's explanation, Stengele said, "Well, I called the captain and told him you was unaccounted for. Had to, man, you weren't answerin'". Stengele didn't really seem at all remorseful, or even worried about the possibility of Rich catching hell for this little incident. "He says you need to call him when you git back."

None of this fazed Rich in the least. He didn't care what the captain thought. He didn't care what Stengele said, or anyone else for that matter. After all, he was a new man — a wealthy man. Now he had to figure out a way to retrieve his new treasure.

Three

Rich awoke the next morning half thinking yesterday had been a dream. Once he realized that it wasn't, his new excitement washed away any leftover sleepiness and replaced it with a childlike energy. He hopped out of bed and began his morning routine to prepare for the day. Only today wouldn't be like the others. Today was the first day of his new life. If he could only figure out how to convert his treasure into wealth and begin that new life. That would be taken care of in time. For now, getting the treasure into the safety of his house became Rich's sole objective. He quickly finished his bathroom routine and headed out to the garage to gather the equipment needed. *"What will I need, and how can I lift such a heavy chest out of that hole?"* he thought. He browsed his lack-luster collection of hand-me-down tools, moving them around on his unused work bench. Spotting a pair of gloves he used routinely for yard work, Rich decided that they'd help protect his hands from rope burn, which jogged his memory of the location of the rope he's never used. But how would he transport the chest to his boat when he got it out of the hole? Rich decided that a beach cart, or wagon, would do the trick. He'd need to buy one, of course, but he looked at it like an investment.

While continuing to fill a small travel tool bag with essentials, Rich explored his mind for solutions to extracting the treasure from the cave. Would it need to be retrieved in portions, or could he get the whole chest out? He thought back to the two beams of wood he had used to get out of the hole and wondered how he could use them as rails for the chest to slide up and out. Just as he was considering making multiple trips back and forth, an idea popped into his head. He'd use a jack.

He recalled a friend using a specific type of jack a few years ago on an off-roading trip they had taken. His friend's jeep had gotten stuck in some mud and no other vehicles present could tow it out. Fortunately, his friend had a *Hi-Lift* jack mounted on the hood of his Jeep. He simply wrapped a chain, attached to the jack, around a nearby tree, and began pumping the lever. The Jeep slowly crept out of the mud, and the day was saved.

That could work! The problem was that there weren't any trees anywhere near the hole of the cave, but he could use an anchor! Anchor to the sand and use rope instead of chains, and the chest will come up the beams with ease. After all, the chest wasn't nearly as heavy as a Jeep, and it wasn't submerged in mud. Piece of cake. *"Now to go buy a jack,"* Rich thought, as he packed the tools into his 1995 Dodge Dakota.

On the drive to the nearest hardware store, Rich kept looking at his watch. He kept remembering that he had to be to work soon. All the excitement kept causing him to lose track of time and forget his responsibilities. *"30-minutes to my shift; 5-minutes in and out of the store; 3 hours at work filing paperwork; and — crap!"* He thought, *"I forgot to call the captain last night!"* There was no doubt he'd receive a stern butt-reaming now, worse than the one he was already prepared for, given last night's temporary absence.

Captain Charles Kelly was a seasoned NCWRC Officer with 26 years on the job. He believed that the organization was growing 'kinder and gentler', and that officers these days couldn't have ever hacked it back when he first started out. This was laughable to Rich because this wasn't exactly the NYPD. Rich himself was admittedly not cut out for regular law enforcement, and maybe not even for his current position, but for Captain Kelly to think the NCWRC was some elite police force; that was humorous. Nonetheless, he's the boss, and Rich would have to face the music.

Rich quickly ran his errands and headed straight for the station. He didn't have many friends at work. Actually, he had only two: Jay Luther, the closest thing to a best friend since he was a kid, and Carol Massey, who was more like a girl he had a crush on, but someone he considered a friend. He considered calling ahead to Jay and asking how the captain's mood seemed this morning, but he quickly dismissed that thought, thinking Jay would just do what he always did and lecture Rich on what it means to be a NCWRC Officer. Carol was more forgiving, but he couldn't bear the embarrassment of being the station's screw-up, so he couldn't call her. He'd just have to walk into the lion's den vulnerable and receive his proverbial lashings.

The captain already had a problem with Rich because of his history of being timid, so he usually talked in a condescending tone, and usually spoke to Rich as if he was using up the captain's valuable time. Even if the captain had initiated the conversation, he looked impatient when Rich talked about anything.

Rich pulled into the parking lot of the station and tried reassuring himself that this was all temporary, and that soon he'd be on top of the world. *"Just get through this day, and go get the treasure,"* he thought, imagining how he'd bring the large chest out of the ground and transport it to his boat. As he headed into the building, his daydreaming began to fade away, pushed aside by the stress of what was about to happen. Confrontation.

He knew that he wouldn't be free from his current life until the treasure was successfully turned into cash, and he could afford to quit this job and disappear. What if it's all too good to be true? What if his dream comes crashing down, and someone else finds out about the treasure? What if it's taken from him and put into a museum? These were all valid questions, and reasons he couldn't count his chickens.

When Rich walked into the front entrance of the station he expected everyone to be staring at him with that *'Ooooh, you're gonna get it!'* look on their faces. But no one really even noticed him as he walked down the hall toward the captain's office. He was somewhat relieved that he wasn't the focus of ridicule, but almost equally saddened because he was so insignificant here.

As he reached the captain's office he knocked on the door frame, standing awkwardly in the open doorway, patiently waiting for the captain to look up from his computer and acknowledge Rich's presence.

After a few painfully awkward and humiliating minutes, the captain finally addressed the timid and nervous Officer. "Get in here, Harris," he growled in a half disgusted, half indifferent tone.

Rich marched forward and stood at attention in front of his boss's desk. He began with the standard reporting procedures, "Good morning, sir! Officer Harris reporting..."

Captain Kelly interrupted, "Cut the shit, Harris. What the hell happened last night? I got dispatch calling me saying you were gone for hours, you can't be reached by radio, and you don't call in. When you finally do get ahold of the station, I get another call saying you're found. Then I awaited your call; the call I told dispatch to tell you to make upon your return." Rich patiently waited for his chance to explain what had happened, but the captain was on a role, and he never gave up an opportunity to humiliate. "Now I know you have my number, and I know you got the word to call me. What I don't know is why you think the rules don't apply to you." The captain felt very authoritative when he spoke this way to his subordinates, but it was almost wasted breath when talking to Rich.

"Sir, I meant to call you when I got back last night, but..." Rich almost completed an entire sentence before being cut off again.

"Don't 'but' me, Harris. You're not in high school. Those excuses don't work anymore. You're an Officer of the North Carolina Wildlife Resource Commission," the captain said with a patriotic emphasis placed upon the title of his fine organization, "you're expected to act like it."

"Yes, sir. I'm sorry, sir — "

"Don't be sorry, Harris," the captain's tone now sounding more like parent scolding a child, "just do what the hell you're told to do, when the hell you're told to do it. Now that's that. What the hell happened to your boat? And your radio? JT says there's nothing wrong with your engine," once again the captain didn't leave any room for Rich to explain himself, or answer any of the questions, "and Officer Bell says there's nothing wrong with your damn radio." Rich waited for a few seconds before speaking as he was almost certain he would be cut off again, but this time the captain was expecting an answer. "WELL?!" yelled the captain.

"Sorry sir... I mean, I'm not sorry sir, I just... Sir...," this was not the answer Rich had formulated in his head during his scolding, "My engine started to sputter on my way back to the station, so I pulled up to a nearby beach," Rich carefully left out the fact that it was a beach on Bear Island. He didn't want to chance anyone knowing the whereabouts of his newfound wealth. "I cut the engine to take a look and see what the problem was, and I tried calling dispatch right away. There was no answer because my radio wasn't working." Captain Kelly looked on and listened skeptically as Rich tap danced his way through his nervous recollection of the events in question. Rich continued, "I didn't see anything wrong, but the engine wouldn't start, and I couldn't get a hold of anyone. My cell phone was dead too."

As Rich continued explaining last night's fiasco, leaving out the pesky details of the millions of dollars' worth of treasure, and the entombed human remains he had found, he decided to account for the time spent in the cave by simply stating that he walked the beach, looking for someone with a phone. After a few minutes of explanation, the captain grew bored with the story, and though he believed Rich was telling the truth, he'd continue to scold. "Enough, Harris," he said as he waived his hand around as if to say it was too much to take in, "you need to keep in mind that I'm accountable for every Officer in this station. You need to check in regularly and check your radio before you go out. Just don't let this happen again." The captain was done lecturing Rich and dismissed him from the office. "Go file your paperwork," he said as he looked back to his computer.

Rich shamefully walked out of the captain's office, still expecting everyone to be pointing and laughing at him, but no one cared. He was glad that wrist slapping session was over and he could now get his work done and get back to Bear Island. As he approached his desk, he noticed an object that he hadn't seen before. As he got closer, he saw that it was some sort of child's toy packaging. He picked up the package to see that it was a pack of children's walkie-talkies. Just then, he heard laughter erupt behind him, and he turned around to see Jay and Carol both extremely amused with their ingenious prank.

"I heard your radio was on the fritz, brother. Thought you should bring a backup out with you on your next shift," Jay chuckled. Carol couldn't come up with anything clever or funny to say, so she simply asked, "What happened Rich?", still smiling from the hilarious walkie-talkie prank.

"Hilarious, guys. Really," Rich said with a smirk on his face. "Look, my engine broke down, and my radio was out. That's it. End of story." He was tired of going over the events in his head and certainly didn't want to chance giving away the whereabouts of his new secret.

"Dude, you know Danny was trashing you to the captain, right?" Jay said, performing his friendship duties by keeping his buddy informed. This was, of course, no surprise to Rich since Officer Danny Bell was the bully of the station. He thrived on making others look bad. "He checked your radio this morning and reported right to the captain when he saw that there wasn't anything wrong with it. I swear, that guy is such a prick."

Jay couldn't stand Danny Bell. Neither could Carol. Neither could anyone, really, aside from his small group of followers. Bell was a bully. He probably wouldn't cut it in a normal civilian job where he would have to treat people with a shred of dignity. He was the typical alpha male, a former high school athlete who peaked in high school. He stays at the NCWRC because of his status, but also because it's safe.

Danny Bell tried to join the local police department right out of high school, but he had injured his knee playing football, and that kept him from being able to pass the physical. He frequently recites the events of the night he sustained the injury, but most of it is fluff. He actually just turned and twisted his leg the wrong way, coming out of a huddle, and tore his ACL. He had been a mediocre player at best, but you wouldn't know that from his stories.

Carol consoled him, "Don't worry about Danny. He's just mad because he's still a child, and everyone else around here has grown up." Rich knew that Carol would be on his side, as usual, and say something nice. Back in high school, Rich had a small crush on Carol, but it never blossomed in to anything more than that. Carol wasn't gorgeous, but she was pretty enough, at least back in high school. He saw her more now as a great friend, and he couldn't imagine anything else.

"Thanks guys. I appreciate you having my back. We all know Danny is a huge prick. He will never change," said Rich. "I wish I hadn't given him the ammunition this time. I swear it really wasn't my fault. I mean, I can't explain it, but both my engine and my radio, oh, and my cell phone, each went dead. Temporary black out or something," he said, trying to make sense of it still. "It was like I entered the Bermuda Triangle or something," he said with a chuckle.

Rich turned, smiled, and gave a friendly nod and wave as he headed to his desk to file yesterday's reports. "Ok guys, I have mounds of paperwork to do," he said, "oh, the excitement of the NCWRC." The three of them shared a sarcastic giggle at the thought of their mundane duties. Rich sat at the desk and began typing.

He thought about his situation. He became excited again at the thought of what he had found. This was going to be a game changer for Rich. He would be a new man after this. Would he include his two friends in his new discovery? He thought about that for a while, as he really did care about Jay and Carol. But for now, he would keep it to himself and move forward as planned. First things first: paperwork.

Four

Rich finally finished filing the necessary reports while chatting with Carol and Jay. He bid them adieu for the day and gave them a fabricated story of how he had to run a bunch of errands. Not that they were even curious about what Rich had planned for the rest of the day, but he liked to think they would want to know.

The drive to the docks where Rich launched and stored his personally owned boat was about 15 minutes from the station. He arrived in 12 minutes this time, driving with his adrenalin pumping. His boat was a 1983, 18 foot center console with a 75 horsepower outboard engine. It was not the prettiest boat on the water, and it frequently had issues, but Rich inherited the boat from his father when he passed away a few years back, so he couldn't complain. It was the same boat his father had taken him fishing on as a kid, so it carried some sentimental value.

Rich finished loading his tools onto the small vessel, untied from the dock, and was on his way. As he made his way through the channels, he again began daydreaming of the first few things he'd purchase. The new boat: the Leopard 44. Such an amazing boat, the Leopard 44. Rich could see himself at the helm, charging forward toward the wide open ocean. He'd sail to some remote tropical island and anchor in a beautiful cove, staring in awe at the crystal clear green water. Maybe Carol would be with him. They could jump into the warm, refreshing water and snorkel around the area. As the vivid visions of Carol's perfect body in a smaller than necessary bikini began forming in Rich's mind, he was jolted back to reality by the loud blast of a large boat's horn.

Rich's heart began immediately racing as he pulled back on the throttle and sharply veered right to miss the large boat coming up fast on his boat's port, or left, side. He wasn't really all that close to hitting the other boat, but his daydreaming had caused him to drift slowly out of his own lane and towards the other boat heading in the same direction.

The other boat's driver shouted some obscenities and threw a finger in the air. Rich was more embarrassed than anything, but he slowed to a very slow crawl to let the larger boat get as far away as possible. Rich was close to his turn to get to Bear Island, so once there were no other boats around, he veered off into the channels which led to Bear. When he arrived to that same spot that held him hostage the night before, this time he gladly beached his vessel into the same spot, hopped off and roped the boat off to a tree.

Most of his tools fit into a backpack, and the heavy jack wasn't a problem because Rich had brought that beach cart he had purchased. He made his way toward the cave, pulling his cart and counting his paces the whole way. After a few minutes of walking, Rich noticed what looked like a small piece of white cloth, possibly part of the shirt he left as a marker, about 20 feet straight ahead. As he stepped closer, he saw that it was in fact the shirt which was now partially covered by some brush and sand. That was ok with Rich because he could see the branches that covered the hole to the cave.

As Rich laid the handle to the beach cart down on the sand and reached down to move away the branches, he couldn't help but get a little nervous that the whole thing was just a dream, or that someone had taken the treasure. He began worrying so much as he uncovered the hole that his heart started to pound harder and harder. Finally, the hole was completely exposed, but the cave was dark. Rich's heart continued pounding as he fumbled around for his flashlight. He quickly shined the light down into the cave to reveal the same familiar gruesome scene of human remains, sticks, swords, and there it was — that beautiful chest of unbelievable riches.

There was no time to waste. Rich had brought an anchor with him to act as the stronghold for the jack to be attached to. He walked about 10 feet from the hole, reached the anchor high above his head with both hands, took a deep breath, and slammed the anchor down into the ground. Wiggling both the rope and the anchor, he ensured that the anchor was securely in place. Surely that would be enough to support the weight of the chest.

Rich connected the other end of the anchor's rope to the Hi-Lift jack and grabbed the other rope from his bag. He attached that rope to the other side of the jack and threw the rest of the rope down into the hole. That would be attached to the chest. Rich tossed the tool bag down into the hole, gave one last look in all directions to make sure he wasn't being watched, and he began climbing down the beams into the cave.

This time Rich was prepared for the darkness of the cave. He reached into his bag and removed a camping lantern; the kind that takes a rechargeable battery. He turned on the lantern and wasted no time wrapping the rope around the chest the best way he could think to attach it.

As he tied and twisted, Rich looked over at the remains that had once lain across the chest. He wondered who this man was. Rich could only assume it was a man by the clothing he was wearing; the same way he identified the two other men and the one woman. *"Who were they?"* he thought. *"They were once alive. They were people. Down here, buried alive? Together. Why?"*

Rich couldn't understand how this scene had come to be. It made no sense at all. The woman lay in front of the chest as if she had been facing the man Rich had moved off of the chest. The other two men were closer to the opening and faced in toward the woman and the man Rich had moved. He kept wondering how these people had died. He thought that if they had just died of hunger or something, they'd be curled up in the corner, but they weren't. Each skeleton was positioned as if they had been killed where they once stood.

Just then, Rich thought back to the daggers by the two men by the opening. They must have had the daggers out for a reason. He stopped tying the rope and stood up to get a better look around the cave at the scene. He noticed sticks all over the place and figured they were fallen branches. He kicked a few around to see if there was more jewelry on the ground. When he kicked near the man by the chest, he kicked something heavy, like a rock. When Rich removed the brush from the ground over the rock, he discovered that it wasn't a rock at all. It was a pistol. *"WOW! This has got to be worth a fortune!"*, thought Rich, as he reached down and picked up the antique piece. It was beautiful. He held the gun in his right hand and quickly realized it was made for a lefty. He switched hands and pointed the pistol at the wall of the cave, turning it over from side to side, admiring its beauty and age. He set the gun back on the ground and covered it with part of the skeleton's clothing. He wiped his prints off of it — he figured he may need to leave it here for when the police would examine how they had died.

Rich summed up what he knew so far about the scene. There was a man with a gun who had been lying across the chest. A woman was in front of him, but she didn't have the gun, so it was confusing why he laid across the chest as if he had been shot. The two men by the cave opening had once held daggers and faced the man and woman by the chest. But the most confusing thing was that they must have all died at the same time. Otherwise, wouldn't they have moved the man off of the chest? There just couldn't be any way that each person was in these final positions had they not died simultaneously.

What happened then? It couldn't have been an explosion because everything inside the cave was still relatively intact, minus the decaying remains and rotting wood. Perhaps it was some sort of poison. But there weren't any vials, or cups, in sight. Maybe the man shot everyone and then himself. As strange as that last thought seemed, it appeared to be the only thing Rich could come up with, that he couldn't immediately disprove. What a sad scene. But why should the treasure go unclaimed?

Rich set aside any of the faint feelings of guilt he had acquired from the unsettling scene surrounding him, and the fact that he was essentially profiting from it. He continued working feverishly on the task at hand. He finished securing the rope around the chest and climbed up the beams for one last check around the area to ensure that no one was around.

When Rich saw no boats or people in sight, he jumped back down into the cave and headed to the chest. He wanted to pull the chest over to the bottoms of the beams to make it easier to pump the jack and lift the chest out of the hole. Rich gave the rope a quick tug, and the chest didn't budge. He conjured up some energy, let out a loud grumble, put all of his body weight into it this time and yanked again, "AHHH!," he grunted, but the chest only moved about a half an inch. Rich's frustration grew as he hadn't anticipated the chest weighing so much. Would the jack even be able to lift the chest out? Each time he pulled, he heard the wood creak and crack. What if he got the chest halfway out of the hole and the wood completely gave out? The treasure would fall everywhere.

Rich decided he'd try the jack and see if it would move the chest toward the beams. He climbed out of the hole and positioned himself at the jack. He could see down into the hole enough to see a corner of the chest, which was enough to know whether the chest would move. Rich grabbed the handle of the "Hi-Lift" and gave it a good pull. This tightened whatever slack was in the rope. He pumped a couple more times, and to his surprise and delight, the chest began to move. He slowly pumped while he watched the chest inch forward, creaking and crunching its way toward the beams. Rich was so nervous that the weight of the jewels and coins would be too much for the old, dried out wood to bear.

As the chest approached the beams, Rich pulled the lever down one last time before the chest would touch the beams. He suddenly heard a crunching noise, like the rope had completely broken through the chest. Even though he didn't want to believe it, that is exactly what had happened. The weight was just too much for the wood to bear.

Thinking quickly, Rich used his backpack to bring the treasure up a little at a time. It would take a lot longer this way, but at least he knew he could still get it all out in one day rather than making multiple trips back and forth to Bear Island.

Rich emptied his backpack out inside the cave and began stuffing as much treasure as he could without it being too heavy to lift. He figured he'd lift it out of the cave himself instead of using the jack in case the bag couldn't handle the weight. As he climbed out of the hole, Rich realized that he was going to be exhausted after this ordeal — going up and down, over and over, and pulling a heavy bag up 15 feet each time. Then he still had to cart the treasure back to his boat, cart it from the docks to his truck without looking suspicious, and then get it home.

Rich performed the grueling task for about 2 hours, sweating profusely, and cursing himself for not bringing water with him. He pulled the last bag of treasure out of the hole and set it on top of the rest on the beach cart. Had it not been for a tarp he brought along, the cart wouldn't have worked at all. The coins would have fallen out the cracks of the sides of the cart.

Rich quickly covered the hole in order to ensure that no one would find the human remains until he could figure out how to wrap up this loose end. He didn't know if he would report it or not. What if someone saw the empty, broken chest, and wondered where its former contents were? Never mind all of that for now. Rich needed to get the treasure back home. Once the area looked as if no one had been there, Rich grabbed the handle of the cart and began pulling toward the direction of the boat.

The cart was much heavier this time around with all the heavy jewels and coins. Rich was having a very difficult time pulling the cart across sand and brush. The long walk back seemed longer due to the increased weight and the fact that Rich was extremely tired. After about an hour of pulling the heavy cart through the sand, he finally reached the boat.

Five

Rich spent the next 20 minutes figuring out how to transport the treasure into the boat and contemplating how he'd get it from his boat to his truck. As difficult as the task had been, Rich got the treasure onto the boat, mostly wrapped in the tarp like a bag. This took a great deal of strength to get over the side of the boat, so he wrapped what he could lift in the tarp, pulled it over the side of the boat, and continued to get the rest with the backpack little by little. Some treasure had to be stuffed into compartments throughout the boat. It was this long, drawn-out calamity of a job that forced Rich's decision to tow the boat home that night rather than try to transport everything again.

Rich pushed his boat from the shore of Bear Island, reflecting on just how difficult all of that work had been. He wondered what he could have done differently and thought ahead to where he would store the treasure at home. But the pure excitement of having found such an amazing treasure had given Rich some superficial strength and energy. He was working from a sort of 'high' that raised his adrenaline and helped him carry out this grueling work. Rich still had no plan on how to convert the treasure into cash. He tried remembering all the movies he had seen where someone had discovered treasures beyond their wildest dreams. He wondered what they had done, but he couldn't remember the pesky little details of how they had actually done it.

Half the day was gone now as Rich putted along the channels on his way to the docks, and thoughts continued in and out of his excited mind. He thought about the Leopard 44, and the cove where he and Carol would one day swim. He thought about cars, and houses, and TVs.

Rich was jolted back to reality by flashing lights and a boat speeding toward him from up ahead. *"What's going on?!"* Rich asked himself,

"Are they coming for me?" His mind began racing. *"What if they find the treasure?"* he thought, *"They will know exactly what happened! I didn't report this! What the hell am I gonna do?!"* He couldn't bear the thought of going to prison, but that's the very thought he couldn't shake from his mind.

The boat grew closer and closer, heading directly for Rich's boat. As it got closer, he could see that it was a NCWRC boat. "Wonderful," he sarcastically whispered. *"This is just what the hell needs to be happening right now."* His heart was racing from fear and adrenaline. How embarrassing. His own crew would be the ones to bust him. Before he could buy a single thing.

As the boat pulled up, Rich could finally see the officer on board. "SIR! CUT OFF YOUR ENGINE AND GET YOUR HANDS WHERE I CAN SEE THEM!" Yelled the officer who was wearing a very large and cheesy smile. Jay looked at the surprised look on Rich's face, and couldn't help but let out a loud, triumphant laugh. "What's up, Richie Rich?" Jay jovially inquired.

Rich's heart still pounded, but he breathed a little easier knowing that it was his buddy Jay playing a trick on him. "What the hell, man?" Rich nervously chuckled. "Why are you flying up on me like that?" He nervously asked, still nervous that Jay would get curious and want to see inside the boat.

"I was skimming the water with my 'binos', and when I saw my boy Rickles tootin' up the way, I figured I'd try and make his butt pucker, HA HA!" Jay laughed, and he continued, "Why'd you get so scared man, you knew it was a station boat?!" He questioned.

"I know man, but you were flying," was all that Rich could think to say. "I didn't know what the hell was going on." He hoped that Jay would lose interest and have the sudden urge to get back to work. "Aren't you on duty, officer?" Rich asked with a nervous smile.

"Yeah, yeah." Jay dismissed Rich's comment. "Hey man, when the hell are we going golfing again?" Jay asked, knowing full well that neither could play worth a damn, but glad to have a friend to play random games with from time to time. Bro-time, he called it.

"Jay, you're the single worst golfer I've ever seen in my life," Rich joked, "and I think I may very well be the second worst."

"All right bro, well have fun fishin', or doin' whatever the hell you're doin'," Jay chuckled. "Some of us gotta work." He turned his vessel to the north and waived to Rich as he pulled away.

"Holy crap, that was close," Rich thought—his heart pounding as he pushed forward on the throttle. After a few minutes more of driving, Rich could see the dock up ahead. He had hoped that no one would be there, and couldn't see anyone from this far out.

Rich pulled his skiff into the dock, and thankfully there was no one around. Finally, a break. He tied his dock line to the nearest cleat and jumped off of the boat. Rich got to his truck as quickly as he could. This was all so exciting. As he backed his truck down the ramp, Rich thought more about how he would exchange the treasure for money. He continued the routine of driving the boat onto the trailer and wondered again how they did it in the movies. It had always just seemed like in the movies they got the treasure and were automatically rich. Of course, it couldn't be that easy.

Rich pulled up to his house, eager to pull the boat into the garage and get started on inspecting each and every piece. His overwhelming desire to examine the treasure was overpowering his physical and mental exhaustion. The strangest feeling washed over him as he backed the boat into the garage. He couldn't tell if it was a feeling of happiness because of his find, or a feeling of greed. Either way, he had his treasure, and no one else knew about it.

The garage was a tight squeeze once the door was closed. There was hardly room to walk around the boat. Rich had random tools laying everywhere with no rhyme or reason to which ones went where. He didn't let that bother him, though; he just hopped up on the boat and opened the tarp. He stood for a moment and drank in the luminescent glow of these beautiful pieces of art. The glimmering coins with some unrecognizable foreign writing, the magnificent golden chalices, the various strands of necklaces; pearl and gem covered; and the many shiny pieces of who knew what, all laying before him.

Rich looked up to a shelf to see an old chest he used for knick knacks and decided that would be a fitting container for such a fine collection of valuables. He grabbed his ladder and climbed up to grab the chest. Forgetting what was even inside, Rich pulled on the chest and underestimated how light it would be. The chest came flying off the shelf and landed on the floor next to the boat. He was lucky he hadn't hit the boat. A few tarps and drop cloths were inside the chest, so Rich dumped them on the ground and took the chest inside the house to the den and laid it in the center of the room on the floor. Rich made trips back and forth from the boat to the chest, bringing backpacks full of jewels at a time until he had transported the entire treasure to the chest. This took Rich about a half hour to do. The whole time he chuckled at the thought of having his treasure inside of a chest.

Staring down at the mound of riches, he tried to estimate the value of the enormous fortune in front of him, but the more he tried to think about it, the more invaluable it seemed. Could this make him rich beyond his wildest dreams? There had to be millions upon millions of dollars' worth of gold, silver, and precious gems. *'Maybe even billions!'*, Rich thought to himself, barely able to contain a confident grin.

He reached into the pile and picked up a piece that caught his eye. It was a large silver bracelet with gems inset all around it. It was like nothing he had seen before. He couldn't even recall seeing anything this amazing in a museum before, though he also couldn't recall the last time he had been to a museum. He rubbed the bracelet on his sleeve and gazed at his reflection sparkling in the silver mirror. Rich inspected the red stones on the side. There were six of the red stones wrapped around the bracelet, and they were shaped like footballs. They had to be rubies. There were also green stones wrapping the top and bottom of the bracelet, but Rich knew nothing about precious gems.

Rich put the bracelet back onto the pile and scooped up a handful of the silver coins. Maybe he could see where this treasure came from and somehow determine its age. The coins made up the bulk of the treasure and there appeared to be thousands of them. He held up a coin and examined its writing.

The coin had a cross in the center, and the writing was unreadable, at least to Rich. Some sort of foreign coins, but they were undeniably silver. Rich knew this treasure was extremely valuable. He daydreamed about all the things that would be possible now with his newfound wealth. He could buy anything he ever wanted. Could this really be happening to him? Was his fantasy finally going to become a reality? The coin he held was so beautiful. Rich admired its beauty the longer he held it. They sure didn't make coins like this anymore. He wondered again how old this treasure was, or where it came from, but his overwhelming feeling of happiness for having stumbled upon this discovery had erased any clear thoughts for the moment. It was a fantastic dream coming true.

Rich put the treasure down and laid on his living room couch; he was exhausted. All the excitement of the day faded as Rich's energy drained and it became apparent that bedtime had arrived. His eyes carried the weight of the day's work, and Rich could no longer keep them open. A great day, Rich thought, as he drifted off to sleep.

Suddenly, Rich found himself in a strange place; a beautiful place, with the salt air all around him, the sun shining more brilliantly than he could remember ever seeing before. He was on a boat of some kind. He looked around to get his bearings and realized that he was on a huge wooden ship, like something out of '*Treasure Island*'. This didn't seem odd at all, though. He belonged there. This was home.

Rising and falling with the swells of the open ocean, the ship felt as if it was dancing to the music of a beautiful symphony. Rich had missed this place. He couldn't remember when he had left, or how long he had been gone from here, but it overjoyed him to be back where he belonged.

Still a little out of sorts, he attempted to get his bearings. He called out to no one in particular, "HELLO!" his voiced reached across the open sea air, "IS ANYONE HERE?!" He looked around and saw no one.

"CAPTAIN!" a voiced shouted from somewhere. Rich looked around frantically, wondering who was calling him. The voice called out again, "CAPTAIN! YOU CALL FER ME?!", but Rich saw no one. He quickly realized that someone was calling him 'captain', which should have seemed odd; it wasn't odd though, it was normal. That's who he was, The Captain.

"RRRRRIIIIIINNNNNNGGGGG!!!!!!!" the roaring screech of an alarm jolted Rich's heart into hyper-drive, and he sprung out of bed. He grabbed the noisy culprit and quickly turned off his cell phone alarm. It had been a dream. Of course it had been a dream, but wow! It seemed so realistic. Rich hadn't had a realistic dream like that in such a long time. In fact, it had been so long that he couldn't even remember the last one that was so real. Did he ever have such a dream as this?

As he thought back to the details of his dream, he realized that those details did not escape him. He kept waiting for the inevitable brain dump that occurs whenever someone tries to recall their dream, but Rich remembered the specifics vividly. He remembered the smell in the air, the details of the ship's wood railing, the sound of the ocean, and even the voice that answered his call. He remembered being called captain. He remembered feeling as if he was home.

Six

After going over the dream in his head repeatedly, Rich finally accepted that it was unusual and move on. He had to figure out what to do with the treasure; how would this be converted into wealth? Rich hurried through his morning routine of pouring a bowl of cereal and nearly expired milk and sat behind his computer. As he stuffed his mouth full of Raisin Bran with his right hand, Rich began typing into a search engine, "How to sell old treas—". But then something stopped him. *"What if someone can see what I've been searching?"*, he thought.

He became paranoid that he was under some kind of surveillance and that whatever he searches will lead the cops right to his door. But wait, wasn't this a little far-fetched? No one even knew about any treasure. When Rich finally sold it all, and suddenly become wealthy beyond anyone's imagination, wouldn't the questions come then? How would he explain what happened without revealing that he took treasure? But now he wondered about the legalities of claiming such a treasure. After all, finders keepers, right? Shouldn't he be able to keep the property he found, which had clearly been abandoned for centuries? But this internal conversation he was having with himself wasn't very reassuring.

Rich decided he'd have to go somewhere else and use another computer to search for the answers to these many questions. He grabbed a couple of the old coins and put them in his pocket. He was rather fond of his newly acquired coins and wanted to keep some on him so he could admire them throughout the day. Rich closed the door of the chest after taking one last look at his new, wonderful treasure. He slapped a lock on the latch. It was a cheap 'master lock' he had used a couple of times at the gym.

Grabbing his keys, he hurried out the door, hopped in his truck and headed towards the library. Rich looked around at the other drivers on the road and pondered how they'd perceive him had they known how incredibly rich he was. "*Ha, if they only knew*", he thought. He looked at the nicer cars in other lanes and imagined how nice his new car would be soon enough. A strange feeling of envy began creeping into his thoughts. He wanted what they had. He wanted that expensive-looking BMW passing him in the left lane.

As the traffic light turned red, Rich crept up next to the beautiful car. As he slowed to a stop, he stared at it; at the driver. The envy was overwhelming now, and he imagined himself getting out of his truck and walking over to the driver's side of the BMW. He imagined knocking on the window as the driver looked up at him, partly in fear, and partly in anger. As the driver rolled his window down, Rich would say in a low whisper, "*I'll be taking it from here*". Was this really happening? Was Rich actually standing outside of the car, ready to do something this insane?

HOOOONK!! The car behind him was lying on the horn as Rich jolted from the daydream and back to reality. The BMW was no longer next to him. The daydream was not only vivid and realistic, but it could very well have happened if Rich pondered any longer. He was feeling these desires, these overwhelming cravings to take what he wanted from anyone and everyone. But he didn't need to. He would soon be wealthier than anyone in this crappy little town.

Finally, having reached the library, Rich sat at a computer away from everyone, and began his search. "Value of pirate treasure", he typed into the search engine. Pages upon pages of "treasure" for sale. From small replicas to genuine relics dating back to the 1700s. The older coins were worn and faded, and come to think of it, looked nothing like the ones he had at home. His treasure was somehow shiny, clean, and not very old looking. It must have been preserved somehow in the cave.

He pondered for a while on how the coins could have been so well preserved, but that line of thinking quickly turned greedy. This meant that the treasure would be worth much more than he had originally thought. Forget about how impossible that kind of preservation would have been. Centuries underground with the salt air working into every crack and crevice inside the cave. But he hadn't considered this. Rich searched page after page, reading here and there about this treasure and that. There was something that all of these pages had in common. Pirates.

The information was vague at best. Rich needed to turn this treasure into cash. He wanted to get to the point where his old life; the one where he was invisible; the one where he had no future; was over. Now he has a future. He would be rich beyond his wildest dreams. He would be more powerful than he had ever imagined. Power and wealth. How did this happen? Why was he the 'chosen one'?

Rich spent the next few hours searching site after site, finding useful information about the laws and regulations on finding things of value. As the day progressed, he felt the greed creeping back into his mind. This time it came with something else. This time he began to feel confident, and though he wasn't really noticing these feelings building, he grew happier because of them. The edges of his mouth began to bend upward into a sort of wicked smirk. It wasn't quite a full smile, but he felt good. Really good. He had to get out of that library. He had to go find some fun.

Night was quickly approaching and Rich felt like taking a break from his boring research and doing something fun. He hopped in his car and drove down the road toward what few bars sat in this small town; he grew irritated. Disgruntled about the fact that he's still stuck in Swansboro, North Carolina. His disgust made its way to audible sounds as he sucked his teeth and spit short insults out at himself. "Worthless. You are freaking pathetic", he grunted, "get out of this shit town and do something!", his tormenting tone forcing an internal struggle. "*Why not?*", he thought. "*Why couldn't I just shoot down to Wilmington for some fun?*". But he knew that he had to work tomorrow, so he had better be safe and stay in the area. What if he didn't wake up on time tomorrow? "*Bitch!*", he yelled at himself, "*don't be a little bitch! Go have fun!*". The irrationality of the thought began to fade, and it started to make sense.

He could do whatever he wanted to do, and right now he wanted to go to a club. Rich pressed the gas peddle down a little harder and purposely missed the turn that would've taken him home. He headed down Highway 17 South toward Wilmington, North Carolina. Wilmington was a much more happening city than Swansboro, and Rich always had fun there. Well, he hadn't really frequented the place, but that's where everyone went on the weekends to have fun; that, or Myrtle Beach, South Carolina, which was about a two-and-a-half hour drive.

As he cruised down the road, his mind drifted from thought to thought, not landing on any thought in particular, until he thought of her. A gorgeous woman he had known for what seemed like an eternity. Her long black hair dancing with the night wind as the sea sang its familiar song. She was wearing a long black dress that waved slowly in the salt air. Her eyes were uncharacteristically blue for her light brown skin tone. She was simply breathtaking. But who was she?

Rich hadn't known her for an eternity. In fact, he hadn't known her at all. But why was she so familiar? Did he ever meet this person? He thought of her again; her thin lips perfectly encased her hypnotic smile. She was the love of his life. But she only existed in Rich's mind.

These thoughts persisted for the next 20 or 30 minutes. Who is she? Where did he know her from? Where could he find her? Then Rich noticed a rugged little bar on the side of the road. He was only about 3/4 of the way to Wilmington, but he thought, "*What the hell? This one'll do*".

The bar smelled like a gym locker room with a hint of must. The house sound system was playing some modern rock song that sounded like every other modern rock song on the radio at the time. Rich looked around and took in the scene. A few of the patrons glared at him, wondering what the hell he was doing at their bar. But Rich didn't care. He was tired of worrying about what people thought. He was tired of having to act a certain way. Go to work, go home, go to bed. Day after day, the same routine. Well, he didn't care now.

As Rich approached the bar, his mouth began to water as he imagined that first sip of rum. Only he didn't drink rum. He actually didn't drink alcohol much at all. Usually Rich would have a few beers when he hung out with Jay and Carol, but that was very infrequent. But tonight was different. Rich knew the taste of rum somehow and was craving it. He looked at the wall behind the bartender; the shelves lined with all varieties of liquor. Rich spotted a few bottles of various brands of spiced rum and decided on one.

"How about some of your finest rum?", he said as he remembered how unbelievably rich he was now. He could afford the good stuff.

"Finest?" asked the bartender, curious as to just what in the hell that meant. Rum was rum, as far as he could tell. You either drank regular rum or spiced rum. "Bacardi or Captain Morgan?" he asked, as those seemed to be the only brands to choose from. Rich had of course never had either, and should have been indifferent in his preference.

"Captain Morgan, eh?" Rich said skeptically, "What ship did he ever captain?" Rich chuckled as if he had just told a clever joke, but the bartender was rather unamused.

"So, Captain?" asked the bartender as he reached for a glass. "You want it straight, or with coke and ice?" he asked as if he were put out by having to perform his occupational duties.

"Straight, no ice" Rich said, as if the very question were an insult to his masculinity. The bartender poured, and Rich took in the room. He had a slight smirk on his face, but it was somewhat sinister, as if he were on the lookout for trouble.

The bartender handed Rich his glass of rum in exchange for the cash Rich had laid on the bar. Rich held the glass up to his nose and took in the aroma of the sweet and sour stench of the spiced rum. His mouth watering a little more as he anticipated the flavor of his favorite beverage. He took an initial swig of the rum and as the liquor ran across his tongue and down his throat; he was refreshed. But this was new to him.

He couldn't remember ever having rum before, but this feeling was different. As if he remembered the taste of rum, but he didn't remember it ever tasting so good.

Rich was delighted to have been reacquainted with his favorite beverage, even though he had never had it. He quickly finished his entire glass and asked for another. The bartender half rolled his eyes as if he had seen this kind of 'showboat drinking' many times before. But he poured the drink, and Rich savored each swig of his rum. He kept this up until he had had about 3 and a half glasses. It looked as if the bartender was going to cut him off just because of how quickly he drank the glasses.

Rich turned around on his stool and faced the room of bar goers. He took large gulps of the rum at a time and felt as if he were the most important person in the whole place. He had an arrogant look on his face while he stared down every man who was glancing his way. He was daring them as if he wanted some confrontation. This was completely out of character for Rich, as he was usually the timid guy who would never want to bother anyone or cause any sort of conflict.

A group of rowdy meat eaters were crowded around a pool table trash talking. They were making fun of each other and a few of the patrons around the establishment. Their attention was turned to Rich because Rich seemed to be standing there like some kind of bad ass who wanted some trouble. "Look at this freaking guy," one of the men said, "He thinks he's hot shit, doesn't he?" They all chuckled at this, but their laughter only drew rich's attention.

Rich started walking over to the men at the pool table. He held his glass of rum in his right hand with arm extended straight downward, walking confidently toward the group of misfits. "Now this sure seems to be quite the jolly conversation," Rich said in a strange accent, not his own. He spoke with a sort of deep growl with a hint of maybe an Irish or Scottish accent, but he didn't know if he had meant to talk that way.

"What?" said the one who appeared to be the leader of the band of thugs. "Son, who the hell you talkin' too?" he said, this time with a much angrier tone. The man and his friends walked toward rich as a group.

"Calm yourself, sonny, I meant nuthin' of it", Rich couldn't believe what he was saying. "What say we have a round of drinks and you can tell some of your hilarious knee-slappers?" Now he must have been completely losing his mind. He was egging these guys on. It became clear that his sarcasm was offending them when their faces all went from looks of confusion to looks of irritation. Rich took a long drink of his rum.

"Dude, what is your deal?" asked one of the men, wondering why Rich wanted to receive an ass whooping.

"Deal? I have no deal," Rich countered, "what sort of deal would you be looking for?"

"What?!" said the leader of the group. Each of the men was ready to pounce on Rich and beat the crap out of him, but part of them was intrigued by Rich's indifferent nature. They wanted to know what he was getting at.

"I'll tell you what, boys. I'll make you a deal," Rich was wondering where he was going with this, as if he had lost total control of his own ability to speak. Maybe the alcohol had rid him of his inhibitions. "Each one of you can profit from this deal," he continued. "I'll take some money out of my pocket and I'll place it on the table behind you," Rich began to fear what he was about to say, but he wanted so badly to say it. "And then I'll go to each of your houses and show your mothers what they've been missing out on for all these years." The entire bar fell silent.

Before Rich could think or react in any way, a fist came full force through air and popped him right on the mouth — 'POP!' He didn't fall, but the blow caused him to back up a few steps. Rich threw his glass of rum on the ground, shattering it to pieces. He threw up both fists, but before he could swing, the rest of the men were throwing punches of their own. Punches were landing all over Rich's body, and all he could do is curl into a ball and absorb them. The men pummeled him, and he fell to the ground. Rich heard glass breaking here and there, people trying to intervene and stop the 'fight'. He heard more fights breaking out around him. He tried hard to gain some footing and get up, but he was now underneath a dog-pile. This went on for a few minutes until the bartender yelled, "Cut the shit right now or I'm calling the cops!"

Most of the fights died down, but Rich was still on the ground after having been beaten all over. The bartender and a few other men in the bar finally stepped in and got the four men off of Rich.

"Is that all you got, lads?" Rich teased, but he was coughing and limping slightly. Clearly, he was not the victor. But the bartender shuffled the men out before the fight could go on. It appeared to Rich that the men were friends with the bartender, and the bartender told them to take a hike before the cops got there.

Rich followed suit and stumbled out to his car. He wasn't that bad off as far as beatings go, but the initial shock of it all had him limping slightly. Slightly intoxicated, he hopped into the car and headed further south. Up ahead, he spotted another dive bar and decided to try his luck here.

Rich walked in the door and ordered some rum. He spent the next few hours drinking and thinking little about the fact that he had to work tomorrow, and then his mind went back to her. The woman with the piercing blue eyes and long black hair. Who was she?

At around midnight Rich stumbled back to his car, far too drunk to drive. He jumped in the driver's seat and headed for home. Still somewhat coherent and, as far as he was concerned, sober enough, he began reflecting on the night's events. Where did this strange persona come from? He felt as if he spoke like someone else and had the blind courage of someone else. For now, he figured it was the alcohol driving his actions, and that it was no big deal. He had fun tonight.

Seven

The next morning, when the excruciatingly painful throbbing in his brain could no longer be ignored, Rich awoke. What had he done? He couldn't remember ever being this hung-over in his life. That is, of course, because he rarely drank and never drank liquor at all. He had little to no recollection of last night's events from the time he left the library. He lay in bed wondering if he had made a fool of himself, or did anything regrettable, but that was almost a certainty given his current state. What if he had slept with some stranger? Though there wasn't a stranger present. How the hell did he get home last night? What time is it?!

Rich quickly looked at his watch and adjusted his blurred vision to focus on the time, which read, '10:23am'. "TEN TWENTY THREE?!" he shouted. Rich leapt out of bed and scrambled to get to the bathroom. "*I was supposed to be in at zero eight,*" he reminded himself, realizing of course that time would no longer be obtainable.

He quickly squirted toothpaste in the general area where he was holding his toothbrush. He got about a third of the toothpaste on the actual brush bristles, and he threw the toothbrush into his mouth, hitting his gums and letting out a muffled and nasally, "Aaaow!" He brushed forcefully for about nine seconds before spitting a large amount of spit, water, and toothpaste mixture at the mirror. Grabbing his electric razor, Rich hurried across the bedroom, picking up uniform items on his way to the front door.

As he opened the door, he remembered that he would probably need his cell phone, so he quickly turned around and ran back to his room. There, on the nightstand, laid his completely dead cell phone. Now he couldn't call in. They must've been calling him all morning. This was not going to turn out well for Rich. He wasn't the most liked individual at the station, so it wouldn't take much for him to lose his job.

Rich jumped in the car and started his way to the station, dressing himself while trying to shave and drive the car simultaneously. As he swerved from side to side and finally got most of his uniform on, he started going over his excuse in his head. This was after all the second time this week that he couldn't be reached. He was sure he would be suspended at the very least. He could not afford that right now, despite the amount of priceless treasure he had back at home.

Rich finally arrived at the station at 10:57am. He couldn't help but be a little impressed with the speed at which he had gotten ready and gotten to work, but there were much more important things to focus on at the moment. His parking job wasn't great; in fact, he parked about a foot over the line to the right of his car, and only halfway into the spot itself. He got out of the car and took off in a mad dash to the front door, as if the measly seconds he would save now would make all the difference in his eventual punishment.

He ran through the front door and darted down the hall, ignoring all the attempts his coworkers made at ridiculing him, and he reached his sergeant's desk. Sergeant Kyle Macon, the sergeant directly in charge of Rich and about three other officers, was about six months to retirement, and didn't have any fire left. He was indifferent to anything that took place within his team of officers because nothing from here on out would change the outcome of his eventual transition to the civilian world.

"Sergeant Macon!" he hadn't meant to say it so loudly, drawing more attention to the situation, "Officer Harris reporting as ordered." The sergeant looked up from his computer screen with an attempted expression of disapproval.

"Harris, what in the absolute shit is going on with you?" the sergeant asked. "Why haven't you been answering your phone?", he continued, "the captain is very upset about this". His monotone scolding was far from convincing, but Rich was still completely nervous about his inevitable ass chewing from the captain.

"Sergeant, my phone died... and that's my alarm... and I..." Rich searched his brain for what should have already been a well-formulated excuse, but what turned out to be verbal diarrhea. "I got home late because... I um..."

"Let me stop you there, Harris," Sergeant Macon interrupted, "I'm not the one you'll be explaining this to." He pointed toward the captain's office, signaling to Rich that he would have to face the big boss for this one; a fact that Rich had already figured.

Rich sighed and made his way to the captain's office, almost dragging his feet; his head hanging a little lower than usual. He hoped that somehow the captain received an important call that required his immediate attention elsewhere. Knowing that to be a complete stretch, Rich took one last breath as a 'free man', lifted himself and knocked a couple of times on the captain's door. 'KNOCK KNOCK KNOCK'

"Yep!" the captain yelled. This was his usual response to a knock on the door and in no way indicated a jovial state of mind. Rich opened the door and poked his head in.

"Sir, it's Officer Harris," said Rich.

"Get the hell in here, Harris," the captain growled in a very irritated tone, "and shut the door!" As Rich walked into the captain's office and closed the door behind him, Captain Kelly started firing away as Rich made his way to the center of the captain's desk. "Well, I'm glad you decided to stop by, Harris. Did your work schedule interrupt something important?" The captain didn't give Rich a chance to answer any of his sarcastic questions or comments, he just kept them coming. "I'm trying to understand why an officer with two years in has the audacity to come in late right after getting in trouble for getting lost or whatever the hell it was you were doing the other night. Harris, maybe I wasn't clear enough when you and I spoke before. You are an officer of the North Carolina Wildlife Resource Commission...for now." That little addition at the end cut Rich deep. "Now I warned you the other day about this shit. Accountability!" The captain slammed his hand down hard on his desk, and Rich couldn't help but flinch. "Now I don't care what your excuse is this time. I don't want to know about your sick goldfish or you running out of gas. And another thing," he said, finally noticing Rich's appearance, "you look like shit! What the hell is going on with your uniform? Tuck your damn shirt in and tie your freaking shoes!"

Rich frantically tucked his shirt in and jumped to the ground to tie his shoes. The captain continued slinging insults and thoroughly counseling the young officer while Rich stood back up. Rich's mind drifted to this morning. He started wondering just what the hell happened last night. This was not him. He was not the guy who partied too hard and missed work. He would never in a million years drink rum. "*What about three hundred years,*" he thought. "*What? What the hell does that mean*". His thoughts were conflicting now, and seemed to be more of a conversation he was having with himself. But what did he mean, 'three hundred years'?

"WELL?!" the captain yelled at the top of his lungs. He was half ready to come across his desk and punch Rich in his already fat lip for not paying attention.

"Yes, sir!" Rich replied, completely oblivious to what the captain was asking. This was all he could think to say, he just said the first thing that came to his mind. 50/50 shot, he supposed.

"Ok then" said the captain. "You get your ass out there and do your damn job and do it right." Captain Kelly didn't pull any punches. He let Rich have it; if only Rich had known what the captain had said while Rich was daydreaming. Oh well, he just needed to count his blessings and get out of there.

Rich quickly got out of the captain's office and headed toward his desk. On the way over, he spotted Officer Bell headed right toward him. "*Great, this is all I need right now*", Rich thought.

"Well, look who decided to come to work today," Bell said, so the whole station could hear. "Must be nice to have your hours, Harris. You take a break on shift and don't answer calls, then you show up a few hours late today; boy, that just seems like a great schedule." Danny Bell was always a prick, but today he actually had ammunition, so you'd better believe he was going to use it.

Rich tried as hard as he could to ignore it, but that was no easy task when the entire station watched and waited for Rich's response. But the response that came was not what anyone, including Rich, expected.

"Thanks Dan, I was wondering when the cliché office douchebag would chime in with his clever and witty comments," Rich said. The entire group of eavesdroppers, along with Danny Bell himself, paused in disbelief.

What in the hell just happened? Rich just stood up to Officer Bell, the bully he feared. This had not been done before, to anyone's recollection.

"What did you say?" Said Bell in disbelief.

"Oh, I'm sorry Dan, were you that inspired by your mindless reciting of obvious events that you didn't hear me?" Where was this coming from? Rich didn't know what had come over him, but his fear of Officer Bell was gone. His confidence, despite his recent ass chewing from the captain, was at a new level.

Officer Bell didn't know what to say or do. While he was trying desperately to conjure up a response, his thought process was interrupted.

"I'll tell you what, Dan, you go ahead and stand here with that look of confusion and think of something else really clever to say, and let us all know when you're ready. I'm gonna go do some work. Since I'm all rested up from my time off."

You could hear a pin drop. The expressions on everyone's faces were priceless. Shocked smiles all around; most people wide mouthed as if to say, 'daaaaaaaaaaaaaaaamn'.

Rich walked to his desk, acknowledging none of his new fans, grabbed his jacket, and headed toward the door that lead to the docks.

Jay and Carol stood by Rich's desk as he passed, looking as happily surprised as everyone else, but they couldn't speak. They didn't know what to say.

No one dared laugh or clap, as was almost expected from the vibe in the room, but a few chuckles could be heard in the back. Officer Bell turned away from the crowd, pissed off to no end, and headed toward the restroom. That just happened to be the direction he turned. Now, to avoid further embarrassment, he would just head to the restroom and hope the crowd disseminated.

Rich walked up to his boat and started untying the dock lines. He was somewhat excited about what he had just done, but not as much as he should have been. It was as if it was natural — like he had always made such sarcastic comments to known bad asses; well, wannabe bad asses anyway.

As he cruised out of the no wake zone that surrounded the station docks, he had a grin on his face- the result of his recent victory. He could feel it. Things were turning around in his life. Despite the hiccups where he was scolded by his captain, Rich was becoming a new man- more confident, more open to doing fun things, more of something else too. He felt different, and not just because of the vast treasure he now had, but seriously different.

Rich reached into his pocket to take another look at one of the coins from the chest. It was beautiful. Its weight alone gave Rich the impression that it was definitely worth a lot of money. He loved it, this magical piece of gold, this shiny symbol of value, of worth, and he wanted more. Not just what he had in the pile at home...more, much, much more.

Eight

The next day was Rich's day off. It so happened that Carol and Jay had the day off too. The three of them had decided a couple weeks ago to go to the boat show in nearby Morehead City, but Rich forgot. He had much more important things to do today. He would take some jewelry from the treasure to some jewelers out of town. Greenville maybe, since that was about an hour and a half away. He couldn't risk anyone accusing him of stealing the jewelry and then following him home.

He sipped on his morning coffee and walked around his living room where he had spread the entirety of the treasure out so as to be able to view it all at once. He really loved this treasure. As he admired the beautiful luster of the various coins and jewelry, his cell phone began to ring. Rich looked down and saw Carol's name, but thought nothing of it and answered, "He Carol, what's up?"

"Where the hell are you, Rich?"

"I'm at the house, why, what's up?"

"Rich, you were supposed to meet me and Jay at his house 15 minutes ago. Did you forget?"

"No, no, I didn't. Well, I mean I kind of did, but," Rich scrambled for an excuse. He really had to get to Greenville and appraise some of his jewelry. "Something came up anyway, I can't make it today. Ya'll just shoot and I'll go next time."

"Are you serious? Rich, we've been planning to do this for weeks. We were gonna make a day of it; all the boats you could dream about, then lunch, then the mall, then dinner and a movie." Carol sounded a little more irritated than usual. "Rich, what is going on with you? You've been distant for the past few days, and no, you're blowing me and Jay off?"

"I'm not blowing you off, I just have to do something today and I haven't been able to because of work."

"What? What is so important you can't wait until Sunday or something?"

"Carol, I promise I will go next time."

"You know what? We're coming over." Carol hung up before Rich could protest.

"Carol, no!" Rich said, trying to convince her, but the other end way silent.

Rich looked around and began to panic a little. If they came over, they would see the treasure. They could turn him in. He could go to jail. As he pondered this, he wondered if he would in fact go to jail for finding treasure. He hadn't really done anything wrong. He found it, so now it belonged to him. But then he remembered the bodies. He couldn't very well justify having left human remains in a cave and not have alerted the authorities.

Rich grabbed his coat and stuffed a few rings and coins in his pocket. He figured he would have to change his plans to keep Carol and Jay from finding his treasure. He headed for the door so he could be outside before they arrived. The range was only a 5 minute drive. As he stepped outside, he saw Jay's truck rounding the corner to his street. Carol looked perturbed in the front seat, wondering what was wrong with her friend.

Rich waved and nodded as if to say, *'ok, ok, you win, I'll go'*. Jay pulled up the driveway and Carol rolled down her window.

"Where do you think you're going, stranger?" she said have joking, but legitimately curious.

"I'm coming, I'm coming. You're right," Rich said, seeming to realize the error of his ways. "I totally forgot, that's my fault. I will pay for lunch. How about that?" Rich said, trying to turn their attention away from his strange actions.

"Well, that sounds good to me," Jay said. He had little interest in the excuse. Jay didn't notice the difference in Rich's actions. He just figured

Rich had other stuff to do. He figured that Carol was a woman, so of course she would make more of the situation than was necessary.

As Rich hopped into the back seat and buckled his seat belt, Carol was about ready to jump out of her skin with excitement. "Are we seriously not going to talk about what happened yesterday?" she said. "What in the hell was that about?" Carol was acting like she had witnessed the showdown of a lifetime, and the underdog was now the favorite.

"What are you talking about?" Rich asked, as if he genuinely had no idea what she meant.

"You made Danny look like a wuss yesterday. You pulled his punk card in front of everyone. Are you worried he's gonna kick your ass now?"

"Danny is nothing more than a bully. He has nothing better to do than feed on the insecurities of everyone around him, but he's really just trying to make up for his own insecurities. Think about it; he has no friends, and we all have each other. He needs his ass kicked is what he needs." These were ballsy words for Rich. Rich, who was the most timid officer in the department. Jay and Carol both listened in disbelief. They had known Rich for years, and they knew he had no backbone. They loved their friend anyway because he was kind. But this was not Rich talking, of that they were certain.

"Are you kidding me, man?" Jay said. "Danny is twice your size and has actually been in a fight. You wouldn't stand a chance. Besides, since when do you stand up for yourself? I mean no offense, man, I'm glad you did, but since when?"

"Since now, Jay, my boy, since now," Rich said, in a slightly different accent. Carol figured the accent was a joke to go along with his insane idea that he could take on Danny Bell.

"Well, you need to be careful," said Carol, "He is definitely gonna want to retaliate now. You made him look like a punk in front of everyone, and he is not going to let that slide."

"You let me worry about ole' Danny boy. He'll be staying out of my way. Of that, you can be sure." Rich's phony accent was no longer funny. Carol wondered if Rich was having some kind of nervous breakdown, but she shrugged it off as they made their way to the boat show.

As they pulled up to the parking area, they saw boats in the distance. Rich got excited about the possibility of seeing the Leopard 44. "You guys think they'll have a Leopard this year?" he asked. His childlike, joyful imagination took hold, and he became more excited about the possibility of seeing such a beautiful boat.

"They have just about everything here," Jay said. "It's the best show, man, I love this thing." He couldn't contain his excitement. None of them were ever in the market for a new boat, but it sure was fun to dream.

Carol liked the yachts the best. She had her eye set on a double decker with tinted windows. She knew little to nothing about boats, but she could see herself laying out on the bow of her dream boat, anchored in a bay in Hawaii, or some exotic location where the water was a beautiful sea green. Jay didn't have a preference, as long as you could fish from it. For someone who spent his days on the water in a small skiff, Jay didn't see there being much joy in boating for fun.

"Man, check out that center console," Jay said, walking quickly like an excited child at the fair. Apparently he did like boats, at least a little. Maybe he could see himself owning one of these after all. "Man, that thing's got to be like a hundred grand or so."

"Damn Jay, settle down, they're not going anywhere," Rich said. Rich was pretty excited too, but he tried to contain his reaction. He had been to a lot of boat shows, but he felt different this time. Was it the fact that he could probably afford almost any boat out here now? "Hey, I bet you could buy it if you took out a second mortgage." The three of them chuckled at the thought.

They walked along the docks, glancing at each vessel and stopping here and there. They were daydreaming at every stop. They each imagined themselves cruising down the Intracoastal on the most glamorous ones.

As they walked along and gawked at the boats, Rich noticed it. About 4 boats ahead on the right. There it is, the Leopard 44. He picked up his pace and headed right toward it.

"Hey wait up," Carol said, taken by surprise. "Settle down, we'll get there", but Rich was on a mission. He had to see it up close. So Carol and Jay took faster steps to keep up with Rich.

"Jeeze, you'd think he was gonna buy one or something," Jay said.

"Yeah, right? Didn't he say they cost like half a million bucks or something?" said Carol.

"Who knows? Whatever it costs, he sure as hell can't afford it."

Rich walked up to the gangplank and started walking right up. He barged right in front of someone who was waiting to go aboard. "Hey watch it man," said the bystander.

Rich didn't even acknowledge his presence. Carol and Jay saw this, and thought it odd for Rich, who was usually very courteous. "Sorry sir," said Carol, on Rich's behalf. "He's just really excited."

As Rich boarded the boat, he began excitedly inspecting it. He grabbed everything he could get his hands on. He tugged on ropes and rubbed his hand down the fiberglass side.

"Some boat, eh, buddy?" A man said. He appeared to either own it, or was a salesman working the show. Rich ignored him and really looked hard at the craftsmanship. "You in the market?" the man asked, half sarcastically.

"Rich, this man is talking to you," Carol said. But Rich continued ignoring everyone. He was in his own world; entranced by the beauty of such a fine vessel. He slid his fingers across a wooden rail, admiring how smooth the surface was. He was oblivious to the world around him. Carol was embarrassed and irritated at this, so she finally yelled, "RICH!"

Rich was jolted back to reality. "What?" he said with a dazed look on his face. He realized then that everyone was looking at him, and that he had completely checked out for a few minutes.

"Rich, what is the matter with you," Carol asked. "First you run someone over coming up the ramp, and now this man has been asking you questions, and you completely ignored him. What has gotten in to you?"

"Sorry, I must've been daydreaming," he said.

"Man, I've seen you daydream," Jay said, "and that was different. You were like another person. You even look different, like the way you move and stuff. It's really weird."

"Ok, I said sorry! Are we all done giving me shit now?" Rich said, a little louder than necessary. He couldn't help himself. He was irritated. More irritated than he had been in a long time. Carol and Jay looked at him in disbelief. Each has a surprised expression on their face. "You know what that was uncalled for," Rich said, "I haven't been feeling well. You two didn't do anything wrong, it's my fault. I'm sorry," he said, and then faced the man selling the boat, "Sir, I'm really sorry about that. Totally got lost for a minute there. This really is a beautiful boat. I would love to come check it out again, I'm just... I'm sorry about that." Rich walked toward the ramp. Carol and Jay still gazing in disbelief. "Guys, I'll be in the truck," he said as he walked passed. "Keep looking, I just have to take a breather."

"Rich..." Carol said, trying to stop him. She wanted to be there for him, but she had no idea what was going on. This wasn't like him. This wasn't Rich. She turned to Jay and said, "What is going on? What is with him?"

"That was totally uncalled for," Jay said. "He flipped out, man. He was in another world, and I'm telling you that was not him. He was moving differently, and when he was yelling, he didn't sound like himself. I mean it, Carol, something's wrong."

"What do we do? Who can we talk to?"

"Who knows, Captain maybe?"

"You think that would get him into more trouble than he is already in?" Carol asked. "I don't want to make things harder for him, especially if he is having some kind of breakdown."

"It might actually help explain why he's been absent lately," Jay said, "like maybe the captain can get him some help or talk to him. I don't know, maybe not."

The two of them contemplated solutions for a few more minutes and then decided it best that they just head home. Rich was waiting at the truck as they approached. None of them said a word. They all got in the truck and took a silent trip home.

Nine

The familiar sounds of the ocean waves smashed against the side of the ship. The smell in the air again reminded him of the hundreds of days and nights he had spent at sea. He walked toward the bow of the ship and he heard the same yell as before, "Captain!" a voice called out. Rich looked around and didn't see anyone.

He called back, "Who's there? Show yer self." Rich's accent grew more like the one he had been adopting lately. His new persona that came with his new confidence had an accent, he supposed.

A man came out from behind a door. His hair was gray and wet-sweaty from working in the sun. His clothes looked like something out of a movie. They were rags; tattered and torn- probably his only clothes. His feet were bare and blackened from the dirt on the deck. He had a large earring in one ear and a small scar on his left cheek. "Captain, where did you go?" the man said. "We ain't seen you around? Thought you left us."

Rich realized that the man was talking to him, as if Rich were this captain. He looked at the man, and without thinking he said, "Don't you be worrying about yer captain, Sammy my boy," Rich said, "I was lost for a while, but this young man is gonna help me find my way home." Rich didn't know what he was saying. The words leaving his own mouth were not his own, but he knew the man, and he knew he was the captain. He looked around his ship... his ship. "Sir, can you tell me where we are?" Rich said as himself.

"Sir? Captain, somethin' wrong? What do you mean, where are we?" The man was confused about his captain's line of questioning. "Captain, your face is startin' to look a little strange; like yer not yer self. Captain, yer not yer self."

Just then Rich felt a vibration that he couldn't identify. It got more intense the second time. The third time it was accompanied by a "RRRRRRRIIIIIIIIIINNNNNNGGGGGG" Rich jumped out of bed and hit his alarm clock. His heart was racing. This was a lucid dream. It was realistic, like the last one. He was on an enormous ship at sea and was the captain of the ship. The man, Sammy, was still very clear in Rich's mind. How could these dreams be so clear? And what did they mean? Rich wondered if there was a correlation between the dreams and the treasure. The more he thought about it, he began to wonder if his recent behavior was related to the treasure in some way. Maybe he was just becoming more confident because he knew he would soon be rich beyond his wildest dreams. And the pirate ship, which is what he assumed he was dreaming about, had to be a subconscious thought from the human remains he found. Those had to be pirates based on their clothes and the treasure in the cave. Come to think of it, their clothes resembled Sammy's. Rich was sure this was explanation enough for everything.

He climbed out of bed and began his morning routine to get ready for work. He added a morning salutation to the treasure in his routine and even rubbed on a few items in his new collection for good luck.

Across town at the station, Carol and Jay were already at work. "I really think we need to talk to the captain, Carol," Jay said.

"Do we even know that there is something wrong? Maybe he's just been under a lot of stress," said Carol.

"You saw him yesterday with Danny, did that seem like our boy Rich?"

"And then he tried to blow us off, which he has never done before."

"Yeah," said Jay, "and what about his temper at the boat show?"

As they were talking it over, Officer Will Stengele was walking by. Stengele was a tall skinny odd fellow who had been at the station for about a year longer than Rich. He was usually the guy who tried to stir up trouble whenever possible. "Hey what happened with Harris yesterday," Stengele said. "That dude finally let Bell have it." He held up his pinky and index fingers in sort of a 'rock on' symbol, "that was awesome, man."

"Yeah," Jay said, trying to think of something to say without bringing negative attention to Rich. "He sure did," was all he could think to say.

"I'll tell you what though," Stengele said, "Bell was pretty pissed. He's been talking about it a lot. Well, not exactly about it, but about Harris. Says Harris is just hiding behind the uniform. Bell thinks Harris is talking a big game cause he thinks Bell won't do anything, cause he don't want to get suspended or something."

"I think we should all just let it go man," Jay said, "Officer Harris has had some things going on in his life, and he's just stressed out." Jay was of course making this up as he had no idea what was going on with Rich. He knew Rich was acting strangely, but wasn't sure of the cause.

"Seriously," said Carol, "I think we're make a much bigger deal than it needs to be. This isn't high school, Stengele. Stop instigating." Carol had Rich's back, like any good friend would do in a similar situation.

"Hey, I'm just sayin' what I heard," said Stengele, "I ain't trying to start anything. Ya'll might want to let Harris know is all." Stengele walked away and went on about his business. He figured they could warn Rich or not, it wasn't his concern.

"Jesus, now what?"

"I don't know," Carol said, "I guess we could talk to Bell." Carol thought about this long enough to realize it was a terrible idea. "But he's a Neanderthal, so that won't do anything. What about Sergeant Macon, or maybe you were right, maybe we talk to the captain?"

"I don't think it would hurt. I mean, the captain might suspend him. Then what? Do we really want to be responsible for that?"

"If that's what it takes to save him from Bell, then maybe. Maybe Captain Kelly is smart enough and responsible enough to actually help Rich," Carol said. "Maybe he will get him help, counseling or something."

The two decided it was best to involve their top leadership and inform Captain Kelly of Rich's recent behavior. They walked across the station, discussing what they would say and who would say what, until they arrived in front of the captain's door.

"Ok, go ahead," Carol said, looking nervously at Jay.

"Go ahead?" Jay said, "Why me? This was your idea. I'm not even sure we should."

"Ugh, fine," Carol said. She knocked on the door and waited for the captain's inevitable and familiar reply.

"Yep!" the captain yelled. There was a very misleading cheerfulness to this answer that led many officers to feeling safe in requesting the boss's time.

Carol opened the door, and leaned in, "Sir, Officers Massey and Luther. We have something we need to discuss with you, sir." She was a confident officer who had done a pretty good job of keeping up with the male officers at the station since she joined. She, Jay, and Rich had all graduated Basic Law Enforcement Training together and joined at the same time a couple years ago. Carol and jay seemed to have more of a knack for this line of work than Rich.

"What is it Massey?" the captain said, "come in."

"Sir, we'd like to talk to you about Officer Harris," she said. Before she could explain her concerns, the captain interrupted.

"Harris?" he said. "He's on his last damn warning. He's about to find himself without a job. What is it this time? If he's done something else, I mean any damn thing else, he's gone." Carol and Jay listened and waited patiently for their chance to talk, but the captain had more to say. "He isn't even that good any damn way. The guy is afraid of his own shadow, he can't even ta—"

"Sir, that's just it," Carol said, completely oblivious to the fact that she just cut the captain off. He stared at her in disbelief while she continued, "he usually *is* afraid of everything and everyone. But something has happened. Ever since that night he came back late," she said as a puzzled look came over her and she looked at Jay.

"Yeah," said Jay. "It has been since then, sir. I don't know something happened. He is acting really strange. He isn't himself. He isn't afraid of anything, really. He stood up to Officer Bell and everything."

"What the hell are you two talking about," said Captain Kelly.

"Sir, he's become a different person," said Carol, "he talks funny, he told Bell off worse than anyone else would ever dare, and he even went off on me and Officer Luther over absolutely nothing." Seriously concerned for her friend, Carol looked at the captain and the captain hadn't seen her this upset before.

"Sir," said Jay, "this isn't like him. He's not late. Ever. You know Ri-, Officer Harris, sir. He might be timid, but he shows up way too early for every shift. He certainly doesn't fail to report in during a shift, and he most certainly doesn't even raise his voice to us, his friends."

"Ok, so what do you want me to do?" the captain said. "What's his problem? Does he have a family? Something wrong at home?" The captain may have been a hardass, but he genuinely cared about his officers no matter how tough he acted.

"We think he's having some kind of breakdown," Carol said. "We think he might be extremely stressed out or something, and he has no other way of dealing with it than acting out like this. I don't know, sir, but he needs help. Maybe counseling or something."

There was of course a limit to just how much the captain cared. "Counseling!" he said. "You think I'm gonna pay for counseling? You think there's money in the budget for counseling? Look at the equipment you all use. You think we got counseling money? We ain't even got boat cleaning money, how we paying for counseling?" This idea was outrageous to the captain. The way they dealt with their issues in his day was by ignoring them.

"Sir, there has to be something we can do," said Carol, "Harris is our friend, and a part of this station."

"Ok, I'll tell you what," the captain said, "he's gonna get some help. He's gonna take some time off. Harris is going on administrative leave."

"What?" Carol and Jay both said, forgetting who they were talking to.

"Sir, please don't do this," Carol said.

"I can't have Harris having some kind of mental episode on the job. He isn't acting right, he's been showing up late, he's telling off guys like Bell, and even his own friends, he's on leave. That's that. You two are dismissed."

"But sir," Carol said.

"Dismissed!"

Carol and Jay looked at each other in shock and confusion. They came to attention as best they could and faced the door. As they walked out Carol gave the captain one last look as if to say, '*you just can't do this to him*', but it fell flat as the captain was already looking down at some paperwork on his desk.

What had they done? They had gone into the captain's office with nothing but concern for their friend, and they ended up getting him suspended. That's what administrative leave really meant. Rich was suspended because of them. Because they meddled in something that was none of their business. This would not go over well. How would they tell him? The captain would surely handle that part, but how would they tell him it was because of them?

Ten

Rich had received the news of his suspension that morning via a phone call from the captain. He didn't react on the phone, he just sort of nodded and said '*yes sir*' a lot, and a couple times said, '*I understand, sir*'. This wasn't a big deal in Rich's mind for some reason. He didn't care. He was glad.

"*Who the hell are they anyway*," he thought. "*I don't need that job. I'm rich. I have my treasure. I have it. It's mine.*" He began to get angry the longer he thought about it, though. Why now? Why didn't the captain just suspend him when he was late? Someone else must have done this. He thought for a minute that it was probably Danny Bell, but decided to wait and find out for sure who he had to thank for this.

Rich wasn't interested in his usual morning routine. He didn't shave and didn't even brush his teeth. All that mattered was the treasure. He wanted to take that trip to Greenville, now that he had the time, and see about selling the treasure little by little. If he could find multiple buyers and sell little by little, there would be less of a chance that someone would find out about his great secret.

Rich reached into the pockets of the pants he had been wearing since the day before, and he pulled out that beautiful coin. How wonderfully magnificent the shine was. He couldn't believe how beautiful all the stuff was. How could he even part with it? This thought had come and gone over the past few days. He wondered if he would even be able to sell any of it. But that was a ridiculous thought since he couldn't be rich until he sold it.

He thought about the woman again as he grabbed his truck keys. He grabbed a small bag he had set aside, filled with various coins and jewelry, and headed toward the door. She was on his mind more and more lately, and he didn't even know who she was. She was beautiful, and he felt like he loved her. Rich wasn't sure if it was something like the dreams he had been having where he was picking up subliminal things throughout the day and dreaming of them at night. Maybe she was someone he had seen somewhere in a movie or a magazine.

He jumped in the truck and started the drive to Greenville, unfazed by his recent suspension. For now, he wouldn't investigate who would pay for getting him suspended. He almost couldn't believe he was actually thinking of retaliating against someone, but he knew it had to be done. And there she was again, the woman in black.

Her face became more defined in his mind each time he thought of her. He realized now that she was Native American. Rich wondered if he would ever meet this woman. He was certain he knew her. And just as vividly as remembering the name of a former schoolteacher, Rich remembered her name- Imala. That was it; he knew it. She was so familiar and so beautiful. He began to say her name in his head, "*Imala*". Then he said it out loud, "Imala". It rolled off his tongue with that deep accent he had used in the bar. Rich wondered why he had reverted back to that accent, but it felt almost more natural than his own normal voice.

He drove on, thinking of her and of his treasure. He thought about his new life, and his new boat. He imagined not having to answer to assholes like Captain Kelly or Sergeant Macon, and he would no longer have to tolerate cavemen like Danny Bell. He wondered if there was room in his new life for Jay or Carol. The thought of them not being a part of his new life didn't bother him. That was strange because before the treasure came along, they were his only friends, and now he almost cared more about the treasure. In fact, that's all he was able to think about; that and Imala.

As he thought of her, he imagined being with her. He thought about what he would say. He wondered what she sounded like, but as he wondered, he could almost hear her calling out to him. "*Is this a dream of some kind*?", Rich thought, "*Why does she seem so real*?" This daydream Rich seemed to be having became more and more real as he thought of the woman, Imala. She looked at him and knew him. Rich drove further down the road, catching himself not paying attention, and occasionally swerving to correct his driving. In his imagination, the woman called out to him. She whispered, but Rich couldn't understand what she was saying.

As Rich listened harder and harder, he began to think that this was a vision of some kind rather than a simple daydream. As he thought of all the possibilities, he noticed that he had veered into oncoming traffic. A car horn blasted at Rich's truck while he did all he could to swerve back into his lane. At 70 miles per hour he was about to hit the other car, head on, when they each turned sharply to their respective right, missing each other by inches. Rich was gripping the steering wheel hard and his heart pounded. Rich was shaken and excited. He had almost run head on into that car because of daydreaming. But rather than fear, Rich was excited. He enjoyed the thrill.

As he approached Greenville and wondered how he would part with his treasure, Rich thought about delaying selling any of it. What if he got caught somehow and wasn't supposed to have the treasure? He pondered this for a while and began mumbling in the accent, "Greenville... Greenville...", he mumbled. "What'll they pay me?", he asked himself, "who'll find out?" He became more and more paranoid. He even started to think his suspension may have had something to do with his finding the treasure. "How could they know?", he asked himself. "Who the hell saw me?", he said with a scowl on his face. "They ain't gettin' my prize. They can sure as hell try, but they ain't getting' it," he said.

Rich looked and talked less like himself and more like the person he was in his recent dreams. He was angry. He stewed over his paranoia and became livid. "Aaaahh!!!! The damn fools'll never get my prize!", he said as he jerked the wheel to the left, sharply making a U turn and heading back in the opposite direction. He pressed harder on the accelerator and reached into his pocket for the coin. He rubbed the coin and stared angrily at the road ahead. Rich felt a strange comfort in holding the coin. He twirled it across the tops of his knuckles, back and forth, unsure of where he ever learned how to do that. Then he began to whistle an old tune he had known from long ago. His anger subsided slightly when he thought about Imala.

Rich drove and thought; wondered and daydreamed; all the way back to Swansboro. On the drive back to his house, Rich decided that he would go out on his boat to clear his head. He felt an overwhelming desire to be out on the water. His inevitable confrontation with everyone at work could wait. He figured that now he had some time to blow off some steam, so why not smell some sea air? He was delighted that he could get his boat to the water so quickly, and just a few minutes after arriving back at the house, he was backing his boat down the ramp at his favorite boat drop.

He squinted his eyes and smiled as he headed out toward the ocean inlet. As he puttered down the channel toward the inlet, Rich noticed the nice houses that lined the waterway. He envied the bigger boats and the luxurious mansions. As he imagined himself living in one of those beautiful castles, he became jealous of the people who owned them. Who were they, after all? What did they have that he didn't have? Most importantly, why didn't he have it? Rich's rage grew as he began to think of how he would acquire the things he wanted. He stewed about these things until he reached the ocean inlet.

There she is- the sea. Rich's boat couldn't quite handle the ocean due to its size, but he always liked to float around near the inlet. He cut the engine and took in the site and smell. He leaned back in his seat and relaxed. The seagulls were singing and the sound of the water filled the background as Rich closed his eyes. He lay there as the boat rocked side to side, taking in the majesty of the ocean an air around him.

He became so relaxed that he started to doze off. Rich decided he had nowhere to be and nothing to do, so it didn't matter if he took a quick nap out on the beautiful water. The sound of the water against the boat was hypnotizing. The smell of the sea air was intoxicating. This was where he wanted to be.

"Billy", the familiar voice of a woman called out to him. Rich was slightly disoriented, but somehow, he knew that the woman was talking to him and he smiled. The thought that he must be dreaming never crossed his mind; he just felt at ease. He opened his eyes and found himself in a different place. He wasn't concerned or startled, but at peace. He recognized his surroundings and thought nothing of it. This was not where he was just minutes ago, but it was familiar. He found himself sitting in a chair on the deck of a ship. "Billy", she said again. Then he saw her. It was her; it was Imala.

"What is this?", Rich asked, "where are we?", but he began to realize the answer. He knew this ship. He knew where he was. "This is my ship", he said as he looked around like an amnesia patient regaining lost memory. Imala nodded and smiled as if she were trying to help him remember. Rich looked at her again. He knew her. He loved her. "Imala, I remember you", he said. He wasn't completely sure what was happening to him, but it was coming back.

"Billy", she said again. Rich wondered for a moment why she continued to call him that name, but just as he remembered her, he began to remember it all. Memories flooded into his head. A feeling of new freedom washed over him as he remembered his power. He remembered his wealth. Like a crawling child learning to fly, Rich felt more alive than he had ever remembered feeling before.

"Aye", he said in a low rumble as an evil smile transformed his face into a sinister grin. "I remember", his confidence overtook him, "I'm Captain Billy Thompson. This is my ship. It was *my* treasure I found. Mine!", he said. He stood and looked around, searching for more things to remember. But the newly found confidence subsided quickly as he still had a cloud of haze surrounding his mind. He didn't remember everything. He didn't know how he came to be in this time; in this body. "But I've been gone. Where was I? Why can't I remember anything?", he asked. He was still out of sorts as he contemplated the impossibility of his existence. How could he remember his life as Rich Harris, and now suddenly remember this old life? He knew he was Rich Harris, but he hadn't always been this person. "How is this possible?" This wasn't the time that Billy had lived in. This wasn't Billy's world. The confusion was overwhelming.

"Billy, it is you", said Imala. She spoke slowly and looked at him in the eyes. "Can you remember?", she said, walking toward him slowly. Her dress flowing with the air as if it were flowing in the water- as if she were a ghost.

He tried to think of his life and how he had come to be here- how he came to be Rich Harris, but he was lost. "I don't know. We were here. But it was long ago. I had a crew. I had a ship and a crew." As he spoke, he became disoriented again. His confusion grew, and he couldn't grasp whether he was Rich Harris, or Captain Billy Thompson. As he looked around, he realized he was no longer on a ship. He was laying down on his small skiff near the inlet. He was no longer in the dream. Was it a dream? He was certain that he had really been on a ship and that he was talking to Imala. As he looked up, he noticed her just beyond the wall of the boat, floating. "What is happening, Imala?"

Just as quickly as he had fallen asleep and saw the visions of this past life, he watched Imala vanish in front of him. But it wasn't simply a vision. Captain Billy Thompson was his name. He had a ship and a crew... and a treasure.

Eleven

Carol kept trying to call Rich on his cellphone, but he wouldn't answer. She was certain that he had learned of the meeting between her, Jay, and the captain. Her guilt was unbearable, but she wanted her friend to get help. She and Jay cared about Rich. They were a group of friends that had become more and more like family as the years passed. That's how Carol knew that something was wrong with Rich. The way he had been acting these past few days was completely uncharacteristic of him. She had never seen him talk to people the way he had done recently. This was not him.

She was beginning to think the worst had happened. She wondered if Rich had become suicidal now that he had lost the only thing he had. As ridiculous a thought that seemed to her, she couldn't help but to give it some validity and attention. She quickly called Jay, hoping that he had heard from Rich.

"This is Luther", Jay answered.

"Jay, it's me," Carol began, "have you seen Rich?"

"No, I was hoping you had", Jay said, now worried more about his buddy. What had they done? What kind of trouble had they caused by simply trying to help their friend?

"I called repeatedly with no answer," she said, "I'm really worried about him, Jay. I think he knows we met with the captain." Carol's concern was affecting her composure, and she started to tear up.

"I'll swing by his house and see if he's there, but I've called him a few times too," Jay said. "Listen, it's not your fault, Carol. Or mine. Rich is going through some stuff, and I wish he'd talk to us about it, but he won't. He's the one who got himself into this mess. I'm not trying to be harsh, I love the guy and you know that," Jay said, trying not to upset Carol even more, "but you can't blame yourself, or us for that matter.

We tried to get him help. We will continue to try to get him help. But he's got to want help." Jay still felt a little guilty. On the one hand, Rich had been acting strange, but on the other hand, Jay and Carol may have contributed to his suspension. Had they left it alone, Rich may still have his job.

"I know," said Carol, "I'm just worried. Can you just let me know if you find him?"

"Of course."

Jay headed to Rich's house, almost certain that he wouldn't be there, and equally uncertain of where he could be. He thought about what he would say to Rich when he found him. He knew Rich would be upset about their meeting with the captain. Who wouldn't be? And what kind of friends would go tattle to the captain like that? Jay had to stop feeling guilty. The important thing was to find Rich.

As Jay pulled up to the house, he saw that Rich's truck was gone. He also noticed that Rich's boat was gone. Jay figured that Rich was out blowing off steam on the water. He decided to call the station and ask for the crew to keep an eye out for Rich.

"North Carolina Wildlife Resource Commission, Officer Dayton speaking, how can I help you?" The monotone voice on the line belonged to one of the junior officers.

"Dayton, this is Officer Luther," Jay said, "I need you to do me a favor."

"Yessir, what can I do for you?", Dayton said with the chipper 'new guy' voice.

"I can't seem to find Officer Harris, and I think he's out on the water on his personal boat," Jay explained, "Can you get a message out for anyone who happens to see Harris, to give me a call?"

"I thought Harris got fired," Dayton said, "talk around the station's that he doesn't work here anymore."

"He didn't get fired, he's on leave," Jay explained. News sure travels fast in a small station. Still, Jay wanted to maintain Rich's dignity by making it sound as if he were simply taking some time off. "Look, Dayton, Harris has been a loyal and faithful officer. He's my friend, and a friend to the station. I don't care what his present status with the station is, I care about his safety," Jay was concerned about how the other officers would treat Harris. "Now all I'm asking is for someone to call me if they spot him. No one needs to go out of their way. Just if you see him, let me know."

"Roger that, officer Luther," Dayton said, "sorry 'bout that. I just heard he was fired is all. I'll get a call out and I'll call you if we see him."

"Thanks, Dayton."

Officer Dayton made the call.

"All units, this is dispatch. Keep an eye open for Officer Harris's personal boat. Officer Luther is trying to locate Harris. Please contact station if you see Officer Harris," Dayton said, "I say again, all units, this is dispatch. Keep an eye open for Officer Harris's personal boat. Officer Luther is trying to locate Harris. Please contact station if you see Officer Harris."

As the call was heard by the patrolling boats, one officer in particular took an interest- Officer Danny Bell. Still nursing his bruised ego, Bell was livid with Rich. He wanted revenge for the way Rich had made him look in front of everyone. Bell wanted to embarrass Rich. He wanted to beat the shit out of Rich. Knowing full well he was capable of crushing Rich, Bell was eager to get him face to face outside of the station.

Officer Bell cruised around the area looking for Rich, but he was unsuccessful. After about an hour of searching, though, Bell was in luck. Though he didn't find Rich, someone else had spotted him, and the call came over the radio-

"Dispatch, this is Stengele, I think I see Harris," Officer Stengele reported, "I'll see if I can flag him down."

Bell listened eagerly, waiting for confirmation of Rich's location. Stengele drove closer and closer to what he believed to be Rich's boat. It was in fact Rich's boat, and Rich was in fact at the helm, and even though he was going very slow, he didn't appear to see or hear Stengele as Stengele called out to him, "Harris!" Stengele yelled, "Station's looking for you bro", he said. Rich glanced over at Stengele, but didn't slow down, or even make an attempt to reply.

"Harris!", Stengele tried again, wondering why Rich was ignoring him. He made another call to the station, "Dispatch, this is Stengele, I see Harris, but he's ignoring me", he said. "what's his deal, Dayton? I ain't got time for this", Stengele said.

"Not sure what his problem is," Officer Dayton said, "Luther wants to talk to him. What's his location?"

"We're at the inlet by the base," said Stengele, "looks like he's headed up the Intracoastal toward Swansboro. I'm supposed to be heading south. Did you need me to follow him?"

"No, that's ok," said Dayton, "Luther just wanted to know where he was. I'll give him a call. Thanks." Dayton picked up the phone and called Jay, but the conversation he had just had with Officer Stengele over the radio was also heard by Officer Bell. That's all Bell needed to hear.

Danny Bell was north of Swansboro, near Bogue Sound, also on the Intercostal waterway. He quickly started heading south in hopes to catch up with Rich. Bell's blood was still boiling, and he couldn't wait to get to Rich.

Stengele was about to turn around and head back south toward his assigned area. He looked at Rich still and wondered why he didn't say anything. He looked strange. Stengele wondered if Rich was ok, but he didn't know the guy very well, so he would leave at that.

*****

Rich, or Billy, drove north slowly, still wondering what was happening to him. He had all of these memories of his life as Captain Billy Thompson, and knew that he was also Rich Harris, but he didn't know how those two facts were possible. How was it possible for him to be so absolutely certain of being each one of these two men? He began to wonder if he was suffering from some sort of mental condition. He wondered if he was having a breakdown or a midlife crisis. Just as quickly as those thoughts rushed into his mind, they vanished. He knew who he was, and he didn't have any interest in some fancy scientific reasoning. He was Captain Billy Thompson. He was a leader of men. A ship's captain. A force to be reckoned with.

Billy decided to go back to Bear Island, where he had found the treasure. His treasure. He figured maybe that island held some answers. As he drove on, he felt more and more like his old self — like Billy's old self, that is. He felt confident and strong. Like he was in charge of his own life, and more. He reached in to his pocket and pulled out a coin. The beautiful silver piece from his treasure chest. He took in its beauty. His eyes glistened as reflected the shine from the coin. He rubbed the coin with his thumb as if to be petting it like a small animal. Billy loved his treasure. He loved all treasures, and he desired much more of it. He wanted it all.

As his boat drifted across the waves in its path, Billy noticed a group of people on a nearby sandbar. He looked on as he pulled back on the boat's throttle. Billy's eyes squinted, and his face contorted. His face looked less and less like the face of Rich Harris, and more closely resembled Billy Thompson. The crow's feet around his eyes became more prominent, and his skin appeared more leathery and weathered by the salt air for at least a decade.

The people at the sandbar wear partying as they do. Playing cornhole, tossing the football around, grilling out, and drinking beer. This used to be the place Rich detested the most. Rich hated confrontation, and he had always known that showing up at the sandbar meant that he would undoubtedly find law violations, and if he had found law violations, he would have to write citations. That meant confrontation. Rich could not handle that. This was not Rich.

Billy began to wonder what he could gain by approaching these people. This was something Billy always wondered. "*What's in it for me*", he thought. His idea wasn't to go write citations. Billy didn't care about the law. In fact, he detested the law. Billy wondered how much he could rob from these people.

He had a look of anger on his face, as if these people were on his personal property. Like they had invaded his territory. But that's what this was now. This was Billy's territory. His property. It was all his. There were around 25 people spread out throughout the sandbar, and each of them were in contempt of Captain Billy Thompson's law.

His boat drifted toward the shore and he pulled back more on the throttle until the engine was at idle. Billy looked around the boat for something to aid him in gaining the attention of his victims. He noticed a bullhorn under one of the seats. This will do nicely. Rich must have had it for emergencies. Rich was prepared like a boy scout. Billy also found one of Rich's jackets that read "POLICE" on the back. This was a little humorous because Rich wasn't really a cop. Not a real cop anyway. Sure, he could write citations, but he couldn't really do much else. Billy grabbed the jacket and put it on. As the boat bottomed out on the sand, Billy walked over to the bow and held the bullhorn up to his mouth.

Twelve

"HELLO HELLO HELLOOOOOOOO!!", Billy snarled into the microphone of the bullhorn. "HEAR ME! ALL OF YOU NEED TO GATHER 'ROUND, I AM THE POLICE!" He projected his authority upon the people of the sandbar. Everyone looked in his direction, but no one was sure what was going on. It seemed very unusual, and Billy sounded like more of a prison inmate than a police officer. As the people stood in their places, staring at this scary-looking man with a bullhorn, Billy couldn't stand their insolence. "I SAID GATHER 'ROUND! NOW GET OVER HERE OR YOU'RE ALL GOING TO JAIL!" He shouted. People began slowly walking in his direction. They looked around at each other in disbelief as if to ask with their expressions, "*Is he serious*?".

As they made their way to him, Billy began his unprepared speech. "GOOD, NOW LISTEN HERE. YOU FOLKS HAVE BROKEN THE LAW!" People looked at each other in more as if to wonder if this was some kind of joke. Billy continued, "NOW I AIN'T GONNA HAVE NO BREAKIN' OF THE LAW, SO GET OVER HERE!"

They gathered in a large group around the bow of Billy's boat. A few of the teenager present began to mumble to each other about how lame this or that was. Some of the older people were beginning to mumble as well. Billy just stared around the crowd and thought. He thought about control, and how much control he had over these people. It was just like in the good old days when Captain Billy Thompson was a known name in the pirate world. People feared him then. These people feared him. Or did they? They kept mumbling and whispering to each other as if this was a big joke.

The crowd was now gathered and standing semi-circle in front of the boat. All within earshot, making bullhorn an unnecessary accessory.

"Folks, there appears to be some sort of confusion as to who is in charge here. You see, I want you to be quiet and somehow you think it's better to run your jibs", Billy said smugly, "I want you to make two lines facing each other with a few feet separatin' ya".

"What is this?", a man in the middle of the group asked, "what are we in trouble for?".

"GET IN THE LINES!", Billy blasted back at him immediately, "I'LL TELL YOU WHAT YOU DONE IN TIME, JUST GIT THERE NOW OR YOU'RE GOIN' TO JAIL!" Billy yelled as he jumped off the boat and on to the sand.

The man wasn't quite convinced, but he made his way toward forming the lines, as did the rest of the crowd. But many of them were still dumbfounded as to why this "cop" was treating them this way. Who the hell was he, anyway?

"You know you can't talk to us like this, man", a woman said, "we have rights. This is a violation of our rights". She stared at Billy in disbelief. Fear kept her in line the same as everyone else. Billy walked slowly down the ranks of people with his hands clasped behind his back. He started to feel like the captain again. The pirate captain. Addressing his victims and preparing to explain that he would be ridding them of all of their belongings. He looked them up and down with an expression of superiority.

"Well I tell ya, there ought to be some kind of laws against drinking and carrying on out here on this island", Billy was referring to the sandbar of course. "I see lots of violations and law breakin' that I think might need addressin'". He reached the end of the group and pivoted around to face about. He looked down the line at the faces of these clueless civilians and thought about how easily he could rob them. He remembered doing this many times before- robbing people. Only in his memories, Billy usually had a crew. His crew would strike fear in the hearts of those they held captive. They would slap people who decided to speak up. They would grab valuables right off the hands, wrists, and necks of their victims. But this time would be different. This time he had no crew.

"Even though there seem to be so many of you who are breakin' the laws of the land", Billy said, "I think we might be able to come to some sort of arrangement."

"Officer, what is going on here?". A very concerned man spoke up after he couldn't stay silent any longer.

Billy stopped in his tracks, which happened to be about 3 steps away from the man who interrupted him. He turned back around to face the man, took 3 steps toward him until Billy was face to face with him. The man's courage vanished as Billy approached and turned to fear. Billy breathed in the man's face, squinted his eyes and looked deep into the man's soul. As Billy leaned in closer and closer, the man began to lean back a bit.

"I don't believe I heard you, friend", whispered Billy, inches from the man's face, "it sounded to me like you just interrupted me, but that can't be true because I don't get interrupted." Everyone fell silent as the tension rose. No one could believe their eyes. What was going on here? This was a police officer clearly abusing his power. This man couldn't do anything to the whole group. Just as quickly as thoughts of defiance entered their collective minds, they vanished from the fear that they would suffer whatever consequences this rugged-looking officer had in store for them.

The silence was deafening. The man began to open his mouth to explain himself. Billy reached back with his right hand and thrust his fist full force into the man's stomach. 'THUD!' The man buckled over in pain and let out a god awful grunt. He sounded like a wounded animal. The crowd gasped in disbelief. They were outraged and terrified. They all started speaking up.

"Hey man, you can't do that!", one of them shouted.

"WOAH! Officer, are you crazy?". Another one joined in.

The man fell to the ground and Billy looked around at all of them. "Don't interrupt me!" He yelled. By this point, the crowd started frantically dissipating. It's as if they all knew he couldn't catch them all and they would try to make a run for it. Billy shouted, "Stop! Stay there and be still!". But no one was listening. They all started running away in different directions. Billy reached down to his right hip to pull out his pistol, but when he felt around, he realized he didn't have one. His authority was gone.

Billy was furious as he started walking toward people and demanding they stop. People were getting in their boats and leaving while Billy made attempts to stop them. He wouldn't lose his dignity by chasing them, as he was already embarrassed that the situation was going so horribly wrong. This was not Captain Billy Thompson. No one would dare run from him. He couldn't believe that he had lost so much respect. Didn't they know who he was? He watched as they all scattered. He didn't bother chasing them. Instead, he stood there and wondered what was next. Did he need to get a crew together? After all, Billy was rich again. He had his treasure. He wondered why he even felt the need to rob those people in the first place. He also wondered more and more how he came to be in this time.

Billy remembered his life as a pirate. He remembered having a crew and sailing the seas. He remembered the drinking, the fighting, the women, and the adventures. He remembered everything but where it stopped and how he came to be here at this time. He tried thinking about it, but the more he tried to concentrate, the more he lost focus. As Billy contemplated these things, he found himself alone on the sandbar. Embattled by his ever changing thoughts of gaining more treasure and re-obtaining power, he thought to himself that he needed to remember what brought him here. This was no ordinary thing, traveling through time, coming to the future.

This was the first time Billy had really come to grips with the fact that he did in fact travel to the future. The future. And what was this strange future? Motorized vessels and motorized carriages. He had somehow eased into this new world as a passenger in Rich Harris's head. He had slowly become the pirate, little by little. That must be how he came to understand some of the things that didn't exist in his time- like a bullhorn.

Billy began to realize that he must not fully be Billy Thompson. How would Billy Thompson know anything about a police jacket, or its significance? He must still be Rich somehow. But that was another plaguing thought in itself. How in the hell did he come into being through this Rich character?

His mind was racing as these realizations began to flood his mind. What sort of magic was this that brought him here. He somehow knew that he was not in his time, but it wasn't until that exact moment that he was completely shocked by his apparent time jump. Billy Thompson's last memory before these past few days were of the year 1720. So what time was this?

As he stood thinking, drifting back in his memories to search for answers, he was interrupted by the sound of an approaching boat. "There he is!", shouted a voice from the shoreline. "Rich!", the man yelled again.

Billy looked over and saw that a boat had parked beside his own. He thought he recognized the faces, but he was out of sorts now. He was shaken from his daze and still stuck between two times in his mind. He tried to mutter something, "Who is it?", he growled.

"Rich, what is going on here?", said a woman Billy didn't know. The boat next to Billy's had two people on it, a man and a woman. Both were vaguely familiar, but he couldn't quite place them. They were jumping down and heading over to Billy. Billy didn't understand what was going on here, so he couldn't very well answer such a stupid question.

"Who's that askin'?", he said.

"Rich, what's wrong?", said the woman, "Where have you been?"

"Rich, it's us man", said the man who could see that Billy, or Rich, was disoriented, "It's Jay and Carol, dude. What's going on with you?", he said.

Billy could surmise from their body language and actual tone of voice that they meant him no harm, and that they were possibly friends of this 'Rich' fellow. He thought about Rich- his host. He wondered again how he came to be in this time, and somehow could feel that he came here through Rich. He could tell that even though he was currently 'at the wheel', that Rich's body is where he was currently. He didn't speak just yet. His face was covered with confusion. Jay and Carol walked closer with concerned looks of their own. They hadn't seen Rich since before Carol had essentially lost him his job. But something was different.

Rich didn't look like himself. The closer Carol got, she began to notice that he almost didn't look like himself at all. His face was weathered, his crow's feet were more prominent than before. He was carrying himself differently. He stood taller, and he looked... angry.

"Rich, we need to talk," said Carol. "We had no idea the Captain was gonna do this to you."

"Man, you gotta know we would never do anything to get you in trouble," said Jay. "We were trying to help. We thought talking to the captain would get you some help. How were we supposed to know he'd suspend you?" Jay pleaded, but he could tell that Rich wasn't listening. Something was wrong with Rich.

Billy's head was spinning as he tried to piece together this strange nightmare in which he found himself. He ignored the two as they talked to him, or Rich, or whoever they were talking to. He started to say something, but he couldn't formulate a word. He opened his mouth and tried to bark something snarky at the two, but nothing came out. Billy felt lightheaded. The world began to spin and before he realized what was happening his eyes were closed and the sound and light were gone.

Thirteen

"Billy", a woman's voice whispered. It was a familiar voice — beautiful and powerful. "Billy, wake up", she said in a sort of whisper. Her voice had a slight echo to it, as if she were speaking across a valley, but that wasn't quite it. Billy opened his eyes and looked around at his new surroundings. As his eyes began to focus, he noticed that this place was familiar to him. He knew this place; this time. He was back in the place he kept awakening to dream of his old life. The impossibility of this was overwhelming.

"What is happening?", Billy groaned. As he once again found himself back in this time, he felt as if he was trapped between two worlds. One minute he is in the place, or time, where everyone and everything seems strange and foreign, and the next minute he is in this place and time. He couldn't quite get his footing in this place... in this body. He was growing irritated by the sporadic jolts back and forth in time. He didn't know if this was real. How could it possibly be real? As he thought about his jumps back and forth in time, he realized that he was himself more and more often. This host, this body he occupied, was no longer at the helm. He could almost control it completely.

"Welcome back, Billy", Imala said. "You have been away a long time". Her voice was dreamlike and distant. Billy looked around at his surroundings. It was his time again. He was on land near a familiar port. His home. He was back in England. His beloved ship was in view at the dock. "We have much to discuss, my love", Imala said. She looked at Billy with a sort of curiosity.

"Imala", Billy said, remembering more about himself, about her. "Imala, where have I been? This is not my body. I remember...", he said, and stopped. Billy thought about the last thing he could remember. He remembered his beautiful ship. He remembered his crew, and his time.

He remembered taking what he wanted, and commanding respect and fear from everyone. He could taste the rum he last drank and smell the salt air from the time in which he now stood. It was as real as anything he had ever experienced. But he couldn't remember the end. He tried and tried and couldn't remember how he had come to be here in this new body- in that new and strange time.

"Billy, you have traveled far. You remember your life. You remember me- your love," she said. As she spoke, Billy realized that as real and solid as everything around him appeared, Imala still seemed distant. She seemed to be floating as if suspended in water. She looked like a ghost. "You left me, my love", she said. "You left me, but you have found me again, and soon we shall be together again", Imala's voice was still something of a dreamlike voice- somewhat of a whisper, and partially echoed.

Billy thought about what she was saying. He remembered her. He searched his heart and mind for the love she spoke of, but could not be certain if he felt it. He knew he was passionate about Imala, but he did not long for her. He remembered parts of his life; parts of his time with Imala. Billy took some comfort in seeing Imala as she was from his time and place. She knew him, and that eased his mind slightly, though he still felt torn between two worlds and had no idea how any of this was possible. Was he dead? Was this Heaven, Hell, or somewhere in between? She may have the answer.

"Imala," Billy said, "where did I go?"

"You have not traveled distance", Imala explained, "you are where you have been since the time you came to my village." Her words confused Billy. That doesn't make any sense. This place is far different from the place he last remembered being. He thought about the waters and how familiar the channels had been, but the structures on land looked nothing like they did where he remembered living. Everything about this place was strange to Billy, the people, the boats, the buildings, the strange carriages. In fact, the longer he thought about it, the more he felt strange and out of place.

"Nothing is the same," Billy said. "This ain't the same place. Is this Hell? Am I dead? Tell me, Imala."

"You are far from dead, my love", she said, "you and I will never die. We are saved from the clutches of death — from an eternity of nothing. We have come here to a new time. You have not traveled a distance, Billy. You have traveled across time." As Imala explained this to Billy, he could feel the time as if he had been suspended for decades, or longer. He felt as if he had been in a dreamless sleep for so long that the thought of it became frightening to him. He suddenly feared that sleep. He didn't how he had come out of it, but wondered how quickly or easily he could slip back into it.

"No. That can't be", he said. "If I am not dead, then how has so much time passed." Billy still did not know just how long it had been since he was last...alive. "Imala", he said, "how much time? How long have I slept?" Was it decades? Things looked so different to Billy that he knew it had been a long time.

"You have been waiting, Billy," she said. But this did not answer his question.

"How long?" Billy said. His feelings were now a mix between irritation and fear.

"You were waiting to find me, Billy," Imala said, again slowing working her way to some explanation.

"Tell me how long it's been, woman!" Billy's patience was wearing thin. He was not someone to toil with, and his infamous anger was beginning to surface.

"300 years have passed, Billy", she said. Billy's heart dropped. His face twisted to display shock and confusion. He couldn't grasp a clear thought. He looked around at his surroundings and wondered how it had been so long, yet he currently stood in his time. "You were lost, but you found your way back", she said.

"300 years", he whispered, looking at the ground now. "300 years... how... when did... where is my crew?", he asked. This was more for his own knowledge, Billy wasn't really all that concerned about anyone other than himself.

"Dead. Everyone you have ever known is dead. Time has taken all but the two of us. You did not care for them, Billy. You did not need them. You need only me. You are the great Cap—"

"Dead", Billy said, interrupting Imala. "Gone. All of them." He began to pace slowly around the grassy area where he was standing. He thought about his men. He had been hard on them. But a pirate can't be weak. He was hard, and he was mean; he treated his crew like dogs. So what did it matter? The only purpose they had ever served was to serve him. Billy wasn't really bothered by the fact that he had left them. He didn't need them. He didn't need anyone. Being along didn't really bother Billy all that much, but he wasn't really alone. "Not everyone...", Billy muttered. He looked up at the ghostly woman with whom he had once shared a reign of terror. "How did you do this, witch?" He asked. His tone was not overly aggressive, but it carried some content. Imala knew that he was a loose cannon. She knew that he was easily irritated, and could turn violent at any minute. Billy remembered the power that Imala had once displayed. How she could carry out various things with her magic — her witchcraft. He thought about the things she had carried out in his name. He remembered her being his... weapon.

Imala could see that Billy could only remember parts of his past — all but one very important part. She had him back, and she needed him to remember all but that one part. She needed him to help her. She needed him to need her again. Imala walked toward Billy, fading in and out as if between worlds. Her ghostly figure glistened in the sunshine. "My love," she said, "I have saved us from death. You ruled the seas once, and you shall rule again. I have always carried out your wishes, your commands. I have a power greater than any other being. Remember my power, Billy. Remember our strength; our magic... remember out power, Billy." Imala reached her hand out to touch Billy's face. Her touch felt distant, as if her hand was not in a solid state upon his cheek. "I brought you back to our time because it is familiar to you, Billy," she explained. "We are not here. This place is no longer as it looks to you now. I have shown you our past, so you may remember who you were. Remember who we were — together. We have come back 300 years after our time to the year Two Thousand and Twenty. Much has changed, my love. But you will rule again with my help." Billy looked up into her transparent eyes.

"With your help", Billy said. He still couldn't grasp it all. The only constant feeling he still had was that he was the great pirate. He relied on no one. Why did he need her help? Captain Billy Thompson took what he wanted when he wanted it. He needed no help.

Imala sensed Billy's irritation with her implication that he needed help. "With my power, Billy," she said. "You are the greatest pirate, the greatest man ever to sail the seas, but these times, they are not our times. You can rule again, but the people are more powerful now. They are more united." She needed him to need her, but she knew that he had to realize that himself. "They cannot be overpowered as easily as they were in the past. My power is what you need. You shall have it, Billy."

Billy thought about the people he had just encountered. He had them at that sandbar, standing helpless. He was about to take from them anything he wished to take. He would kill anyone who stood in his way. He had them, and he felt like himself again, commanding their obedience. He could tell they were different than the people he used to terrorize. He could sense more defiance than he was used to receiving. It was easier in his time to strike fear. "These people do not fear me," he said, "not as they once did. It's as if they don't know the nature of a pirate. I ordered them to listen, and they had no fear of death."

Could that be it? Maybe they just needed to see that he was a killer.

"They do not fear pirates because they have not seen a real one in centuries," Imala explained. "The world has defeated the pirates of old. They have united and defeated the terrors of the sea. You are the last, Billy. You are the only one left, and you are the one who shall take back this world. You will make them see that man is weak. They need to be ruled, Billy. These people are sheep, and you will be their master. The world will be yours. Riches beyond what you have ever imagined. You can have it all, anything and everything your heart desires. You will need the ancient powers that I possess, Billy. With my powers, you can overcome any enemy. You can wield the power yourself, Billy." Imala skillfully manipulated Billy as she painted the picture of his ascension to greatest. He needed to know that her powers were necessary to carry out his will. The part that caught his attention was that he could wield this power.

"What do you speak of, Imala," Billy said, "How can I have the power?" The most familiar of Billy's personality traits had thrown him off whatever train of thought he may have otherwise had — greed. The thought of having Imala's power in his own hands was intoxicating. He remembered her great power, and how she could simply wave her... arm... or her hand... or something, and make objects move, or burn, or whatever she wished. She could seek out treasures and pull them from the ground by simply pulling back her... hand... or something. There was something missing. What was it? What did she pull back? Or move or shake? Billy couldn't quite remember what Imala had used, but he remembered that there was some object that she used for her power. It wasn't just from her, but she was the witch. Billy looked at Imala floating in front of him. She didn't have whatever it was.

"I will reunite us and complete the spell upon the solstice." Imala spoke of the spell for the first time, and for a second she worried that Billy would remember everything. Imala started to open her mouth to explain this to Billy, but at that moment, Billy felt a slap across his face. He was instantly jolted away from this time, and out of his dream.

Fourteen

Billy opened his eyes as if waking up from a long sleep. He saw two images hovering over him he couldn't quite make out. His eyes began to adjust, and he started to make out the two fuzzy shaped people standing over him. It was those two idiot friends of the asshole he now inhabited. One of them must have slapped him to wake him up. That'll need to be punished.

"Rich," Carol said. She was clearly afraid, as if she thought she may have lost him. "Rich, it's us, Carol and Jay." "What happened, buddy?" Said Jay. "Are you ok? You passed out, man. And you look God awful." Carol slapped Jay's arm, scolding him for his unfiltered comment.

"Jay!", Carol said. "Rich, are you ok?" She noticed even more that he did look terrible. He looked very different from his usual self. His face was distorted and strangely shaped. Rich almost looked like a different person. She wondered if he had some kind of stroke or something along with his apparent nervous breakdown.

"Get back!" Billy shouted. He sat up and shook their hands off of him. Carol and Jay each looked shocked, both at the sight of their friend, and at his erratic behavior. Billy stood up slowly as Carol and Jay watched, wondering what was going on.

"Take it easy, man," said Jay. "Take it slow. You should sit down for a minute. You just passed out man." As Jay pleaded, Billy stared at him in anger. Billy looked at both of them and thought about how easily he could gut them both where they stood. These fragile sheep.

Before Billy could speak the threatening words he was about to speak, a nearby boat grabbed everyone's attention. The boat was pulling in to the sandbar fast. The boat's roaring engine quickly came to a quiet idle as the boat came to a near stop and drifted closer to shore. Billy,

Carol, and Jay stared at the boat, wondering who could be pulling in so aggressively.

"Well, well, what the hell's goin' on here?" The boat's driver shouted. "Looks like y'all are up to something. Is this civilian up to something officers?" It was Danny Bell. His condescending tone was recognizable as soon as he spoke. Carol rolled her eyes. This couldn't be good. The last thing they needed was for Danny Bell to show up here. Especially right after Rich had been hassling all of those people. And since Rich was suspended, this could really put him in a bind. "Looks to me like he may be drunk," Danny said. "Looks to me like he drove here on his boat... drunk." Danny was of course grasping at straws, but he hated Rich, especially after Rich made him look like a fool in front of everyone. He was willing to find anything he could to ruin Rich.

"What do you want, Bell?" Jay said.

"Looks like y'all need a real officer to look into this situation since y'all are friends with this guy who is clearly breakin' some laws." Danny stepped down from his boat and pulled it a little higher up onto the sand. He walked his anchor over and slammed it into the sand.

Carol knew they needed to deescalate whatever was about to take place in order to save Rich's job. "Danny, we're just talking to Rich, that's it. He's not drunk," she said, "he just doesn't feel well. Please, just leave us alone."

"Leave you alone?" Danny said. "I'm an officer of the law. You want me to ignore what's going on here?" Danny knew this was a long shot way to play the situation, but he really just wanted to antagonize Rich. He wanted to make Rich pay for being a smartass. He wanted to teach Rich a lesson.

Billy stood there watching the situation unfold. He wasn't impressed by the asshole who was approaching. Billy wasn't intimidated. He could tell that the man approaching had some quarrel with the body Billy was inhabiting, and he was always up for a fight.

Danny walked toward the three with a very cocky demeanor. Carol and Jay were standing on each side of Billy, ready to break up whatever scuffle might take place here. They could both see the look in Danny's eyes. They knew he was looking for a fight after what Rich did to Danny at the station.

"Take it easy, Bell," Carol said, "that's enough." She held a hand out as if to halt him. Danny slapped her hand away violently. This surprised Jay and pissed him off at the same time.

"Woah man!" Jay said, "What the hell is your problem? Cut the shit, Bell." Jay walked in between Rich and Danny and held his own hand up to halt Danny, but Danny swatted Jay away even harder. Jay stumbled to the side as Danny seemed to walk right through him. Danny was very strong, and both Jay and Carol could feel his strength when he had pushed them to the side. They knew they wouldn't be able to stop a fight at this point, but they each continued to shout at Danny in an attempt to stop him.

Billy raised his hand toward Jay and Carol as if he were telling a dog to heal. He welcomed this potential fight. He needed this fight. Billy looked at Danny as Danny stepped up within inches of Billy's face — a real intimidator move Danny had used many times before on many people. Billy was of course not intimidated at all. In fact, his adrenaline began to rise. His rage was being as it had done so many times before. Billy was notorious for fighting, and he was a force to be reckoned with.

"Let's see how clever you are now, Harris," Danny said, "you don't have your audience this time, and the Captain ain't here to save you either." Danny stared at Billy, ready to pounce at any second. He noticed Billy's weathered face making Rich look much different from usual. He didn't ponder this too long because his desire to beat Rich up was more of a priority to him at the moment. "You've been awful ballsy lately, Harris. And I don't give a shit if you are going through some nervous breakdown bullshit, you done messed with the wrong guy this time, dickhead." Danny noticed that Rich wasn't acting like his usual coward self. He wasn't backing down, or even backing up. In fact, Rich hadn't flinched at all. He stood his ground. This sort of standoff typically throws a bully off of his game, but Danny was determined. He knew he could take this wimp.

Jay and Carol stood in anticipation, each wishing somehow they could stop this from happening. They were too weak to fight Danny, but so was Rich. They knew he was about to receive the beating of a lifetime, and there was nothing they could do out here on the sandbar with no help in sight.

"Got nothing to say now, I see," Danny said. "What's the matter chicken shit, don't have the balls to say something to me now? You were pretty chatty when you had the station to back you up. Well, I'll tell you what, I'm gonna wipe that smug look off your goddamn face for good. How about that?" Danny just knew his threats would intimidate Rich this time. It didn't matter anymore though. This was it. Time to shit or get off the pot. Danny suddenly reached far back with his right arm, his fist clinched tightly. He swung forward as hard as he could, landing the punch directly across Billy's left cheekbone.

Danny's fist impacted Billy's face like a wrecking ball through a building, causing Billy's head to turn sharply upon impact. But his body hardly moved. Billy absorbed the punch like a pebble falling gently into a creek. It was as if it simply moved his head and nothing more. Billy didn't fall or move much at all. He slowly turned his head back forward. His eyes looked devious and sinister. Billy had half a smily on his face when he looked back at Danny. Carol and Jay looked on in shock. They flinched harder than Billy did when they watched the punch occur. Now they wondered how Rich was still standing. Danny was strong enough to knock Rich's head off, but he just stood there and absorbed the thunderous punch. Danny was shocked too. He thought for sure Rich would've been knocked out cold after a punch like that. He gave it everything he had. There was now a tinge of fear in Danny as he was now fairly uncertain as to how he would be delivering this beating after all.

Billy's creepy smile became more prominent as he was once again face to face with Danny. "That all you got, lad?" The last time Billy said this was back at the bar after he received his ass kicking. At that time, though, he was more Rich than Billy. Billy was back, and he could feel it. He licked his lip and tasted the slightest hint of blood. "I suppose that makes it my turn," he said. Billy didn't rear his arm back, or choreograph his moves in any way. He quickly reached forward and grabbed Danny by the throat. His hand moved so quickly that it startled everyone present. They each flinched at the sudden movement. It was almost a supernatural speed. Billy's hand made a loud slap noise as it connected with Danny's throat. The look of utter confusion on Danny's face was incredibly satisfying to Billy. Then the next apparent super nature ability was displayed. Billy lifted Danny completely off of his feet. Danny weighed 220 pounds, so this was no small feat. Carol and Jay couldn't believe what they were witnessing. This couldn't be happening. Their timid friend who was afraid of his own shadow not only took a punch that would make any boxer stumble, but he was now lifting a 220 pound man off of the ground with one arm. Was he on steroids? How in the world was this happening? The fear in Danny's eyes as he grabbed onto Billy's wrist was intoxicating to Billy. Billy held Danny there for a few seconds and then quickly pushed forward and downward, slamming Danny onto the ground hard. Danny impacted the sand so hard it created a small crater, and sand flew out from all sides of him. Each move caused the two onlookers to flinch, but they didn't know what to do or say. They just watched in shock as their friend appear to man handle this mountain of a person like he was a rag doll. Danny let out a loud grunt upon impacting the ground. The wind was knocked out of him as he slammed to the ground. Billy held Danny's throat tightly, choking Danny, but not completely restricting the airflow. Billy knelt next to Danny's limp body, pinning him down to the ground with one arm. He leaned in next to Danny's distraught face and whispered, "don't seem like this is gonna be much of a fight to me, boy." Billy's voice was scratchy and low — certainly lower than Rich's. His slight accent cause Carol, Jay, and even Danny to wonder just what the hell was going on with this guy. Why was he talking like this? Why was he acting like this? How in the hell was he doing this?

"Ahhghgg," Danny gargled, trying to form words.

"What's that, boy? I can't quite hear ya," Billy answered, taunting his prey.

"Bbbcch," Danny was scared, shocked, but also pissed. He wasn't used to having the shit kicked out of him. He wasn't used to being thrown around. "Bbbcch," he tried again.

"Speak up!" Billy yelled. He let a little pressure off of Danny's throat. He was a little curious to hear what his little rag doll had to say.

"Bitch!" Danny yelled in a pinched and baffled sound. "Bitch! I'm gonna kick the shi—"

"Bitch, you say?" Billy said. "You'll be kicking the what? You'll be beating me bloody, I suppose. Ohhh, my little bag of skin and bones, you won't be kicking anything. Not no more." Billy raised his left fist high behind his left shoulder and brought it down like a hammer to Danny's face, breaking Danny's nose. The strike was violent and loud, but it didn't satisfy Billy's lust for blood. He raised his fist again and brought it smashing down to Danny's face. Danny's body was limp as Billy repeatedly punched with his left and finally switching to his right fist. Carol and Jay, appalled by what they were witnessing, each launched at Billy and each grabbed an arm to stop him. They felt Billy's strength as they did the best they could to subdue him, each shouting at him to stop.

"Rich! Stop! You'll kill him!" Carol said.

"Jesus Christ, Rich!" said Jay. "Stop it, man! Stop!" They fought as hard as they could to slow the punches. They were eventually able to stop Billy. Both Carol and Jay were now using all of their strength and energy, and it seemed as though Billy could have kept going if he wished, but that he grew bored with beating the living hell out of Danny. Billy paused for a moment. He had a satisfied look on his face while Jay and Carol both looked completely terrified at what they had just witnessed. Still holding Billy's arms, they wondered if Danny was still alive. Billy shook their arms off of his harshly and stood up. He looked down at the pitiful scene — two sissies scared about seeing a man beaten to a pulp. What had this world come to? This was routine in Billy's time. Carol immediately began checking Danny for signs of life while Jay looked at his friend who he no longer recognized. "Get the hell out of here, Rich," Jay said. "You better pray that he's ok, man." Billy considered finishing the job and even adding the two sissies to his list of victims, but he had grown bored with this and decided it was time to get back to work doing what he does best.

Billy walked back to Rich's boat as Carol and Jay desperately attended to Danny, hoping he was still alive.

Fifteen

Calls about the incident on the sandbar had been coming into the station. People were complaining that an officer was holding people against their will. Some said they felt as though he was impersonating an officer, but they were too afraid to test him during the incident. They were of course talking about Rich... about Billy, taking control of the crowd at the sandbar.

Officer Stengele was attempting to contact Officers Luther and Massey on their radios, but to no avail. He then attempted to contact Officer Bell as he had been told that Bell had headed toward the sandbar. No one was answering their radios. "*Here we go again*," Stengele thought, thinking back to when Officer Rich Harris wasn't answering his radio the night his boat had allegedly broken down. After attempting to contact all the officers he knew who were near the sandbar, Stengele decided that he needed to inform Sergeant Macon that there was a problem. Stengele got up from his desk and walked over to Sergeant Macon, who was watching videos on his computer. "Uh Sergeant?" Stengele said, "We got a small issue."

Sergeant Macon quickly clicked his browser window closed and gave his attention to Officer Stengele. "What's up?" He asked.

"We've been getting calls about some kinda incident at the sandbar," Stengele said, "but I can't get a hold of any Officers in the vicinity." Stengele always tried to talk like a cop from a TV show.

"What kind of incident," Macon asked. "What's going on? What do you mean you can't get a hold of anyone?" Sergeant Macon's questions came out quicker and quicker as his panic began to build. He knew he would get in trouble somehow if he couldn't handle this without having to involve the Captain.

"Some folks been calling in saying some Officer from our station was holding them up at the sandbar," Stengele explained, "and that he was yelling at everyone and demanding they listen. Real weird stuff. I got no idea who coulda done that, but I was thinking—"

"Yelling at everyone?" Macon said. "Who the hell would do that? Bell maybe? Nah, he isn't that stupid."

"I as thinking maybe it wasn't even one of ours. Maybe like someone just saying they were a cop."

"Who's on it?" Macon asked. "You say you can't find anyone out that way? Where's Luther? Or Massey? Or Bell? You can't find any of them? That's not right. Goddamn Harris would be next to call if he wasn't suspended." Macon seemed to have a realization right when he said the name 'Harris'. Stengele looked at him right at that moment as they both realized something at the same time.

"Harris?" Stengele said. "You think Harris may be involved? That guy is afraid to talk to people, much less yell at anyone."

Macon thought about it for a split second and realized Stengele was right. In the years that Macon knew Harris, he knew that Harris was a weak and timid man who was not capable of yelling at anyone.

Just then the radio bussed alive with a familiar voice. "Dispatch, this is Officer Massey, over" Carol said frantically.

Officer Stengele and Sergeant Macon ran over to Stengele's desk, and Stengele grabbed the radio. "Go for dispatch." Stengele said.

"Stengele, we got a problem," Carol said sounding out of breath, "Officer Luther and I are headed in with Officer Bell. We have to get him to a hospital, there's been an... accident." Carol wanted to say incident, but she still clung to the idea that she could keep Rich out of trouble. Although after all of this she didn't see how that would be possible.

As Stengele prepared to ask questions that wouldn't help the situation at all, Sergeant Macon grabbed the radio out of his hand. "Massey, this is Macon, what the hell is going on?" Sergeant Macon said.

"Sergeant, Officer Bell has been beaten up pretty badly," she said. She tried to dance around the subject of the beating, but there just wasn't any way around it. "Sergeant, Bell and Harris got in to a fight at the sandbar and Harris beat Bell unconscious." As Carol explained this Sergeant Macon and Officer Stengele stood and stared at the radio in disbelief. Harris was not capable of beating up a blind middle school girl, let alone the toughest guy in the department. "Bell threw the first punch, Sergeant," Carol continued, "Bell instigated the fight, Harris was defending himself. Bell came there looking for a fight, and he punched Harris in the face. Harris retaliated and beat up Bell." Silence fell over both sides of the radio as everyone digested this information. Carol and Jay were also still completely surprised by what had unfolded. Macon and Stengele couldn't believe what they had just heard. It seemed like a few minutes had passed before Carol go back on the radio. "Sergeant, are you there?" she asked.

"I'm here Massey," Macon said. "What's... where...," he couldn't quite formulate the question he wanted to ask, "where are you taking Bell, what's your current location, and how is Bell doing?" Macon asked.

"We are currently heading up the New River, just went under the 172 bridge," Carol listed as many details as she could, "heading to Hadnot Point. We're taking him to base because it's the closest hospital, and he is not looking good." Carol was referring to the Marine Corps Base, Camp Lejeune, where there happened to be a Naval Hospital. The sandbar was located very close to the base, so this was the closest hospital by far.

"Not looking good?" Macon asked, "What's that mean, is he ok? Is he going to make it? Jesus Christ." As Macon released the 'push to talk' button he considered the severity of this situation. One of his officers had beaten another of his officers to the point where he could possibly die...

"He's breathing," Carol said, "but he's not conscious. I'm sure his nose is broken... Sergeant, he looks bad."

"Roger that," Macon said, "Get there quickly, and keep me posted Massey. Call as soon as you get there."

*****

As Billy pushed forward on the throttle, he felt the power and speed of this modern boat. Even though Rich's body and mind were the reason Billy was somewhat familiar with modern things, he was becoming more and more himself, and therefore Rich was fading away. Therefore, the things that Rich knew were no longer helping Billy all that much, and he began to struggle with understanding much of the world around him. The houses looked strange, the boats, some people even operated small boats that only one person could operate, with only one seat that they straddled. Billy had no idea what a jet ski was. He cruised through the waters, uncertain what his next move needed to be. Before Imala had explained to him that he had been suspended in time for the past 300 years, all Billy cared about was his treasure, and acquiring more. Now he knew there was more he needed to do in order to continue living his life the way he intends. He needed to get the power. He needed the power that the only witch he had ever know, Imala, had once controlled. Billy had no idea how he was going to do this, but he would figure it out.

Billy thought back to the docks in 1720 where he spent some of his time in between "runs" as he called them back then. He thought of his time here back then. He remembered that he hadn't lived in this area very long back then — only a few years. It was coming back to him slowly. He thought back to the waters he and the crew navigated. These same waters, at least in some way. He thought about the towns he would terrorize when he decided to port. His crew crowding around him at every establishment they entered. The crew was a rowdy bunch of drunken misfits, each loyal to Billy because they each feared death. They also enjoyed living the pirate life, though. As long as they worked for Captain Billy Thompson, they could reap the rewards; the women, the money, the alcohol — anything and everything they wanted... as long as the Captain didn't want it, was theirs for the taking. Billy thought about his ship. His beautiful ship. He remembered stealing that very ship from... from someone. He couldn't quite remember everything. He took it nonetheless, and he was Captain.

All of this daydreaming and drifting up the intra-coastal, and Billy was no closer to a plan, to finding an answer to how he could gain the power he needed. Did he need to find Imala? Billy was lost for the first time in... 300 years.

*****

Carol and Jay pulled into the dock at Hadnot Point and were greeted by a group of military Emergence Medical Technicians. In the Navy, they were known as Corpsmen. The Corpsmen put Danny Bell onto the gurney and rolled him to the ambulance. As the Corpsmen loaded Danny into the back of the ambulance, Carol and Jay jumped in to ride along. The doors shut, and they were on their way. The Corpsmen began checking all vitals and assessing the damage done to Danny — damage that looked like it was inflicted by four or five men, certainly not just one.

“Broken nose,” one of the Corpsmen said, “broken jaw, broken cheek bone, collapsed eye socket,” he continued. The list went on, but it appeared aside from the broken bones, Danny would be relatively ok. He’d live... with a messed up face that may take some time to get back to normal.

Carol called Sergeant Macon to update him on the situation. She told him that Bell would be ok, but had some broken bones. Of course she downplayed it a little, so as not to stir up too much concern. Macon had talked to the Captain about the situation by now and had more questions for Carol. “About this ‘incident’ at the sandbar,” Macon said. Carol knew he was no longer talking about the fight between Danny and Rich. “Just what in the hell happened there? Some officer was holding people hostage or something?”

“Sergeant, we don’t know...” Carol began to explain, “we don’t really know what happened there. We were driving around looking for Harris, and saw a bunch of boats leaving the sandbar, so we headed that way. When we got there, Harris was standing there...” she considered holding back the part about him looking crazy and passing out. What if he was on drugs or something?

"Keep talking, Massey," Macon said.

"He looked like... confused or something. I'm not sure what was happening or what had happened, but we called out his name as we pulled up," she said, "and he passed out."

"Passed out?" Macon said. "What the hell do you mean? Was he the one we got the calls about? Was Harris the one harassing people? Was he drunk or something, or on drugs?" He was firing his questions rapidly, as he tends to do when he is nervous and has no answers.

"I don't know what was said about an incident," Carol said, "I just know that's what we saw before he... before Officer Bell arrived."

"Captain Kelly is pissed Massey," Macon said, "we got calls about an officer assaulting civilians, and here we have two officers fighting at a sandbar... one putting the other in the hospital!" Carol listened as she had no answer to any of this. She wasn't sure how Rich had come to look the way he did, or to do the things he did. She wasn't lying when she said she didn't see the other incident, so she had no idea if Rich had in fact harassed or assaulted civilians. Nor could she think of any possible reason he would ever do so. But he certainly wasn't acting like himself. "Where the hell is Harris?" Macon said with as much authority as he could muster.

"I'm not sure, Sergeant," Carol said. "He drove off after the fight while Officer Luther and I were checking on Officer Bell."

"Well, I'll tell you this much, Massey," Macon said, "you'd better goddamn find his ass, and find him soon. You and Luther look wherever the hell he hangs out. Go to his house, go to his boat... find him. When you do find him, I want you to call the station, and then I want you to arrest him. Do you understand me?"

"Sergeant—"

"Arrest him!", Macon yelled. "This guy is coming in and answering for whatever the hell he has done. I don't give a shit about any kind of nervous breakdown!" Sergeant Macon had learned from the Captain that Harris had been suspended for his recent pattern of unacceptable behavior. The Captain's opinion was that Harris was having a nervous breakdown, which seemed to be the common thought around the station. Even Carol and Jay felt as though that was an accurate assessment.

"Yes, Sergeant," Carol said. She got off the radio and turned to Jay. "He's in serious trouble, Jay. I don't know what's going to happen to him, but we have got to find Rich... and arrest him."

Sixteen

As the day turned into night, Officer Danny Bell was waking up in a hospital bed at Camp Lejeune Naval Hospital. He slowly opened his eyes... or eye, rather. His right eye socket had been shattered, so he could only open his left eye, and not very wide. He was in excruciating pain that became more apparent the more time had passed. He could see the IV in his arm, and eventually he could feel the bandages around his head and on his face. Danny didn't remember anything after arriving at the sandbar at first. He was confused as to how he arrived in this room and was not sure why he was in pain or what had happened to him. He had glimpses of his altercation with Rich, and then it all started coming back — he was beaten to hell by that weakling Rich Harris. Danny felt enraged and embarrassed. He would never live this down. For a bully, it is probably the most humiliating thing that could happen — being beaten up by one of your victims. It had happened. This was real. Danny wondered how badly he was hurt. He reached up to touch his right cheek and as his fingers gently pressed his skin, he quickly pulled his hand away and let out a quiet yelp. "Ahh!" That certainly hurt more than he thought it would. This upset Danny even more. His hatred for Rich, and now this was just too much. Danny would never live this down. He would never be respected again. How could he ever be taken seriously as a tough guy again? He wanted to get even. He wanted to get the advantage. He wanted to destroy Rich Harris.

A nurse entered the room as Danny contemplated his situation. "Well, hello Mr. Bell," the nurse said, "I'm happy to see you awake."

"Where am I," Danny said. "What hospital is this?"

"You're at Camp Lejeune Naval Hospital, Mr. Bell," she said. "Your friends dropped you off here about 3 hours ago."

"Friends," Danny chuckled, "I'm guessing you mean the assholes who were there. They aren't my friends. Those assholes witnessed a civilian assaulting an officer." Danny's fury grew as he thought about the scene for a minute. Maybe that's what he would pursue. Assaulting an officer could be something that could get Rich locked up. That would be somewhat satisfying to Bell, but it didn't quite ease his mind. First off, that was still embarrassing, saying that he was assaulted by a civilian, let alone this particular civilian. Secondly, it didn't come close to the punishment that Rich Harris deserved.

"I'm terribly sorry, Mr. Bell. I didn't mean to upset you. Just letting you know you arrived about 3 hours ago."

"What's the damage? What's broken?"

"I better let the Doctor fill you in on that, let me go—"

"Nurse," Danny said, "What is broken? Just tell me what's broken. Tell me when I can get out of here."

"Sir, I can tell you your nose and cheekbone are broken, but I don't have all the details. I don't know when you can be released. Let me go find the Doctor. He can explain everything to you. That important thing is that you are ok," she said with a forced smile.

"Ok," Danny said sarcastically. "Do I look ok? I sure as hell don't feel ok." The nurse politely nodded and backed out of the room while Danny was still complaining about how he looked and felt. "Ok, she says. Can't tell me what the hell is broken. What kind of hospital is this?"

*****

Carol and Jay were headed back toward the docs. Rich was not at any of his usual hang out spots on the water; the radios had been buzzing all day looking for him. They had headed toward the station after leaving the hospital so they could get to a car. Carol thought Rich would likely be at home after a day like today. Jay agreed. The two officers reached the station, quickly tied the boat down and headed to one of the station cruisers. Jay jumped in the driver's seat and started the car. Carol buckled her seatbelt and wiped a tear away from her face. They rode in silence as they headed toward Rich's house, both contemplating everything. How had it come to this? This was their best friend, and now they had to arrest him. This was completely insane.

"Can you try his cell again," Carol said.

"I keep calling," Carol said, "no answer. Same with texts. He's ignoring us, Jay."

"How's this going to go?" Jay asked. "We just show up and say, 'Hey Rich, it's us, your best friends in the world, the ones who got you suspended. We need you to come with us. Oh, and by the way, you have the right to remain is—"

"I don't know, Jay," Carol said. "This is all crazy to me too. I don't know what we do. He's not going to come with us willingly. Did you see his face?" Carol thought about Rich's twisted, wrinkled face. He looked like he had aged 10 years, got way too much sun.

"Yeah, it didn't look like Rich at all," Jay said. "How does that happen? Drugs? We'd know if he was on drugs, right?"

"I don't know," Carol said. "What kind of drugs make your face change that quickly in such a short amount of time? You think Rich is on Meth? I don't think so. It's like he had a stroke or something." She thought more about Rich's behavior. "And what about his strength? Have you ever known Rich to be that strong?"

"I know, I couldn't believe it. I've worked out with that guy, and he couldn't lift a twenty-pound dumbbell if you paid him. And the rage... he was... he was crazy with rage." The two rode in silence as the image of Rich choke slamming Danny replayed over and over in their heads. They both realized that they were losing their friend. Whatever this was, drugs, a nervous breakdown, it was going to ruin Rich's if he continued down this path. His life was in decay.

"Rich, it's Carol," she said to Rich's voicemail, "Please Rich, you have to answer... or text back... we have to talk, Rich. This is bad. Please call me back. Jay and I are on our way to your house. Please talk to us Rich." Jay listened and shook his head as if to say it was no use to even leave a message.

Jay pulled the car into Rich's driveway. The car wasn't there. "Welp, he's not here," Jay said. "Maybe out on the boat still?"

"Probably, but how the hell can we find him out there?" Carol said. "This is our best bet at a clue of some sort. Or maybe he will come back here."

"So what do you suggest, we just sit here and wait?"

"I don't know, maybe we go in. Maybe we can see if anything inside will give us a clue as to why he's acting this way. Maybe drugs are inside."

"Carol, be serious. We're cops. We can't just walk into a suspect's house to look for shit like that, even if he is our friend."

"I'm aware of the law. I know... I know it's stupid. This is Rich though, Jay. This is our best friend. This isn't just some suspect. Plus, sitting here won't do much either. I'm pretty sure if he sees us here, he's gonna turn around and take off. If he wanted to see us, he'd return a call or a text."

"Jesus Christ," Jay said. "I can't believe we're even considering this. This can end our careers, you know. This... this right here can get us canned. What if we do find something? What then? We can't use any of it if it's found without a warrant."

"I know, Jay. Jesus Christ, don't you think I know these things? I'm trying to think through this. I don't care about evidence to convict him, I'm thinking about finding evidence, as friends, not as cops, in order to help him. You're right though, this will end our careers if we go in. Mine... it'll end mine."

"What the hell is that supposed to mean?" Jay asked.

"It means you need to leave. You and I will split up to look for Rich. You leave me here. You can't be implicated if you had no knowledge of me going in—"

"Carol," Jay said.

"Just listen," she said. "You and I went separate ways to try to track him down. I will go in and find out what I can find out, and I'll call you when I'm done, or if I find something. This way you had no knowledge of me breaking any laws, and you can't get in any trouble. I will take the risk myself." Jay was shaking his head throughout Carol's recitation of the plan. "You go to Rich's dock and see if his boat is there. Just wait there until I call you. That way if he returns on the boat, you'll be there, and I won't be caught in the house." Jay listened, but ignored Carol. He wasn't about to let her do something so stupid. He wasn't about to let her ruin her career. At least not alone.

"Ok," Jay said. "Let's go." Carol stopped talking and looked surprisingly at Jay. She wondered what he was getting at. "Let's go in," Jay said. "I'm not leaving you, Carol. He's my best friend, and that's that. We're in this together. If you go down, I go down." He almost couldn't believe he was even speaking the words, or that he was going to go through with this. "I mean, maybe Rich won't press charges since it's us." They both laughed nervously.

*****

The Doctor entered Danny's room with an obligatory smile on his face. He had been informed by the nurse that this particular patient was abrasive and was demanding to know when he could leave. "Mr. Bell," the Doctor said, "I'm Doctor Allen, how are we feeling?" His chipper demeanor annoyed Danny.

"We?" Danny said. "I don't know about you, Doc, but I feel like a bag of smashed assholes." Danny's colorful language wasn't anything Doctor Allen hadn't heard before, but it didn't get any easier to be professional when patients spoke to him this way. "What's broken, Doc? How bad is all this, and when can I leave here?"

"Mr. Bell, I can certainly understand your frustration." He said. Danny almost jumped in and accused the good Doctor of not knowing his asshole from a hole in the ground, but he figured he'd let the man speak. "I am happy to say that your injuries are not life threatening." Doctor Allen sat down at the computer in the room and pulled up Danny's file. "You have a nasal fracture; you have a zygomaticomaxillary fracture, which means your right cheekbone is fractured; you've suffered an orbital fracture to the right eye — this means that the bones around your eye socket have been broken," the Doctor continued to list

Danny's injuries in a very 'matter of fact' way. "You've suffered a concussion..." he said. Danny wasn't really paying much attention to his injuries, he just wanted to know how bad it was.

"Ok ok, Doc, how bad is it?"

"Well, Mr. Bell, it's not ideal to have these types of injuries. 'Bad' is a relative term. It's bad in a sense that you may lose vision in your right eye. Now I don't know if that will be permanent at this stage, but there is a good chance you won't regain vision." Danny's factored jaw dropped at the thought of being partially blind for the rest of his life. He thought about all the consequences of such an injury — a lack of depth perception, which would make driving harder; he can't golf or play on the station softball team anymore... just then his thoughts landed on a very big consequence... his job. You can't be a blind wildlife officer.

"I'm gonna lose my vision?" Danny said.

"Mr. Bell, I'm trying to tell you that you may lose your eye completely." Danny could feel tear welling up in his non-bandaged left eye. A lump began to form in his throat. Danny was on the verge of crying. For the first time since he was a kid, he felt the helpless tears of a sissy who showed emotions. This feeling of helplessness was accompanied by rage. Danny's rage was building to a new level, even for him. "I'm waiting on some tests to come back, and I will have a better grasp on the likelihood of that, Mr. Bell. For now, just be thankful you're alive. You were in pretty bad shape when your friends dropped you off." There it was again. Friend's. Danny's tear was now impossible to hold back. He almost made an audible crying sound, which would have really set him over the edge. Doctor Allen could see that Danny was not taking this well and needed to be left alone. "I'll be back as soon as I have the tests back, Mr. Bell. Rest up."

Seventeen

Carol knocked on the door, though she knew it was merely a formality. Rich wasn't home, she's knew that. Jay looked around to see if anyone was watching them getting ready to commit their first 'B&E'. Carol grabbed the knob and shook it to find that it was locked.

"I'll go around and check the back," Jay said. He walked around back as Carol peaked into the living room window. She couldn't make out anything inside because Rich had closed the curtains. She wondered if he had purposely done that to conceal drugs or something. She couldn't believe she was actually thinking that there could be drugs in Rich's house. Around back Jay tried opening the sliding glass door with no luck. It was also locked. He tried each window nearby, and they were each locked.

Carol was checking the windows in front, wondering why Rich hadn't given her or Jay a spare key. After all, they were his closest friends. Although that was kind of a funny thought at this point, as they were attempting to break into Rich's house. She thought about the spare key idea and decided to check under the mat. Nothing. She checked any spot near the front door that looked like it may have a key. Just then, she heard a smash — it was the sound of shattering glass. Jay had lost interest in trying to find ways to get in. He had broken a window in that back near the den. Carol ran around back to see Jay climbing awkwardly into the window.

"Jay, what are you doing?" Carol asked. "Are you crazy?" She quickly scanned the area to see if anyone had heard the noise and was watching them break into Rich's house. Jay fell to the floor inside the den. He jumped to his feet and looked around the house quickly to see if anyone was there. It was dark inside because all the curtains were closed, so Jay couldn't see much. He went to the sliding glass door and unlocked it.

Carol slid the door open and walked in. "You broke the window?" She said. "That was loud, Jay. Not to mention the fact that there is no way we can hide the fact that we broke in now."

"Shhh," Jay said, "we're in, aren't we?" They paused momentarily and listened for any signs of trouble. Carol walked over and opened the curtains covering the sliding glass door and the light flooded into the den. Jay and Carol watched the light pour in and their attention was immediately drawn to the center of the den floor. There, in the center of the floor, was a piece of furniture neither had ever seen before — a large chest. They looked at each other in shared confusion.

"You ever seen that before?" Carol asked.

"Nope. You?"

"Never. What do you think is in it?" Carol began to image all kinds of things, but figured it was some kind of chest filled with memories from Rich's past. A place to keep your old 'Letterman's jacket', your yearbooks, old pictures.

"Porn," Jay said. "Gotta be porn." Carol slapped Jay's arm as Jay laughed at his answer. "Well, you never know is all I'm saying."

"It's probably just an old 'memories' chest. You know, to keep old pictures and stuff," Carol said. Jay was looking it over as she spoke.

Jay pointed to the lock. "Memory chest, huh?" He said. "I don't know anyone who keeps their memories locked up unless they've got some skeletons in the closet... or in the chest in this case."

"Should we break the lock?" Carol said. She had a very troubled expression on her face, as did Jay. They both knew that it was a violation of Rich's privacy.

"I don't know," Jay said, "I mean we're in kind of deep already, and it's really for his own good, right?" He was trying to convince both Carol and himself that they needed to see the contents of the chest. Carol, looking even more worried, shook her head. She was having second thoughts. "Rich put a guy in the hospital, Carol. Danny could've died. You saw him. That could be considered attempted murder. And now he's nowhere to be found. We need to find him. We need to help him, and if this is a clue of why he's acting the way he is, then we have to look."

"If we look in this chest, and it turns out to be drugs... or body parts..." Carol thought about what she had just suggested, and began to cry, "then it will NOT be admissible." Not that she would ever want to convict Rich of anything.

"Admissible," Jay said, under his breath. "I'm going to get a hammer." He walked out to the garage, and Carol didn't stop him. Her curiosity was now winning a battle with her conscience. After a few minutes, Jay returned from the garage with a hammer. He stood in front of the chest and took one last look at Carol as if he was waiting for her to stop him. Carol hesitated, then nodded.Jay swung the hammer down hard on the latch and almost took the latch completely off. The next swing broke the latch off completely. One more look at Carol, who was on the edge of her seat with curiosity.

"Open it," she said.

Jay reached down to the lid of the chest and slowly lifted it. The light shining through the back sliding glass door hit the treasure and amplified its glow. The treasure reflected the beams of sunshine like a disco ball, and the light filled the room. Jay and Carol stood in silent shock, staring down at this beautiful collection of jewels and couldn't tell if they were dreaming, or if they were really looking at a treasure chest.

"Holy shit," Carol said without realizing she said it out loud.

"Holy shit is right. Holy shit. Holy—"

"What..." Carol couldn't form a rational thought. "What is... is that... is that what it looks like?"

Jay tried to contain himself, but was just as dumbfounded as Carol. Never in their lives had they ever seen such relics, such beautiful jewels and coins, such valuable stuff in one place. Not even in a museum. "It looks like a treasure chest," he said, not believing the words that just escaped his mouth.

*****

Billy looked out over the water and breathed a deep breath of the salty air. The night was always a better time to sail. He thought about this and remembered that he wasn't actually sailing. He wasn't sure if he liked this new technology of a boat that moves on its own, but then that removed his need for a crew — at least somewhat. He would still need some muscle to help rough people up. Or would he? With Imala's powers, Billy wouldn't need anyone. He thought about how he would take Imala's power. This would be a question he would need to pose in a delicate way when he saw her again. He struggled with the thought of having to be diplomatic. When he wanted something, he took it. But this was different. Imala was the most powerful witch he had ever come in contact with. That's what drew him to her those years ago. Back then, Imala was just learning of her abilities, but after a couple of years, she was able to move entire ships at will. That's how they were able to get the treasure. Billy's thoughts landed on the treasure. He remembered that he got the treasure with Imala's help. She was his key — the weapon he used against... against what? Against who? He couldn't quite remember everything.

Calls continued coming over the radio for Officer Rich Harris, but Billy ignored them. He couldn't figure out how to make the contraption shut up. The station was calling all boats in the vicinity, asking if anyone had seen Officer Harris. They even broadened their reach to include the coast guard, but no one had seen him. This was good for Billy because he didn't want to be found. He realized that everyone was looking for the body Billy was inhabiting — this 'Rich Harris' fellow.

Floating quietly through the channels near Hammock's Beach State Park, a small local island close to Bear Island, Billy looked around for any lights on the nearby water. He knew lights could mean boats, and boats could mean trouble. Billy was familiar with hiding out and being pursued. Billy wasn't sure what everyone wanted with this Rich Harris, but figured it must be because he hasn't exactly been himself lately. No matter. He had to find Imala. He had to find her source of power, whatever that was.

"Imala," Billy whispered, closing his eyes. "Imala, come to me." He wasn't sure if simply asking her to appear would work, but it was worth a try.

The sound of a nearby conversation rattled Billy, and he opened his eyes. There were lights approaching quickly. Billy stopped his boat and floated, wondering who was approaching, assessing the threat. The boat wasn't slowing. It was as if they didn't see Billy's boat. Maybe they were just civilians passing through. Of course. The boat got closer and closer, and the men onboard eventually saw Billy's boat. They slowed down almost to a stop.

"Woah, sorry bout that," The driver said. There were two men on the boat. They appeared to be passing through, but they sure did try hard to focus on the image of Billy as if they were wondering if it was the missing wildlife officer.

Billy stood up and stared hard at the driver of the boat, ready for a fight. He clinched his fists and prepared to leap into the approaching boat. The occupants of the other boat looked confused at Billy's stance.

"Hey man, we said sorry. You alright? You need help or anything?" The man realized Billy was in a NCWRC boat.

Billy could see that they had no quarrel with him, and that they really were just passing by. He still didn't want to waste an opportunity. "I could use a hand actually," he said in his best 'wolf in sheep's clothing' voice.

The other driver pulled closer to Billy until the two boats were right next to each other. "Sure officer, you broke down? Need us to call someone? We can tow you to the ramp if you want."

"No, I ain't broke down, lad. I just need a favor from you boys." Billy reached into the pocket of the police jacket he was still wearing and grabbed the grip of the flare gun he had found earlier in a compartment on the boat. He didn't know it was a flare gun since he had never seen one before. Billy pulled the flare gun out and aimed it at the driver of the other boat. "I'll be needin' your money."

"Woah man! What's your problem?" The two men raised their hands instinctively and flinched at the site of the flare gun. "Is that a flare gun?"

"Your money, gentlemen. Toss it over."

"Dude, do not shoot that at us, man. Aren't you a cop? You can't point that at us, man."

"Your money! Or you'll be tasting lead, my friends."

"Lead? What are you talking about, man? That's a flare gun. That thing will start a fire man. Someone can get hurt. This isn't funny." The driver turned to his friend. "Ron, call the cops." The passenger reached into his pocket and pulled out his cell phone. He prepared to dial.

Billy grew impatient. He was getting more and more upset with this time. No one took him seriously. It was time to spill some blood. He pulled the trigger. The flare shot out of the gun and hit the driver in the chest hard. Both men jumped back out of fear and disbelief. The flare ricochetted off of the man's chest and landed in the boat, burning so brightly that everyone had to look away. The men screamed and yelled, confused and upset that Billy had shot a flare into their boat.

Billy was taken aback. Once again surprised by something strange in this time. How had the bullet bounced off of the man, and how had it started a fire after impact? He saw the men flailing around on their boat, disoriented. Billy didn't wait any longer. He jumped onto the other boat, which was catching fire. He grabbed the driver and began beating him as he had beaten Danny, without mercy. The passenger yelled and attempted to help his friend. Billy grabbed the other man and began pummeling him as well. Swinging his fist from man to man, back and forth, Billy continued to punch both men's faces, one at a time, until they both laid almost limp. Each moving slowly and ready to cooperate with their vicious attacker.

Billy got up and caught his breath, the boat burning more and more. He searched around the side of the boat that wasn't ablaze. "Where's your loot, boys?" He looked for anything of value, but found nothing. The men groaned and held their faces. He quickly started to search the men's pockets where he found their wallets. Billy shoved the wallets into the pockets of his police jacket and quickly jumped back over to his own boat. As he pulled away, he watched the boat become engulfed in flames.

Eighteen

"We have to report this," Jay said.

"Report this? What even is this?" Carol answered.

"You think it's real? It looks real."

"I guess so... I mean yeah, it looks real." But how... where would this... where would this have come from?"

"I've never seen a treasure up close. I thought that was only in the movies." Jay said. He reached down slowly to pick up a coin.

"Stop!" Carol said. Jay jumped nervously. "Don't touch it. If this is stolen, then your prints will be on it. Don't touch anything else. This is serious, Jay. This has to be stolen."

"Right? It has to be. You're right, you're right. Don't touch." Jay began wiping the chest with his sleeve to erase his finger prints.

"Hang on a second," Carol said. She reached into her pocket and pulled out her phone. "Open the lid back up. I'm gonna get some pictures of this and we're gonna find out where it came from. Rich is in deep shit, Jay." She snapped a few pictures of the various treasures. She got some closeups of the coins and other items in case they had some identifiable features showing.

"Jesus, this is big, Carol. Like where the hell could he have stolen this from? The queen of England?"

"These coins are old. Like, really old. This is from a museum or something. It has to be. We just need to find out where it came from, and who is possibly looking for it. Why hasn't it been on the news? Why aren't the police looking for this? How long has he had it?" They both sat and thought for a minute. "Who the hell is he, Jay?"

"Let's get out of here. I don't need the cops showing up and putting us away for life."

They exited through the front door and locked it behind themselves. They jumped in the car and Jay drove away. Carol took out her phone and began searching the internet for any recent news of missing treasure. "Where do we even go?" She asked.

"I don't know, the police station? Ask if anyone's missing a treasure?"

"Be serious, Jay. I'm searching for anything on a missing treasure. I don't know of any museums in the area. But come to think of it, what museum would have that much valuable stuff in one place like that? It had to be worth millions of dollars. Do you think he's been collecting it for years? Like maybe he's a cat burglar or something on the side." The thought of that was ridiculous, but with Rich's strange behavior lately, Carol and Jay felt like they didn't even know him.

"Well, let's find out what the coins are. Maybe that will tell us something. Search for coins with certain markings."

"Ok, I typed coins with crosses on them. It's got a bunch of images, but none of these look like our coin. I'm gonna try 'treasure in North Carolina'."

"Or missing treas—"

"Woah," Carol said. "It's all about pirates; a bunch of metal detecting sites. What's that about. Is that a thing people do here, look for pirate treasure with metal detectors?"

"Could be, maybe that's how he got it all. Does he have a metal detector?"

"There is no way in hell he found all of this... in one place... no way in hell. No way he wouldn't have immediately told us about that. Maybe that's a start, though. We could ask a metal detector person if they know what the coins are."

"Good idea. That's a start." Jay drove toward town as Carol searched local metal detecting clubs. She clicked on the first one she saw — *NC Dirt Detectives*. Perfect.

Carol called the phone number listed on the website and spoke to one of the members of the *NC Dirt Detectives*. He agreed to meet up in the morning at the Dunkin' Donuts in Swansboro.

Carol and Jay met up the next morning at the station and headed toward the Dunkin' Donuts in Swansboro. They pulled in to the parking lot and as they were parking; they saw one other person in the Dunkin' Donuts. Carol walked up to the man sitting at a table along with his latte.

"Are you DJ?" Carol asked.

"Yep, you must be Carol," the man said as he stood to shake her hand.

"Yes, and this is my friend Jay." They finished the handshaking ritual, and each took their seats.

"So what can I do for you," DJ said.

"We're a little unfamiliar with metal detecting," Jay said, "so, basically, you guys just go look for treasure and stuff?"

DJ chuckled and shook his head. "Well, not exactly. We look for history for the most part. There's two basic kinds of detecting, or digging, or hunting, as we also call it — beach hunting, and dirt digging. Those guys you see on the beach are looking for rings, other jewelry, anything a tourist or beachgoer may have dropped. Sometimes we find class rings, sometimes we can even track down the owner and return jewelry. The other kind of hunting is dirt digging. This is where you'd go to an old farm or an older property and get the owner's permission to hunt their property. Usually we find old civil war relics and stuff — musket balls, uniform buttons, things like that. No one really hunts to get rich. It's more to find old cool stuff."

"Back to the beach," Carol said. "People find coins and stuff? What kind of coins?"

"Oh yeah, all the time. Mainly clad — that's what we call modern coin that's only worth it's face value, but sometimes older coins, like silver ones. On dirt digs you find more old coins, but there's old stuff on these North Carolina Beaches. There's a lot of history here."

"DJ, can you tell us what kind of coin this is?" Carol said as she turned her phone screen toward him to show a close-up picture of one of the coins.

"Looks like a Spanish Reale. Did you find one?" DJ suddenly became very excited at the prospect of seeing a full Reale up close. He knew some guys who have found pieces of them before, but never one in such great shape.

"No, a friend of ours may have found a couple—", Carol started to say.

"A couple?! Holy crap! Those things are worth some money!" DJ's inner nerd was on full display.

"How much money?" Jay asked.

"I don't know exactly, but they're super rare to find. It's like finding pirate treasure or something because they're so old—"

"Wait," Carol said. "Pirate treasure? What do you mean? Is there really pirate treasure?"

"Sure there is. They've found all kinds of stuff. Caches of coins and jewels and stuff pirates used to steal and hoard. There are people who hunt for treasures — groups and stuff. But it's super unlikely."

"So how do we know where the coins came from," Jay asked. "like these ones in the picture?"

"No real way to tell if it's only a couple, but that's a pretty lucky find. Your friend should post those pics on our Facebook page. My group would really like to see those. Also, there's a site called *ID Me* that you can post pictures of stuff you're not sure of and then people post what they think it is. That's more for like relics and stuff."

"Suppose there *was* some kind of treasure discovered. How would someone find out where it came from?" Carol feeling as if she might be giving too much information decided to clarify, "I mean my friend only found the couple of coins, but hypothetically, if someone found a whole treasure, what then? What do they do?"

"Well, there'd definitely be taxes to pay. You can't just claim a ton of money and not cut Uncle Sam in on the deal. I guess they could look at historical sites, or... oh, I know. They could go to the local Historical Society and read about the history of the area where they found the treasure. Again, though, super unlikely. Like no one finds entire treasures. They've all pretty much been discovered, and it's usually by an archeological group of some kind. Haha, everyone who gets in to metal detecting does a little research on that in the beginning. We all find out pretty quickly that it's not realistic."

"Ok, well DJ, thank you so much for the information," Carol said. "We'll pass it along to our friend. I'd love to try the detecting thing sometime." She was being polite.

"Hey, anytime. You guys should come check it out, we have a group hunt coming up next month."

Carol and Jay said their goodbyes and headed to the car.

"So we're totally going to that, right?" Jay said, sarcastically. Carol smirked and got into the passenger seat.

"Ok, I think we need to check out the local Historical Society, and also the library," Carol said.

"Library? For what?"

"They may have books on old coins. The Historical Society will have historical books of the area, but the library has other area history. I don't know, it's all I can think of right now."

"You know what my mind keeps jumping to? Pirates. Can you imagine? Pirate treasure. And that's totally what it looks like. Or at least what the movies have made it look like. What if this is some kind of pirate treasure, Carol?"

"I don't know where the hell it came from, but if it's real, then I doubt Rich has a legitimate reason for having it in his den."

The Swansboro Library was not a large building. It was actually about the same size as the local ABC store. There were plenty of books for a small town, but Jay and Carol doubted that they what find anything they needed in such a small library.

"At least they have computers," Jay said.

"You hop on a computer and start searching for anything on missing treasure, stolen treasure, museums missing treasure, I don't know, something. I'll go look for books with coins, jewels, anything distinguishable in these pictures." The two got to work searching.

*****

Billy looked down at his treasure chest — the broken latch on the ground in front. A panic came over him like a blanket as he considered opening the lid and seeing an empty chest. He quickly reached down and flung the lid open hard, almost breaking it off of the chest. The brilliant glimmer of light blasted out like an explosion, and Billy's heart was at ease. His precious treasure was intact. He was still extremely concerned at the fact that someone had been there. He walked around the house to see what had been touched. First noticing the broken window, Billy wondered why nothing was taken. "*Maybe they seen my treasure and knew they shouldn't mess with a man who had such a haul*," he thought. Nonetheless, this meant that someone knew that Billy had a treasure. Someone knew exactly where to find it.

Billy knew he had to hide it. He needed to transport it somewhere no one would ever find it. For a split second, he thought of how easy it would be to move if he had Imala. "Imala," he said out loud. "Imala, I need you. Where are you, witch?"

Nothing. Billy grew angry at the fact that someone was forcing him to have to move his treasure. Whoever it was was going to get their throat cut for sure. Billy wasted no time. He began transporting the treasure back to the boat by first dumping the nearly thousand pound treasure out on a tarp in the den and taking the empty chest to the boat in the garage. He made trips back and forth with a heavy backpack, transporting the treasure little by little until the whole thing was inside the chest and on the boat.

*****

The next morning Danny was greeted by the 'good news fairy' — that's what he called Doctor Allen. "I'm afraid I have some bad news, Mr. Bell. We have to remove your eye," The Doctor said in his best 'I'm terribly sorry to have to tell you this' voice. Danny sunk in the bed. That was that. All hope was gone. "You see, the ocular cavity—"

"Save it, Doc. I don't give a shit. Doesn't matter. That's it, there went my career." Danny stared at the wall with his left eye and pondered life. Doctor Allen thought it best to let him sulk — he would have time to explain it later.

"I'm terribly sorry, Mr. Bell, I know this can't be easy to hear," Doctor Allen paused again and then chipped up as if he had an epiphany, "I do have some good news — your Captain is here to visit you." The Doctor smiled a very uncomfortable smile, which Danny answered with a look that shot daggers at the Doctor.

"Terrific," Danny said. The Doctor left the room and minutes later Captain Kelly strolled in. Danny would have rolled his eyes if he could.

"Officer Bell," Captain Kelly said, "I'm so glad you're ok."

"Captain." Danny wasn't in as jovial a mood as everyone else appeared to be.

"Listen Bell, I'm sure this can't be easy. I'm told you may lose the eye. I'm sure you've already thought about what this means for your career—"

"I am losing it, sir. Doc just told me. I know that means I'm done."

"Well now, I know it's not something you want to do, Bell, but medical retirement isn't too bad, pay wise. Bell, you've been a great officer, and we are going to hate to lose you, but at least you'll have a pension." Danny was growing more enraged as the conversation went on. Captain Kelly continued, "and we're gonna throw you a big party to send you off ri—"

"I don't want a party. I don't want a ceremony. No need to go stand in front of a bunch of assholes who never like men while they pretend to be sad that I'm leaving."

"Officer Bell, it's customary when an officer retires—"

"But I ain't retiring, am I, sir? I'm being forced out because some shitbag got a lucky shot and broke my eye bone or whatever the hell it's called. With all due respect, Captain, I don't give a shit about that. I don't give a shit about any of those assholes. I'll collect my pension like the cripple I am, but I ain't going back to that station. Not ever."

Captain Kelly would have spoken much harsher under different circumstances. No one spoke to the Captain that way, but this was different. He knew Danny was taking this hard. Sometimes you had to let people say what they mean. That last part about the lucky shot reminded the Captain of the other thing they needed to talk about. "Speaking of the 'lucky shot', let's talk about Harris for a second. How did that whole thing go down, Bell?"

Danny knew Harris was going to get what was coming to him, but he was going to be the one to deliver Harris's punishment. "It was just a fight, sir. It got out of hand."

"Bell, you're laying in a hospital bed with your face broken to shit. You're going to lose an eye. This was far more than a fight that got out of hand."

"I'm not pressing charges."

"Well now, that may not be up to you at this point. There will be an investigation on this. I want to know who started it, I want to know everything. For now, you rest up, son. I'm very sorry about all of this, Bell. I'll be back by to visit in a few days."

Nineteen

Danny woke up from the surgery, slowly opening his remaining eye. He wasn't quite clear-headed yet, but he knew he had lost it. He could feel nothing on that side of his face, but he knew it.

"Mr. Bell," the nurse said. "You're awake. The surgery went well, sir. Let me go get the Doctor." She began to walk toward the door, hoping she could make it out before he spoke.

"My eye… it's gone." Danny reached up to feel the gauze over his eye. The nurse didn't want to suffer this man's wrath again, so she rushed out to get the Doctor.

Danny's rage began to build at the thought of being a cripple. This was it. His job, his life, it was all over. He didn't feel like much of a man anymore, and he had Rich Harris to thank for that. Rich Harris — the biggest pussy the station had ever seen — that Rich Harris. The guy who was afraid of his own shadow and could fight his way out of a wet paper bag. Danny thought back to Harris's comments at the station when Harris humiliated him in front of everyone. He thought about the sandbar and how he had punched Harris hard enough to knock him out cold, but how he just stood there as if he had gotten punched by a child. How had he done that? What was this guy on that gave him such strength?

Danny lay in bed, thinking of all the things he wanted to do to Rich Harris. He had never wanted to hurt anyone so badly in his entire life. He had never before felt such a strong desire to kill someone.

*****

Billy made sure to grab one of Rich's handguns before he left the house this time — a Baretta 9mm. That other strange orange gun he had used didn't have quite the effect he was expecting. He wasn't exactly sure how to operate this gun, but at least it wasn't orange. He had grabbed knife he found in the garage as well — at least knives didn't really change much over the years. Billy certainly knew how to gut someone if the need should arise.

As he cruised around the small cluster of islands searching for a spot to burry his loot, he tried thinking of how to summon Imala. He concentrated on her and tried speaking to her with his thoughts, but that wasn't working. He cut the engine and slowed to a crawl, drifting through the channel. He closed his eyes. He concentrated harder, focusing on the image of Imala's face. She really was quite beautiful, and Billy was attracted to more than just her power. Much of that attraction was an infatuation with such a powerful woman. There was something about a woman who was possibly more powerful than a man.

"Imala," he said out loud, "Imala, where are you?" He waited patiently, which wasn't an easy thing for Billy Thompson to do. "Imala, come to me." His frustration grew and his anger took hold. "Imala, where are you? You have to come here now. You have to show me the magic, woman. I need the power. IMALA! Answer me, witch!" Such a degrading tone had been a normal way of speaking for Billy. He never cared how he sounded to others. He spoke the way he wished to speak. Even when they were together, Billy spoke to Imala this way. He didn't think of it as degrading, and neither did she. It was simply how it was.

A nearby bush began to move as if an animal had been spooked. Billy looked at the bush and quickly drew his gun. A figure stood slowly. It looked like a bear standing to attack from where Billy sat on the boat. He pulled the trigger and heard nothing. Billy hadn't known how to chamber a round, or even take the safety off in order to shoot. The shadowy figure seemed out of focus and it moved toward him slowly. Billy stood and drew his knife. This would surely finish the job. As the image grew closer, Billy could see that it had a familiar face. This was not an animal at all, it was the ghostly image of his beloved Imala.

"Do not fear, my love. It is me," she whispered as she floated closer.

"Fear? I have no fear, woman. I'd have killed you if this pistol worked."

"You cannot kill me, Billy. It is as I said — we are beyond death. We are immortal."

"Where have you been? I've been callin' you. I need the power. I need it Imala, time is runnin' out." She could hear a hint of fear in his voice, as if he were afraid of being caught — the only thing he had ever feared.

"Billy, I am here," she said, "but I fear that I may not be for long." Imala knew that Billy would fear losing her because he would lose her magic. She desperately wanted him to need her again.

"What do you mean? What does that mean?"

"I don't know how much longer I can stay in between realms Billy."

"But you said we was immortal. You said we didn't need to fear death no more."

"You do not need to fear death Billy, you have been awakened and brought to this time through a vessel, but I have not. The spell must be completed upon the solstice, or I will fade from this world, my love." She was uncertain if lying to Billy was such a great idea, but part of what she said was true. She needed a body to gain a footing in this time and place, and the only person in this world who could help her was Billy.

"Completed? Solstice?" Billy didn't remember the spell, but he knew Imala was responsible for their having cheated death. They had planned to become immortal when they found out how, but Billy didn't remember that part of history. "What do you mean, you didn't complete the spell? What's gonna happen to me, Imala?"

Imala realizing her opportunity to manipulate Billy to help her, she said, "Without me, you will cross back over. You will not be dead, but you will not be. Without me, the spell is not complete, and you will fade away into eternity, Billy."

Billy squinted his eyes and looked down, pondering an eternity of nothingness. How could that be? He was finally back, and it could all go away. He didn't remember the 300 years of nothingness, but that was enough to scare him. He knew he didn't want to fade away. He tried harder to think about the details of how they found the spell. "Where... where did we get the power to get here, Imala?"

"It is unimportant, Billy—"

"Where'd we get it? How does the magic work?" Billy said sternly.

"I make it work, Billy. You know that I am a witch."

"Then how were you gonna help me 'wield it'? Wield what Imala?"

Billy didn't remember it. She would need him to find it, to save her from an eternity in a cave. "My staff, Billy. It is my weapon, *our* weapon."

Billy instantly remembered her staff — it was an old, weathered gray staff with four vine like tips that swirled at the end like a fire. It was said to be crafted from the trunk of a 1000-year-old tree and enchanted by the witches of Imala's tribe. Imala had taken the staff when she ran off with Billy. The memories of Imala holding the staff and performing great magical feats came rushing back to Billy. She used it to capsize ships, burn villages, flood entire towns, move the treasure... it was used to steal the treasure.

Billy remembered meeting Imala for the first time — it was 1717, and he had just arrived to the coast of North Carolina. Imala was 22 at the time, the youngest of the witch's in her tribe. Billy was only 27, so there wasn't much of a difference in their ages. He remembered that he wasn't a ship Captain at the time, but just another face in a crown of pirates. His Captain... what was his name... his Captain had given the men some well-deserved shore time. They usually got rowdy with the townspeople and took what they wanted. There were rarely any murders during these stops, as the Captain didn't want to be caught and hanged as a pirate. Unless there was looting to be done, there'd be no killing. Billy had always thought this showed weakness, but he did as he was told. He remembered walking by the center of the small town and seeing a slave auction taking place. Among the slaves was a beautiful your girl who didn't look like the rest. Billy had never seen a Native American before, but she piqued his curiosity. There was something about her that drew him to her. Billy had only ever see black slave at these auction blocks, which seemed odd to him, but skin color wasn't the difference he noticed in this girl. It was as if she was calling to him with her mind. He remembered walking over to the girl who looked at him, approaching as if she made him come to her. "*What's your name, girl,*" Billy had asked her.

"*Imala,*" she had answered. She left a slight smile on the end of the word as it left her lips. This drew Billy in.

Billy remembered the auctioneer walking over to him, talking to Imala and saying something like, "W*hat do you say, son? This one here's a real hellfire. She put up quite a fight. You better watch yourself.*" Or something along those lines. The girl looked at Billy and seemed to talk to him with her mind. He could feel her pain. He somehow knew how she was taken — much further inland, near her village, a group of men grabbed her when she was far enough away from her people, but how could Billy know that? He remembered being completely mesmerized by whatever was taking place. He remembered wondering how she was doing this.

"*You want to come with me*?" He had asked her. She had simply nodded. Billy looked over at the man and said to let her out. The man started walking over and let Billy know that this one wasn't like the rest, and therefore would be more expensive. This didn't concern Billy because he had no intention of paying. *"Let her out."*

"Now just a minute son, that'll be—"

Billy drew his pistol and pointed it directly at the man's nose. The man quickly unlocked the cage and let Imala out. Billy could hear him mutter something under his breath, "*G.... P....*", but Billy couldn't quite make it out.

"*What was that, sir?*" Billy had asked the man.

"*I said, God damn pirates,*" the man clarified. Without any hesitation at all, Billy re-aimed the gun at the man's face, pulled the trigger and blasted away most of the man's head. The townspeople screamed and ran. It was pure chaos. Billy hadn't considered how mad his Captain would be for defying him. But Imala eased his worries. He remembered not to fear anything any more.

Billy remembered staring into Imala's eyes and then letting her go. He had saved her, as she had asked him to do... in her mind. Billy headed back to the ship along with the rest of the crew. He had surely alerted the authorities of the area that pirates were in the area, so they would need to get out to sea. Imala had run off as some pirate grabbed Billy and pulled toward the direction of the ship.

Billy remembered standing in front of his Captain explaining what had happened. He remembered the strong backhand come across his face as he dropped to the ground, humiliated in front of the crew. "*Take him to the brig, Sammy,*" he remembered the Captain saying. "*Seems Mr. Thompson don't know how to follow orders. I'll need to be teachin' him a lesson.*" He remembered being taken below and making small talk with Sammy on his way down. And then he remembered the turning point in his life.

That night, as Billy sat in his cell wondering when and how he'd be killed, he heard someone approaching down the steps. He jumped to his feet and looked out to see the beautiful girl from the town. How had she gotten past anyone to get to this point? This must be a dream. "*Imala,*" Billy had said as she approached. She was holding it, the staff. That was the first time Billy had ever seen the staff.

He remembered Imala reaching up and pointing the staff at the cell door. It was magic. Magic before his very eyes. The staff flashed a flicker of light, and Billy could hear the lock unlocking. His cell door opened and Billy stepped forward toward Imala. That was how it all started. He remembered that was how they took the ship and he became Captain. Imala was his weapon.

Jolted back from his memory to the present, Billy looked at Imala again. "The staff," he said.

Imala thought that Billy was completely capable of double crossing her, so she didn't want to send him for the staff without first having her 'vessel'. She would need him to procure a body — a woman. "Yes, Billy, you remember it. That is how I will give you the power. You can wield it, but you must learn. I must teach you." This was partially true. Imala was a witch, so she had the ability to work the magic of the staff more than any living person, but this staff was enchanted by many witches, and was powerful beyond belief. Billy could find a way to use it if he found it. Or worse, he could destroy it, and trap her in limbo for eternity.

"Where is it?"

"You must not touch the staff, Billy. It has to be recovered by me though the vessel." Her fear was growing. Billy wasn't much for rules. She didn't know if she could convince him. She would have to hurry before he remembered everything. "If anyone else finds it, we could be lost forever."

Billy thought about where the staff could be, barely hearing Imala speak. He wondered if he could use it without her. He had an internal battle over whether he would look for the staff, or try to bring Imala back. He didn't think it could hurt having her around again. She was his companion, and his weapon.

"What do I need to do?" Billy said.

Imala, relieved that Billy was going to save her, showed no signs that she was misleading Billy. "You must find a woman. This woman must be the first to touch the staff. It is only then that I will be able to enter her body. You must hurry. Once the solstice has passed, it will be too late. You have but one more day, Billy. We will then perform the spell at dawn tomorrow, completely, and the world will at last be yours."

"A woman. Any woman? I can just go snatch a woman up from another boat."

"I would prefer a beautiful woman as this is the body I will occupy, Billy."

Billy thought about this for a second and realized he knew exactly one woman — that friend of his host's body.

"I know of a woman, but I don't know where to find her. That friend of this *Rich Harris*. Kinda fitting, I think."

"I will help you, my love."

Twenty

"Says here, piracy was pretty big in this area," Carol said. "It's funny how everyone glorifies pirates and how awful they were in real life. How many schools' mascots are pirates? They were murderers, rapists, thieves — it's crazy. Jesus Jay, look at this," she said, pointing to a picture in an old book on piracy in North Carolina. It was a picture of similar coins and jewels they saw in the chest in Rich's den.

"Wow, that's it. That's exactly it."

"Well, it's not exactly it, but they look about the same, Jay. I think this is what we're dealing with. Can you freaking believe this?"

"Pirate treasure. That's what we're dealing with? I just want to make sure I understand you. Pirate treasure, that's what is sitting in Rich's den?" Jay took a deep breath and let it out slowly. "There could be another explanation—"

"Look, I know this is crazy Jay, but what else could it be?"

"Ok, I'll bite. Where'd he get it? When did he get it?"

"I don't know," she said as she looked down at the table, feeling as if she was no closer to finding the answers to any of her questions. "Did you turn up anything of missing money or treasures or museums or anything?"

"Nothing. Like nothing at all anywhere. Nothing's been stolen that I know of."

"So if no one is missing it, then it could be that Rich found it, right? Maybe everything is ok, and he just found it."

"Then why would he be having a nervous breakdown, Carol? The guy would be over the moon if he had found it. He'd certainly tell us about it. There's no way. I have a bad feeling about this."

"Jay, when did Rich start acting strange?"

"Seems like right after he broke down that one night."

"I agree. And where did he break down?"

"Can't remember. Wait, you don't think that's when he found it, do you? That's crazy, he'd have told us. Maybe he's paranoid. What if we just talk to him—"

"Because that's been working so well. Hey buddy, we broke in to your house and found your pirate treasure, can we talk?" Carol pulled her cell phone out of her pocket and called the station. After a few rings, Officer Stengele answered. "Hey Stengele, it's Massey. Listen, where did Harris say he had broken down that night when he didn't check in?" She listened and nodded. "No, nothing yet, just putting the pieces together. Thanks, Stengele." She hit the "end," button, put her phone in her pocket.

"What'd he say?" Jay asked.

"Bear." Carol sat thinking about Bear Island. "You think he found a treasure that night?"

"Maybe he finds the treasure, and gets it home, and doesn't want to tell anyone because it might be illegal to own it or something?" Jay tried to make sense of it. "But then he'd just need to search it on the internet to see that he could keep it. Wait, can he keep it? Maybe that's it, maybe it would be owned by Hammock's Beach State Park since they own Bear. Jesus."

"That could be it. Or we could be completely out of our minds and it might not be a completely ridiculous thing like a pirate's treasure. I mean Jay, there were millions of dollars worth of gold and silver in that chest. Weren't all the big treasures found? What's even still out there?" Carol got up and walked up to the counter. "I'd like to check this book out," she said, handing it to the staff member working the computer.

Jay logged out of the computer and followed Carol to the desk. "So let's go to Bear," he said.

"It's a big island Jay, what would we look for?"

"Oh, yeah, true. Well, so then what do we do?"

"We start by finding Rich."

They left the library and hopped back in the car. "Sooooo, where we headed?" He asked.

"I guess we can go back to the house and see if he's back. You know he's not going to leave that much money lying around." Carol was grasping at straws, but it was all they could do.

"We wait down the street or something until he pulls up? Go confront him about it? Call for backup? Arrest him, like we're supposed to do?" Jay asked.

"I don't know, just go."

Jay pressed the gas and headed toward Rich's house.

Carol was thumbing through the pirate book some more on the drive to Rich's house. "Well, there was definitely a lot of piracy around here. I'm not sure why people lived here if this is how bad it was in coastal towns. I mean, people stop in every couple of months and rough up a town, and the town doesn't defend themselves?"

"Different times, Carol. The police weren't all that advanced or equipped to handle much, and the townspeople didn't have many moving options I imagine."

"Yeah, I guess," she said. She saw some rough drawings of pirates of the time — all looked roughly the same, scraggly and mean. She read something about how they were looked at like modern day gangsters are looked at now. "The most notorious of the pirates in NC was Edward Teach, better known as Blackbeard," she read. "Yeah, he's probably the most famous one I've ever heard of."

"Same," Jay said. "You know they found the Queen Annes Revenge out at Bogue." Jay was referring to Blackbeard's ship, which was located in like the late 90s. Jay couldn't quite remember when or where he had heard that.

"Really?"

"Yeah, it was some shipwreck company or something. Anyway, they have divers go search the wreckage. They got the anchor and stuff." That was about the extent of Jay's pirate knowledge. Despite having lived in the area his entire life, he just wasn't all that interested in pirates.

"Did they find any treasure?"

"Not sure."

Carol and Jay parked far enough away from Rich's that they were sure he wouldn't see them. They looked like real cops on a stakeout. Carol kept reading the book while Jay stared out the window and thought about all the possibilities this money could bring if it were legitimate. He thought maybe Rich would share it with them since they were such great friends.

*****

"Where the hell is he?" Doctor Allen asked.

"I don't know, Doctor, I just came in to check on him, and he wasn't here." The nurse said, sure that she would be reprimanded for losing a patient.

"He left. Unbelievable. He's in no condition to be out and about, but you know what? That's not my problem. The guy doesn't want to follow my medical advice, so be it. Call Captain Kelly and inform him that his Officer has checked himself out and is no longer under our care."

"Yes, Doctor."

*****

Billy Thompson wouldn't be in any history books, because no one would ever remember he existed. Imala took care of that. Beginning with the former Captain of Billy's ship, Billy had Imala erase any memory of his having killed the Captain. That's how the crew remained loyal to him after he became Captain. He remembered taking his place among the great pirates of his time with Imala by his side. He was unstoppable. He would steal what he wanted and she would help him. The crew was happy because they were oblivious to most things that went on as long as they were fed and had plenty of rum, plenty of loot, and plenty of women. Billy made sure to keep his crew happy.

Part of him wanted the fame that came with being a great pirate, but Billy was smart enough to know that he could have more with a certain amount of anonymity. This would normally make it hard for a pirate to demand respect and strike fear into people's hearts, but Billy had Imala. He didn't need to be like the rest. Billy remembered that this anonymity began to eat away at him. He remembered that he was the greatest pirate of his time, and he couldn't bask in the glory of it. But anonymity was the key to success for a pirate; that and having a powerful witch by your side.

Billy headed back to the dock to go find the woman. His treasure sat with him in the small skiff. He stared at it often. He loved his treasure more than anything else in the world, and he wasn't about to leave it again. He would need to find this woman, and help Imala finish the spell. Then they could continue where they left off in 1720. But he still couldn't remember it all. He still struggled with the end. How had they come to this time?

Imala had vanished again, as she had done more and more recently. Billy wondered how he would summon her again once he found the woman. More importantly, where would he stash his treasure while looking for the woman. Billy slid the chest under a cubby used for storing a cooler. This would hide it until he returned with the woman. He decided he would take her back to Bear Island, where his treasure was stored the first time.

Billy thought about Bear Island — the cave. He knew that was the place it all happened, but couldn't remember details. He couldn't remember details because he was still Rich at the time he discovered the treasure, but Billy didn't know that. Billy didn't know that his rotting bones were at the bottom of the cave, along with Imala's. He didn't have any idea how he had come to this time.

He pulled into the dock and tied his boat up. He ran up to Rich's truck and began his drive to the house. He figured he'd look for clues there, since that's the only place he knew how to find at the moment. It was miraculous how the transformation from Rich to Billy gave Billy some knowledge of the certain things that he was doing during the transformation — driving being one such thing, both this truck, and Rich's boat. But it didn't help with all things. Had he actually fired a gun during the transformation, he might know how to operate the one in his pocket. Cell phones are also a mystery, which is why Billy left Rich's cell phone at the house. He had no idea what it was.

As Billy pulled in to the driveway, Jay spotted his car. "Carol, it's him!" He said.

Carol looked up to see a man resembling their friend getting out of Rich's car. "Jesus, Jay, look at him. He's not himself. He looks terrible."

"So, do we arrest him?"

"We talk to him first, but then, yeah, I think we have to. We'll get this all cleared up. Let's go."

The two walked slowly up to the house. As they approached the door, they felt nervousness setting in. Carol put her hand up to the doorbell and hesitated. She finally pressed it, and called out, "Rich, it's us. Carol and Jay."

Billy didn't know what the bell sound was, but he could hear her at the door. His prey had come to him. This was going to work out perfectly for him. Billy slowly approached the door. He knew she wouldn't go willingly. He peaked out the front window and saw the man with her. It was that other idiot friend. Billy figured he'd kill the man and take the woman — should be pretty easy.

Not one to be trapped as these two were clearly trying to do to Billy, he decided to go around back and sneak up on them from the side of the house. Billy grabbed the gun, which he still didn't know how to use, out of his pocket. He slipped out the back door and tiptoed around the side of the house. He could see Carol and Jay standing at the front door, neither expecting a surprise. Billy aimed the gun at Jay as he walked up behind them.

"Well, isn't this lucky," he said. Jay and Carol quickly spun around and faced Billy.

"Jesus, Rich!" Carol said.

"What the hell are you doing, man?" Jay said.

"Rich, it's us," Carol said, "It's your friends. Put the gun down." She tried to reason with him, but she could see that he was not himself.

More than ever, she could tell that the Rich Harris they knew was not the person holding them at gunpoint.

"Get over here, woman," Billy said.

Jay tried to step in between Billy and Carol, but Billy reached the gun back and pistol whipped Jay in the face hard. Jay went to the ground immediately. He held his nose and cried in agony. "What the hell is wrong with you, Rich?" Jay cried.

"I said come here, woman."

Carol was terrified. She didn't know what Rich was capable of. She slowly stepped toward Billy and he grabbed her arm forcefully, pulling her toward the truck. "Stop it Rich, what has gotten in to you? We know about the treasure Rich, we're here to help you."

Billy stopped in his tracks. The treasure. Of course. They were the ones who broke in. They were the ones who wanted to steal his treasure from him. He pointed the gun back at Jay. "I'll kill him right now. What do you know, woman?"

"No, no, please, Rich! Nothing, nothing," Carol pleaded, "we found it, but we don't want it, it's all yours. Please, please don't shoot him. Please. I'll do what you want. No one is going to take it, Rich. It's all yours."

Billy knew he couldn't shoot Jay, but he did need to do something about him, so he didn't run off and get back up. Leaving a dead body here may not be the best idea either. "Toss your guns over in the bushes," Billy said.

Jay reached into his holster and did as Billy commanded. Billy grabbed Carol's gun and tossed it into the bushes.

"Now get in the truck," Billy said, still pointing the gun at Jay and still holding Carol's arm with the strength of a vice. He walked the two over to the truck. "You drive," he said to Jay as he and Carol got in the passenger side. Billy stuck the barrel of the gun into Carol's side when they got in the truck. "Try anything, and she becomes a memory. You hear me, lad?"

"Yeah, ok, Rich. Jesus Christ, man. What is wrong with you?" Jay said.

"Head to the dock where I keep my boat. Now."

As Jay pulled out of the driveway and away from Rich's house, the excitement of everything taking place took his attention from the other cars on the road, and he didn't notice the car following him..

Twenty-One

"Dispatch, I got a lead on Officer Harris," the radio chirped. Officer Stengele jumped up from his micro-nap and grabbed the radio.

"This is Stengele. Who's this? What do you got?"

"Yeah, this is Officer Dayton, I had someone come up to my window and say that they seen a guy matchin' his description down near Hammock's Beach talking to himself. I'm in my truck, or I'd go myself."

"Nope, we got it, thanks Dayton." Stengele immediately made the next radio call out. "All boats in the vicinity of Hammock's Beach, be on the lookout for Officer Rich Harris, last seen near Hammock's Beach." Billy had already gone from that place, all the way to Rich's house, and was now headed back to the docks to go to Bear Island by the time the call came through.

"Harris again?" A voice answered back, "sounds to me like a trend with this guy. I'm near there, this is Johnson. I'll call if I see him."

Captain Kelly answered his phone. It was the hospital calling to inform him that Officer Bell had checked himself out. "Thank you nurse," he said, and hung up the phone. He picked it back up and dialed Officer Bell's number. The phone rang and rang, but Bell didn't answer. The Captain figured he wouldn't answer. He knew how upset Bell was about losing his eye, and subsequently his job. "Stengele!" He yelled out his open door.

"Yes, sir!" Stengele shouted back, jumping up from his chair. He ran over to the Captain's door.

"Find Bell. Have someone call his house, his cell, hell have someone go to his house."

"Sir, is everything ok? Is he out of the hosp—"

"Find him, God damnit. Jesus, this whole department is falling apart. I got an officer who starts losing his mind, so I suspend him, then he goes and assaults another officer, allegedly, and now I got a one eyed pissed off officer leave a hospital against the Doctor's orders. Christ almighty, this shit is gonna get my ass canned." Captain Kelly felt as if he was losing his grasp of the station. He had already had to alert the local law enforcement units about his missing officer, who assaulted another officer. That was embarrassing enough to have to tell another department. Now Bell was missing, but then again, Bell was probably just upset about his job, or his eye, and went home. "Yes sir, I'll call Dayton. He can swing by Bell's—"

"I don't need a play-by-play Stengele. Get it done. If you talk to him, tell him I'm pissed, but I understand, tell him he's allowed to leave, but it's stupid, tell him — just tell him to call me."

"Yes, sir." Stengele scurried out and went to his desk. He grabbed his phone and called Officer Dayton. He didn't want to hear any more smart ass remarks about missing officers. The Captain might blow a gasket if he heard anything else like that on the radio. Stengele explained the situation to Dayton as best he could, and Officer Dayton headed to Officer Bell's house.

*****

"Rich, come on man, talk to us," Jay said.

"Rich, Rich, Rich," Billy answered, annoyed at the sound of the name. "Listen fella, I know this may come as a shock to ya, but I ain't this 'Rich' fella you keep referrin' to." Carol looked over to Jay with a worried expression. She looked back at Billy.

"It's us, Rich. You know us. We're your friends—", she said.

"There you go again, girly. I think you may be hard of hearin'. Maybe you two are just a little slow. I s'pose I can see how it'd be confusin', me looking like yir friend, but I ain't him."

"Why are you talking like this, man? For God's sake, you're freaking us out." Jay said.

Carol and Jay each thought the worst, that their dear friend had completely lost his mind. Now here they were being held hostage with no clear way out of the situation. Carol thought maybe Rich suddenly became schizophrenic or something. That would explain his erratic behavior, and why he was talking the way he was. But it didn't account for Rich's face, or his strength. This was something more than some mental disorder.

Billy ignored them and looked around at the world around him as they headed down the road. He wondered what some of the things were; a teenager on a skateboard was completely foreign to Billy. He looked at the lights of the signs in front of stores. None of it looked familiar to him. "300 years," he said under his breath.

Carol looked at him. "What?" She said.

"Keep goin'. We're going to yir friend's boat. Not another word or I'll carve out your eye." Something told them he was serious. They fell silent and didn't dream of making a peep. Billy had more to say, though. "It's been 300 years. Don't make sense to you cause you've never seen magic like the magic of my time." Carol and Jay could feel the reality that their friend was completely gone setting in. They listened in silence at the wild story Billy decided to tell them. "See, I ain't from this time. You two fools don't know that cause the magic brought me here." He figured it made no difference if they knew who he was since the man would be dead soon enough and the woman would become Imala. Who would they tell? Who would believe them if they did tell. Billy hadn't been able to piece it all together yet, and it felt good to reminisce about his former glory. After all, Billy hadn't gotten any of the credit he deserved because no one had ever heard of him. Surely he could brag a little. "Sir friend, this '*Rich*' fella you keep yapping about. He's the one that found my treasure. I don't come from this time. Last year I remember before coming back was 1720." Fear of death began to flood through Carol as she could hear the mad rantings of a lunatic. This was not her friend. "I'm Captain Billy Thompson — the greatest pirate who ever lived, cheater of death, and Captain of the... the..." Billy's memory wasn't quite back fully. He grew frustrated. "Blast it all the shit!" He yelled. Carol and Jay flinched, each believing they were about to be shot. "Just keep moving!"

Jay pulled into a parking spot near the docks, and the three got out of the truck. Billy grabbed Carol's arm and motioned Jay to walk toward the boat. Carol let out short cries as Billy's hand was hurting her arm. Jay was desperately trying to think of a way out of this. He thought about how he could lunge at Billy, who he still thought was Rich, and wrestle the gun out of his hand, but that thought seemed to end with him getting shot. They got onto the boat as Billy untied from the cleat. He climbed in and pushed the boat away from the dock. They each sat down, Billy motioned for Jay to take the wheel. He was smart enough to keep the man busy, so he could try anything.

"South side of Bear Island," Billy said, instructing Jay where to drive the boat. We're gonna have a little history lesson today, folks. I remember where my treasure was buried, and that's where we're gonna put it for the time being. Seems that may be the best place for it since it stayed hidden for 300 years. I don't need no one stumblin' onto my loot no more." Billy looked Carol up and down. "You'll do just fine, girly." Carol didn't know what to think. This was insane. They were being led to their deaths by their closest friend.

One of the things pirates always did when heading out to sea was to watch behind them to see if they were being followed. This was no different. Billy kept looking back to see if anyone was behind them, but he saw no one. He was in the clear.

As they headed toward the south side of Bear Island, they had to pass by Hammock's Beach where Billy was spotted earlier, and where there happened to be a boat, operated by Officer Johnson, the smart ass from the earlier radio call, waiting for a Rich Harris sighting. Jay could see the bow of Johnson's boat up ahead, but decided not to say anything. This could be their chance to end all of this. As they got closer, Billy looked ahead and saw the boat. He jammed his gun into Carols ribcage. "Friend of yours?" He said.

Jay didn't want to take a chance with Carol's life, so he was partially honest. "I'm not sure. It may be one of ours," Jay said. They got closer, about 30 feet away, and Officer Johnson could see them approaching.

"You better get rid of him, or he's a dead man." Billy said.

"He's looking for us, Rich... Billy... or whoever you are. He's doing his job. I can tell him we have you — ", Jay said.

"Tell him what you gotta tell him, but get rid of him, or he dies." Normally this wouldn't have been an empty threat. Billy couldn't risk drawing attention though until after the spell was complete. He knew that killing the man in the boat would surely bring others, and if he didn't have the staff, or Imala, he risked disappearing back into the dark depths of eternity. As they came closer, Johnson picked up his radio and called the station, letting them know he saw someone approaching that could be Officer Harris, but he couldn't quite make him out.

Jay could see that it was in fact Officer Johnson. "Hey Johnson, it's Luther and Massey. We've got this all under control. Already called it in, you can go ahead back to the station." Jay called out.

Johnson looked at him, puzzled. This was a very strange encounter. If they did in fact "have him", then why is he sitting awkwardly next to Officer Massey, and why was his arm hiding under his jacket? "Uh, hey Luther, you guys ok?" Johnson asked.

"Yeah man, we're good," Jay tried to signal with his eyes and eyebrows to alert Johnson that something was out of place, "we're taking him in now."

"The station's the other way," Johnson said, still puzzled at the scene he was witnessing. He placed his hand on his weapon, but didn't draw it.

Billy could tell something was wrong and that the other man didn't believe what he was being told. Billy stood up and pulled Carol up with him. He held the gun up to Carol's head and pulled her in front of himself.

Johnson drew his weapon and pointed it at Billy. "Woah woah woah!" He yelled. "Easy Harris!"

"Woah man, don't do anything crazy," Jay yelled. Jay dropped from his chair and held his hands up. "Please Ri... Billy... Captain, don't do it, please, man."

"Now you listen to me, lad. You're gonna toss your pistol into the water right now, or this young lady is gonna have her thoughts splattered out of the left side of her pretty little head." Billy said.

"Do it Johnson, throw down your gun," Jay said.

Officer Johnson had the same amount of police training as just about everyone else in the North Carolina Wildlife Resource Commission, but not one scenario helped in this particular situation. He was in a full panic — his gun now shaking as he pointed it. He realized he was not equipped to handle this.

"Do it, boy, or I'm shooting both of them, and I'll gut you and chum these waters without a second thought."

Johnson believed this and slowly lowered his gun and tossed it into the water.

"Good boy," Billy said, "now pull up your anchor." Billy said. Johnson complied and slowly pulled the anchor in. Carol was crying, wondering which moment would be her last. Once the anchor was inside the boat, Billy pointed at the dock line on Johnson's boat. "Now throw us the line." Johnson did as he was told and tossed Jay the dock line. Billy pointed his gun at the water. "Now jump in."

Johnson was compliant; he sat on the edge of his boat, threw his legs over the side and jumped in. Billy turned to Jay. "Tie the line, we'll be taking the boat with us. It ain't exactly the fleet I had in mind, but it's a start." Billy joked. "Now keep going, and you there in the water," he said, "if we're followed, or found, you can bet your ass these two will be fish food." He looked back at Jay. "Get going, boy. Get us to Bear Island."

Jay looked at Johnson treading water as they drove the two boats away. He was thankful that Rich hadn't killed Johnson, something Jay now thought he was completely capable of doing. Maybe his friend was still in there somewhere. Maybe they still had a chance.

All the commotion had captured Billy's attention. That was fun to him, not as fun as killing the man as he wished he could have done, but fun. What he hadn't been paying attention to was the fact that they were being followed.

Twenty-Two

"Johnson, this is Dispatch, do you read me?" Stengele said. "Johnson, are you there?" Stengele was trying to get Johnson back on the radio. He had called in a possible sighting of Officer Harris, but now he wasn't answering his radio. It could have been nothing, but protocol wouldn't allow Stengele to blow this off. "All boats in the vicinity of Hammock's Beach, please call in if you get eyes on Officer Harris or Officer Johnson." This really wasn't Stengele's week, or the department's week for that matter. It seemed like everyone was missing; first Harris, then Bell, now Johnson, and what about Luther and Massey? They hadn't checked in for quite some time. Stengele once again figured he'd better keep this off of the radio. He picked up his cell and dialed Officer Luther.

Jay felt his pocket vibrate. Rich hadn't made them throw their cell phones, only their guns. Jay became excited about this lifeline, but he knew he couldn't answer the phone. Not with Rich watching his every move.

Stengele hung up and dialed Officer Massey's number. Her phone rang loud enough to startle both her and Billy. Billy had never heard anything like it. It resembled music, but it was louder than any music box Billy had ever seen. He aimed his gun at her. "What is that?" He asked, trying to mask his nervousness.

Carol figured that this might be her last chance to save herself. She picked up the phone slowly and showed Billy. "It's ok, it's just my cell." Billy didn't know what that was. He thought it might be a weapon, so he was on edge and aimed again. "Wait," Carol said as she held it out in front of her. She hit the 'answer' button, but didn't put it up to her ear. She slowly laid the phone on the deck. Stengele was talking, but no one in the boat could hear him.

"What's that thing?" Billy said, ready to shoot — still unable.

"It's ok Harris, it's ok. You can put the gun down. We're almost at Bear Island's south side. You'll get what you wanted." Carol said. This talk was strange even to someone who wasn't from this time. Billy was confused. He reached his foot up and slammed it hard onto the phone, smashing it into pieces.

Carol talked enough for Stengele to alert the Captain who was already gearing up to go out that way since Johnson's initial call. He had three other boats of two-man teams of officer in the ready as well. The four boats left the station, heading for Bear Island's south side.

Jay slowed the boat down a little more every couple of minutes in hopes that someone would be able to catch up to them if they slowed enough. Billy was still frazzled by the noisy magical device, but he could tell they were going slower. "Move it, sonny. If you wanna live to see another sunset, you may want to get where we're goin' quick." Billy said. He planned on killing Jay anyway, but threats were second nature to Billy. Jay sped up slightly. The four boats leaving the station were at full throttle, heading straight for Bear. They drove in a staggered line, speeding past other boaters on the water. People looking on from afar, wondering what was going on that had this many wildlife boats heading to at the same time. Must've been a drug bust, some thought.

Billy, Jay and Carol were approaching the south side of Bear Island as Billy pointed to the spot where Rich had first landed the night he had found the treasure. Billy couldn't remember that, but he remembered where he had parked the small dingy he, Imala, and two of his crew had parked when they initially brought the treasure here to hide. He also knew how many paces the cave would be.

Jay pulled the boat onto the sand. The three jumped off of the boat, Billy holding the gun on them as Jay pulled the boat up onto the sand and set the anchor. Billy looked up toward the Island. He could see both east, ocean facing side, and the west side of the island from where they stood. He remembered the paces and knew to stay in the center while walking. As he was looking up and studying the island, he hadn't been watching Jay, who had crept up behind him.

Jay jumped up as high as he could and landed on Billy's back. As he jumped, he swung down hard on Billy's right arm, knocking the gun from his hand. All his weight and all his might slammed onto Billy, and Billy fell to one knee. He immediately gained footing and, with Jay still on his back, he stood as if Jay were a child. The two wrestled and shuffled, Billy reaching back for Jay, trying to get a good enough grip to throw him off. Billy would kill Jay just as soon as he could swing him off of his back. He finally got a good hold with his right hand on the back of Jay's neck and he pulled forward as hard as he could, slamming Jay onto the sand hard. Billy pulled his knife out instinctively and drove it toward Jay's throat. Just then a gunshot rang out, and a bullet hit the ground near Billy's foot. Billy held the knife near Jay's throat. He and Jay looked up to see Carol holding the gun. Billy wondered how she was able to make it shoot.

"Get off of him," she said with tears in her eyes. She aimed the gun right at Billy's head. Billy knew that he would be shot if he made a wrong move. He slowly lowered the knife and set it on the ground.

"Easy girly," Billy said. "You don't want to go doing that if you ever want to see your precious 'Rich' ever again." This would be a last ditch effort for Billy, but Carol didn't understand the threat, so it had little effect. "Put the pistol down and I'll spare your lives. We just need to get up here and I'll show you how to save him." Since Jay and Carol knew nothing of the spell, and still saw their friend — albeit very strange looking, but there nonetheless — speaking to them, this still meant nothing to them.

"Now, Rich. Get off of him." She said sternly. Just then, four boats acmes swinging around the west side of Bear Island, all with lights flashing as they came to the south side. Carol's tears were blocking her view, so she wiped some away while still locked onto Billy. Jay slid away slowly and then got to his feet next to Carol. The Captain got on the bullhorn. "This is the North Carolina Wildlife Resource Commission," he said, wishing he could simply say 'the police', but knowing that wasn't completely accurate. "Officer Harris, lay down on the ground, face down." The officers on all four boats had guns drawn as they jumped off their respective boats and pulled them up onto the shore.

Billy slowly laid onto his stomach on the sand. Time was running out, and now he has lost the woman, the treasure... the treasure. He hadn't quite lost that. No one knew it was on the boat. Carol and Jay thought it was still at Rich's house.

The Captain approached while the officers all pounced on Billy and cuffed him. He reached up and laid a hand onto Carol's still aimed pistol. He slowly guided it down. "Easy, Massey. It's alright, we got him." He said. He walked over to Billy while the officers stood Billy up.

"Officer Harris, you are under arrest for the assault of Officer Bell, and for the robbery and attempted murder of two civilians, as well as for arson—"

"What the hell?" Jay said.

"Seems Harris here beat two men up on their boat, took their wallets and set fire to their boat while they were still in it. They jumped off before being burned alive." Captain Kelly said. Jay and Carol looked on in shock.

"Oh my God," Carol said, "I think I'm going to be sick."

"Easy, Carol," Jay said as he put an arm around her. The two sat on the sand as the officers led Billy back to their own boat. "Take it easy, it's gonna be ok."

"Massey, Luther, we're gonna need statements from you both," Captain Kelly said, "and would you mind bringing his boat back? We'll need to take it in for evidence."

"Yes sir," Carol said, "also Captain, our weapons... he made us throw them into the bushes at his house."

"Go ahead by and grab them, don't go in the house obviously, but we got a little time. We're gonna get him back to the station for questioning. I imagine he'll want to contact his lawyer—"

As the Captain spoke, Carol remembered the treasure sitting in Rich's den. She considered telling the Captain at that moment, but for some reason decided she'd wait. She still held out hope that this was some kind of nightmare that she would eventually wake up from, and that Rich was still able to be saved.

Captain Kelly and the other officers pulled their boats away from shore as Carol and Jay were walking toward Rich's boat. They watched Rich or Billy as he sat handcuffed on one of the station boats. Billy was staring up toward the center of the island still. It was as if he knew something they didn't.

Carol and Jay each tuned to face the center of the island, both looking for some clue. They were wondering what Rich was looking at. They were wondering why he had brought them back to Bear in the first place. There must be something here.

"What do you think?" Jay asked.

"Just a quick check?" Carol asked.

"I mean, there's got to be a reason he brought us here."

"I agree, but what the hell could that possibly be? The treasure is at his house."

"What if there's more, Carol? What if that wasn't all of it?"

"We should check it out."

The two walked toward the center of the island. Jay took a look back at the beach to see that Captain Kelly and the other officers were gone, and that Rich's boat was still parked. Carol pulled out her cell phone and dialed Stengele's number.

"Hey Stengele, it's Massey," she said.

"Yeah, Captain Kelly said they got him. Sorry Massey, I know y'all are friends."

"Never mind that. Listen, I need you to see who is on land and can swing by Rich's place. They can NOT go in, Captain's orders, plus we'd need a warrant, but mine and Luther's weapons are in the bushes in the front of the house. Harris had us throw them in there. Can you have an officer go get those while we wrap things up here?"

"Yeah, no problem, Dayton is in a truck. What did he say to you guys—"

"Thanks Stengele, Gotta go." Carol hung up the phone. It was no time for gossip.

Neither of them knew what they were looking for, and the sun was dropping lower in the sky. If they didn't find a clue soon, they'd have to come back tomorrow.

What Jay and Carol hadn't known as they walked further inland, was that the person that had been following them was watching from a distance as everything unfolded on the island.

*****

Danny watched as Harris held Massey at gunpoint. He was waiting behind another small patch of land for his opportunity to attack, but since Harris was armed, he couldn't just go in guns a blazing. Danny saw Luther jump onto Harris's back. He watched as Massey picked up the gun and held it pointed at Harris. He even saw the four approaching station boats with lights blaring coming up to the island. He saw the Captain and the other officers arrest Harris. This part was almost too much. Danny wanted his revenge, and now the Captain was having Harris arrested and taken away. Danny waited patiently for the four boats to leave. He would follow Massey and Luther when they went back to Harris's house. Then he noticed that they weren't going to Harris's house. He saw that they were walking inland.

Once Massey and Luther were out of view of the beach, Danny decided to drive over and park on Bear Island. He pulled the boat up next to Harris's boat and pulled it ashore. He set the anchor in the sand and walked over to Harris's boat. He looked inside, but didn't see anything of use, so he decided to follow Massey and Luther to wherever they were going. Danny's curiosity was piqued.

He started walking toward the direction the other two had been walking, careful not to be spotted. Further and further inland and the terrain became more vegetated and hard to walk through. He saw Massey following Luther further inland. They were far enough away that he could quickly drop down into the brush if he were spotted. He noticed they had stopped and were pointing at something ahead of them as they had a conversation that he couldn't hear.

*****

Carol and Jay looked at the white cloth on the ground and wondered what it was. Jay reached down to pick it up.

"Looks like a shirt," he said. Jay knew that Bear Island was a popular camping spot, but that was on the north side of the island. The brush on the south side made it uninteresting to visitors.

"Look," Carol said as she pointed a few feet in front of the shirt. There was a pile of sticks covering what appeared to be a large hole in the ground. It looked as if someone had haphazardly thrown the pile onto the hole to cover it, but didn't do a very good job of it.

Rich hadn't really done a good job of covering up after himself after he had found the treasure. He left the shirt, and he didn't cover the hole complete. He hadn't cared at the time though because he had the most important thing he needed from the cave... or so he had thought.

Twenty-Three

As Jay lay headfirst into the hole, looking down with Carol's cell phone as a light, he could see the beams that Rich had used to get up out of the hole. "Looks like there's something down here, Carol."

"What do you see?"

"I'm gonna climb down these beams. I can't believe there is a cave here. I don't know how this isn't flooded with water."

"Easy Jay, I don't know if you should be going in all the way—". As she spoke, Jay was already easing himself down the beams and onto the ground inside the cave. "Great, thanks for listening," she said sarcastically.

"Jesus Christ!" Jay shouted.

"What? What is it? What do you see?"

"Carol. You gotta get down here. You gotta see this."

Carol thought about the danger of jumping down into a strange cave in the middle of an island, but that thought lost the battle to her curiosity. She quickly grabbed onto the edge of the hole and lowered her feet down. She grabbed onto the beams and lowered herself into the hole.

As Carol reached the ground, she looked up around the cave and saw that there were bodies in various places. She let out a short, excited screech, but contained herself. "Jesus."

"Yeah, I know, and they're old as shit. Like no flesh whatsoever."

"What the... how old do you think... who were they?"

Jay and Carol walked around looking at the bodies and examining as best they could without touching any of them. They noticed their clothes didn't look like any modern day clothes. Jay noticed that one was holding an old-looking pistol. "Oh my God, look at this." He pointed at the gun. "That thing has to be a couple hundred years old."

Carol noticed a large rectangular spot with much less dust and dirt than everywhere else in the cave where there seemed to have been something missing. "There," she said, pointing at the spot. "He must've gotten the treasure from right there. Jesus, Jay, this is really happening."

Jay looked around at the bodies and again took note of their clothing. The old pistol — he started putting it all together.

"Ok, I'll say it," Jay said, "Rich found a burned pirate treasure, and these are dead pirates." This ridiculous sentence just came out of his mouth, and it was true.

"Not all of them," Carol said, looking quizzically at the one against the wall, a few feet away from the one nearest the spot where the treasure once laid. "Look at that one. It's not dressed like the others. This must've been a hostage. Looks like a dress... I think this one's a woman."

"There weren't lady pirates?"

"I'm not saying that, I'm just saying that this one isn't dressed like a pirate. I don't know." Just then, Carol saw the dust on the ground begin to move as if the wind had shifted, though there was no wind inside the cave. The dirt swirled and shifted, drawing Carol's attention slightly to the right of the skeleton that appeared to be a woman. She noticed a pile of sticks, but among them, something out of place. She saw that one of the sticks was not like the others. It was a weathered gray stick that looked long, like a staff. It had points that looked like the shape of a fire's flames, and they swirled together at the tip. Carol felt drawn to it. She walked over to it, knelt down, reached out her hand—

"Stop," Jay said, "We're not touching anything, Carol. This is a crime scene." But Carol couldn't stop. She reached down and grabbed the staff.

As she touched the staff, the surrounding dirt blew away in all directions as if it had exploded, but it hadn't. Carol slowly stood as the cave walls seemed to be shaking slightly.

"Damn it, Carol, you know this is a crime scene, and now you've contaminated it." Jay began to notice the shaking of the cave walls becoming more prominent. He could see that Carol was ignoring him. "Carol!" he shouted.

Carol snapped out of whatever daydream she was in. The walls no longer shook. She looked at Jay as if she had just been woken up from a dream.

"What the hell was that?" Jay asked.

"I... I don't know... I felt..."

"Look," Jay said, "behind you on the ground." He pointed to an object that had been uncovered when the dust moved. Carol turned around and looked down at what appeared to be a rolled up piece of paper.

"It's old. Really old," she said, "should I touch it?"

"You're already touched that tree branch, you may as well. Just be careful," he said.

Carol knelt down and picked up the paper. It looked like an ancient scroll from a movie. Little did they know, it was just that. She placed the staff down against the wall of the cave and began to unravel the paper. Jay walked over to have a look. He looked down at the branch Carol had picked up while Carol was opening the paper. He reached down to have a look for himself.

"Stop," Carol said, "Do not touch it."

Jay was taken aback. What the hell was she talking about? She had already contaminated the scene. Who cared if he touched it at this point. "Jesus, ok, it's not a big deal. You want your prints to be the only ones on it, suit yourself" Jay couldn't tell that Carol was being protective over the staff.

She studied the paper. It had symbols and words. She could tell this was extremely old, but had no idea of its actual age or origin. It was written in another language that Carol certainly couldn't read. She handed the scroll to Jay. "Any idea what language this is?"

Jay gave it a look. "Yikes, not a clue, but it's old as hell."

Carol felt drawn again to the staff, and she reached over and picked it up. She held it as Jay examined the paper. He turned the paper over to look at the back, and Carol caught another glimpse of the words on the front. They appeared to be readable now, as if the ink on the paper had somehow changed. "Wait," she said, "Let me see that again."

Jay handed Carol the scroll.

"I can read it," she said.

Jay looked down at the same words Carol was looking at, the same words they had been the whole time, and wondered what she was talking about. "It's another language, Carol."

Carol read the words, but did not speak them aloud. She somehow knew what would happen if she did...

Souls through love forever bound
Eternal grip shall not release
Upon the solstice and on this ground
Unshaken spirits will not cease
Blood of the body forever ties
That which the soul is truly drawn
Unending passion hears the cries
Sealed forever by the dawn

"Well?" Jay said. "You can suddenly read whatever language this is. What does it say?"

"It's some kind of ancient language that isn't spoken anymore. I don't know how I know that." Carol said, not knowing where her knowledge had come from.

"And you somehow know how to speak it?"

"I don't know... I guess... I just..." Carol, confused about her new knowledge, took out her phone and began typing the words. She hit search and got a bunch of random results that had nothing to do with anything, really. "Nothing."

"I have an idea. I have a friend who's a history buff. Email it to her and see if she can help. I would, but our pal Rich destroyed my phone. Her email address is... are you ready?" Jay said, but Carol wasn't ready to type yet. When she finally gave the 'go ahead,' nod, Jay said, "queenbee69@hotmail.com."

"Please tell me you're joking."

"Oh, and put on there that you're my friend, and that my phone is destroyed. Yeah, I'm serious, that's her address. She's a weirdo. We used to sort of date. Anyway, she knows all kinds of useless shit about history. I've even heard her talk about caveman stuff — hieroglyphics and shit like that. It's worth a shot."

"I guess." Carol hit send. "And now we wait." Carol began to lose interest in the conversation rapidly. A little too rapidly. "I need no one's help..." she said, without thinking.

"What?"

"I didn't mean to say that," she said. As Jay looked at Carol, he could visibly see a new color begin to wash over her face. Her eyes seemed to change to a darker color.

"Carol, are you ok?" Jay watched Carol's face as it began to distort. "Carol?"

Carol shook her head hard. Everything seemed normal looking again to Jay. "I'm ok," she said, but she wasn't very convincing.

"Carol, what the hell was that? Your skin... your eyes changed color, they turned like really blue... what was that?"

"Must have been the lighting in here. It's getting dark, we need to get the hell out of here. We can alert the police of these bodies, and we need to get to the station to give our statements."

"Lighting my ass, that was strange. I saw what I saw." Jay thought about the other person he knew whose face looked distorted from what they normally look like. He began to wonder if he was losing his mind. So many strange things had been happening around him for a while now. He thought for a split second that it could just be him. "You're right though, we need to get going."

They walked over to the beams and got ready to climb back out. Carol took one last look around the cave.

"You got that scroll thing still?" Jay asked, "Make sure you grab that. That thing could be a clue or something." Carol nodded and patted her pocket where she had stored the scroll. She held the staff tightly.

They began climbing up the beams. Carol struggled as she was only using one arm as she was holding the staff in the other. Jay got out first and reach down to help Carol. He pulled her out, and they stood looking at the cave opening.

"Should we cover it up?" Jay asked.

"Yeah, we don't need anyone falling in there, or even finding this place."

"So, leave the shirt?"

"Unless you have a better way for us to find it when we show the police where this is."

Jay placed the white shirt back a few feet from the hole, so he could easily find it, but so that it was away from the hole enough that if someone happened to stumble upon it, they may not actually find the cave. They turned toward the south side of the island to head back to the boat. As they turned around, the first thing they both saw was a man holding a gun aimed at them. The man had a patch over his right eye.

"Well, well," the man said. "If it isn't the crime fighting team of the century."

"Bell?" Jay said. "Holy shit man, what happened." Jay knew full well what had happened to Danny, but was asking in a rhetorical way.

"What happened?"

"I didn't men—"

"What happened? I'll tell you what happened, asshole. That sonofabitch prick friend of yours got a lucky shot in and hit a man while he was down." Danny believed so deeply that he was superior to Rich Harris in every way, so the only way this could have possibly happened was if it was luck. Forget about the absorption of such a hard punch, or the almost superhuman strength Rich possessed at the time; it had to be luck.

"Put the gun down, Bell," Carol said, "it's us, you can see that now, so stop pointing it at us."

Danny didn't flinch. He smirked and kept the gun aimed. "Where is he?"

"Danny, I'm serious. Put the goddamn gun down, or you're going to be charged with endangering the life of an officer, assault with a deadly weapon, do you really need charges like that? Now I'm sure you're going through a difficult time, but you don't want to threaten us and make it worse." Danny kept the gun pointed. "Goddamnit you started it, Danny! You went to the sandbar looking for a fight. You did. Not Rich — you. And he beat you up, and now you're pissed. Well, oh well."

Danny pulled the hammer of the gun back with his thumb. Carol swallowed hard, and Jay took a step forward, holding out his hand.

"Ok, ok, easy Danny," Jay said, "let's all just take it easy, man. It's ok, we're on the same team here, man. We're on the same team—"

"Same team, huh? What team is that, Luther? The North... Carolina... Wildlife... Resource... Commission? Well guess what, dickhead, that's where you're wrong. I ain't a part of that "team" anymore." He made air quotes when he said the word.

"Oh shit man, I'm sorry to hear that," Jay said, though he wasn't sorry at all. Everyone hated Officer Danny Bell, and this news was actually good news.

"Seems that losing an eye makes me medically disqualified to be a wildlife officer. So your good buddy Harris has ended my goddamn career. I know that prick is on drugs or something. There is no way you get that strong out of nowhere. Tell you what though, that asshole took my life away, and now I'm gonna take his life away."

"Woah, woah, Danny, listen to yourself," Carol said, "that's not the answer. Killing Rich won't solve your problems."

"I'm not just gonna kill him, Massey. You two shitbags didn't stop him, did you?"

"Jesus Bell, listen to yourself," she said. "If you're trying to scare us, you have. You can stop now. We're scared. Now stop." She grew tired of cowering. She quickly became unafraid. She quickly became very brave.

"Trying to scare you? Ha!"

"Then do it," she said. Jay looked at Carol like she was speaking gibberish. "Why are you talking so much?"

"Carol, what the hell are you thinking?" Jay said. Carol began to look like she did in the cave. Her skin tone seemed darker, and her eyes turned a piercing blue.

"Listen to your friend, Massey," Danny said. "You think I'm the kind of guy that makes idle threats?" He was hesitating, but only so he could work up the nerve to do it. Danny did want to kill them, but he had never killed anyone before, so he knew it would be tough at first. His life was over, so he had nothing left to lose.

"Do it, Bell. Stop being so weak. You have always been weak. You could never be Billy because he is stronger than you will ever be."

"Billy?" Danny said, confused. "Who the hell is Billy?"

"You are half the man he is, Bell. You are weak and small, and you can not harm us."

Danny was becoming infuriated.

"Carol, who the hell is Billy?" Jay said.

Danny aimed the gun directly at Carol. She squeezed the staff. He had never shot a weapon using his left eye before. He was right-handed. This was the first time he had realized he might miss whatever he is aiming at. He looked down the barrel with his left eye, holding the gun awkwardly in his right hand.

"Danny, please man, she doesn't know what she's talking about." Jay said, fearing for Carol's life. "Danny, please."

Danny applied a slight amount of pressure to the trigger. He stepped closer to Carol to make sure he didn't miss. Carol began to smile slightly.

"Do it, Danny."

Danny felt a calm come over him. He moved closer to Carol. He held the gun up to her forehead. No way to miss now. He applied pressure to the trigger. He pulled back as hard as he could on the trigger. He waited for the feeling of a small explosion in his hand, but it didn't come. He looked at his hand and his trigger finger hadn't moved; in fact, it couldn't move. He tried to pull the trigger, but his finger wasn't doing what his brain was telling it to do. He wasn't paralyzed, but he couldn't pull the trigger.

Carol was squeezing the staff. She pointed the staff down to the ground, and Danny's hand, along with the gun, lowered at the same time, pointing to the ground. "You are weak. You are no man." Jay watched in complete shock. Danny was terrified that he was unable to control his actions. He opened his mouth to say something smart when a sudden "THWACK!" Had come across his face. Carol had swung the staff so hard it knocked Danny out cold. The concussion played a part, of course, but it was still a hard hit.

"Holy shit, Carol, he could've killed you. He was going to kill you." Carol stared around at the beach around her as if she was seeing it for the first time. "Carol, are you listening to me? Carol?"

"Do not speak. I wish to look and to think."

"Carol, are you ok? What the hell is going on with you?"

She turned and looked at Jay. "What?" She said. Her face was not quite back to normal, nor was her skin tone.

"Carol, what is going on? What is wrong? Ar you ok?"

"I feel strange, Jay. Like I passed out or something." She held her staff, and for now, her footing in this world. Imala was fighting hard to take the wheel.

Twenty-Four

Billy sat in a small room, which was the closest thing the station had to a cell since it wasn't actually a police station. He was cuffed to the table and patiently waiting for his big escape to enter his mind. He was thinking of how he would spring himself before he was to be hanged as a pirate. Of course Billy didn't know that that sort of thing didn't happen anymore. He felt like a caged animal nonetheless.

Captain Kelly and Sergeant Macon entered the small room and sat at the two chairs opposite Billy. "Harris, you have been read your Miranda rights. I will ask, would you like to wait for your lawyer, or would you be willing to answer some questions?" The Captain asked. Billy just stared quizzically at the Captain. He only understood a couple of the words in those sentences. "Harris, do you understand your rights, and would you like to answer questions?"

"Rights? Lawyers? Questions? You know what I did and who I am or else I wouldn't be sittin' here."

"Harris, why are you talking so strangely? This is not a joke. You're facing serious charges," Captain Kelly said.

"Why are people calling me all these different names," Billy said, "Rich this, Harris that." He looked the Captain in the eyes. "Don't make no difference what you call me for the time being. Soon you'll be addressing me by my proper name."

Captain Kelly and Sergeant Macon looked at each other in disbelief. Rich Harris had clearly lost his mind. This was not the officer they knew a week ago.

"Harris, why are you doing this?" Captain Kelly asked, "is this because of the suspension? All you had to do was take some time off. You would've had your job here waiting for you. You had to go and assault an officer. And Frankly I don't care who started the goddamn fight. You put the man in the hospital. He lost an eye. Then you go and allegedly rob a couple of fishermen and burn their boat down? You're looking at attempted murder here, Harris. You could spend years behind bars. Years! Is it temporary insanity you're shooting for with this act? Is that it? Well, I hope that works out for you. We're transferring you to the county sheriff's department. They'll be handling the investigation."

Billy was looking around the room, uninterested in Captain Kelly's little speech. He wanted to yank hard on his cuffs to see if he could break free, but he thought it better to just wait and formulate a plan. His irritation was growing. No one was taking him seriously. They didn't know what Captain Billy Thompson was capable of.

"Ok, just answer me this, Harris," Captain Kelly said, "was it you that robbed those fishermen?"

Billy looked up at the Captain and smiled. "Finally got something right."

"Jesus Christ, why would you do that? And you set their boat on fire? Left them to die?"

"They ain't fish food? I gotta stick around longer next time, make sure to finish what I started.""God damnit, Harris! This is not a game! You could've killed those men. It's a miracle they made it off the boat. Now this is not you. I've known you for a long time, son," Kelly shifted to the father figure approach, "and I know this isn't you. Now tell my why you did what you did — with them, and with Bell."

"I'm growing bored of this. It's time you let me out of here before all of you get to see my bad side."

Captain Kelly and Sergeant Macon looked at each other again. The Captain signaled to Sergeant Macon that this interview was over. The two stood and exited the room.

*****

"What do we do about him?" Jay said, pointing down at Danny Bell as he lay on the ground, out cold.

"I don't know. Can you throw him over your shoulder?"

"Are you serious? Look at me and look at him. Does that seem possible?"

"We gotta go, Jay. I can't explain it, but we have to find Rich. We have to."

"We can't just leave him here, Carol. Are you seriously considering that?"

"We drag him away from the cave on our way to the boat, get him far enough that he can't find it if he wakes up, I'll call the station when we get to the boat and they send someone to come get him. I have to see Rich. Now." Carol felt an overwhelming internal struggle and a need to find Rich. The need was greater than any logical solution to their current problem. "Or you can figure it out, I'm going." Jay could see that he wasn't going to change her mind.

"Ok, ok, let's at least pull him away from here. This is insane. I can't believe this." Jay grabbed Danny's right leg and Carol, with one hand, grabbed his left. The two began to pull Danny's limp body toward the boat. Splitting the 220 pounds between them made pulling the body much easier, but it was still difficult across the brush and sand.

They pulled him about 100 yards, and Carol was ready to leave him. "Ok, that's far enough, let's go," she said.

"Jesus, Carol," Jay said, wondering what has gotten in to his friend, "You're really ok with abandoning him here. I know he's an asshole, but this is crazy."

"What about the fact that he tried to kill me, Jay?"

Jay had no answer for this, and could see her point — at least a little. They dropped his legs and started hiking toward the boat. "You couldn't have left that damn thing in the cave?" Carol wouldn't put the staff down. "You know, when this is all over, we're gonna have a long conversation about all of it. I think we all need psychiatric help. First Rich, now you're acting strange, I feel like I'm losing my mind. This is all too much."

As they got closer to the boat, Carol took out her cell phone and called the station, as promised. "Stengele, this is Massey. Officer Luther and I are on Bear... I know, just listen. We're heading back now, but we need you to send some units here to get Officer Bell. He's knocked out... just listen... he's knocked out, but he tried to kill us... no, I'm not kidding. We had to leave him, it's important that I get back now... because we have to get back, and we couldn't carry him by ourselves. Listen, it's really important. We took his weapon, so he's not armed, but he is dangerous. He's lost it, Stengele, he was gonna shoot us." Carol went back and forth with Officer Stengele while Jay untied the boat and they both jumped in. Stengele immediately hung up and ran into Captain Kelly's office, where the Captain was on the phone with what appeared to be the sheriff's office. Sergeant Macon was waiting patiently by the Captain's desk. "What is it, Stengele?" He asked.

"Sergeant, I need to talk to the Captain—"

"Can't you see he's on the phone? What is it?" Macon asked in his best authoritative tone. Captain Kelly looked annoyed at both of them for continuing their conversation there in the office while he was clearly on an important phone call.

"Officer Massey just called from Bear—"

"They were supposed to be back by now—"

"I know, Sergeant, that's what I said too. Anyway, her and Luther are headed back, but get this... Bell is knocked out cold and they left him at Bear."

"What was he doing at Bear Island? He's knocked out? How did that happen? Why would they just leave him there?"

"I know, I know. Anyway, apparently Bell tried to kill them!" Stengele couldn't wait to get that part out. He tried for the best shocking affect he could get, and it appeared to have worked. The Captain looked up, and Macon looked over at Captain Kelly, who would certainly be taking over the conversation from here.

"I'll call you back," Captain Kelly told the person on the other end of the line. He hung up the phone. "What the hell did you just say?"

"Sir, Massey said that Bell pointed his weapon at her and Officer Luther and tried to kill them. I guess they knocked him out cold—"

"Pointed his weapon... what in the hell is... do you mean to tell me..." Captain Kelly had officially lost control of his officers. "And they left him there?!"

"Yes, sir. I guess so. She told me to get some units there—"

"Call her back right now, tell her and Luther to stay with Bell. They need to restrain him—"

"Sir, I tried that. They're already headed back here. She said she had to get back here—"

"God damn it, that's it! She's done. Luther is done. I'm gonna have their badges... Now! Do it now! Get someone there now and get his ass back here. What the hell has gotten in to this department? I want to see Massey and Luther the minute they step foot in this station." The Captain was pacing behind his desk. Macon and Stengele waited to see if he had anything else to say. "What the hell part of NOW did you not understand? Go, Stengele." Stengele ran out of the office and got to work. "Macon, get on the phone with the Sheriff's department. Tell them to come get Harris. I've got to make some calls. I have a feeling I'm going to be retiring soon whether I want to or not." He picked up the phone and shewed Macon out of the office.

Billy sat cuffed to the table. He knew his way out of this was through Imala. "Imala," he called out. He looked around the room and waited for his witch to appear. "Imala, come to me." Nothing. He yanked at the cuffs, which did nothing but hurt his own wrists. "Why do you not come when I call you, witch?" Billy looked around the small room and was still painfully alone. He sat and pondered ways to escape, but nothing came to mind. He began to wonder if this is all that would come of his 300 year jump through time — dying by rope shortly after arriving. It couldn't be. This is not the way Captain Billy Thompson meets his end.

The four Sheriff's deputies that entered the room might have seemed like a bit of overkill any other day, but after Officer Harris's display of beast-like strength, no one was taking any chances. They walked over and uncured Billy from the table and rebuffed his hands behind his back. Billy didn't put up a struggle as he was being escorted out o the building and into the police van out front. He would bide his time.

*****

As Jay drove the boat, he remembered the scroll and the fact that they knew nothing about its origin or the meaning of the words."Hey, check and see if my friend emailed you back."

Carol was staring off into the distance, not paying attention. Darkness was falling all around them.

"Carol, did you hear me?"

She snapped out of her daydream. "Sorry, what?"

"Check to see if my friend emailed you back."

Carol took out her cell and opened her email. "Nope."

"She just doesn't know who you are, maybe she thinks it's spam. Oh well, we can take it to the historical society or something."

Carol put her hand over her pocket and felt the scroll. She didn't want to take it to anyone. She didn't want her precious scroll being seen by another human being. Just as quickly and naturally that thought came to Carol, she wondered why she felt that way. It was strange, but she really didn't want anyone to have her scroll... *her* scroll. She felt the same way about the staff when Jay had tried to hold it. Why did she feel this sudden attachment to inanimate objects? "Let's just get to Rich, quickly."

"Yeah, I know, I know. Although I don't know why. He's going to be taken to jail, and there isn't anything we can do about it."

"He needs me — us. He needs us, Jay."

"There you go again, acting like a weirdo. I tell you what, we need to take some leave after all of this."

They pulled into the dock at the station, and Officer Dayton was already at the dock to meet them. "Captain wants to see you both in his office," Dayton said.

"Yeah, I figured that was gonna happen," Jay said. He started walking behind Dayton. Carol looked at the building to see if she could see Rich in the windows. "Carol, come on." She followed behind. When they got inside, Carol didn't see any signs of Rich. Dayton lead Jay and Carol into the Captain's office where Sergeant Macon and Captain Kelly had been waiting. "Sir, Officers Luther and Massey reporting as ordered—"

"Cut the shit. Sergeant Macon, escort these two to the interview room. Leave your guns here. Oh, that's right, you don't have them. Where is Bell's gun?" Jay reached into his pocket and took Bell's gun out and handed it to Captain Kelly. "Massey put that stick down and go with Sergeant Macon."

Carol looked at the Captain and didn't move. She was conflicted. On the one hand, she had never defied her Captain before, but on the other hand, she felt as if she could not let the staff out of her site.

"Massey! Put the goddamn stick down." Carol reluctantly set the staff to the side, propped up against a wall behind her. She took some comfort in knowing that no one really ever went into the Captain's office. "Good, now what else do either of you have on you? Empty your pockets."

"Sir, are we under arrest?" Jay asked.

"Empty your pockets, Officer, that's an order. You're under arrest just yet. We're gonna ask you some questions and we will see if I decide you need to be detained after that. Now empty them and then follow Sergeant Macon to the interview room."

Carol slowly took the scroll out and set it on the coffee table in the center of the room.

"Jesus, what the hell is that?" The Captain said, "You guys are out here playing '*Dungeons and Dragons*' while this station is falling apart." The four of them went into the interview room, leaving the staff and the scroll behind.

Twenty-Five

Three boats arrived at the south side of Bear Island to retrieve the unconscious Officer Danny Bell. They each set their respective anchors in the sand and began to walk inland. They walked about 50 yards and didn't see anyone. They stayed in the center of the island as instructed as that's where they were told Officer Bell would be. The four spread out to cover more ground, but as they made it further and further inland without seeing Officer Bell, they thought it best to call the station.

"Dispatch, go ahead," Stengele said.

"Yeah dispatch, we're out here on Bear, and don't see Bell anywhere. We've gone back and forth a couple hundred yards up the island. It's getting pretty dark, but he's definitely not where Massey and Luther said he'd be."

"Hang on a sec," Stengele said. He went over to the interview room and knocked on the door. Sergeant Macon opened it and Stengele explained what he was just told. Sergeant Macon told Stengele to have the men keep looking, and if they don't find him within 30 minutes, they would contact another agency for assistance.

"Ok you two, let's hear it — what in the hell would possess you to leave a hurt officer unconscious on an island?"

"Sir, Officer Bell attacked us — ", Jay said.

"Ok, so you subdue him, you don't god damn leave him. And what do you mean he attacked you? Why the hell does he have any beef with you? What was he even doing there? How'd he know you were on Bear Island?"

"Well, sir, I don't know why. I guess because we're friends with Harris. At least that's what he was talking about. He's really upset over getting his ass kicked by Harris... a fight which he started, sir — ", Jay said. Carol said nothing. She just sat and stared at the door.

"Massey, why are you being so quiet? Did you say he pointed the gun at you? Look, I'm not trying to be an asshole here, I hope you're ok. However, I just finished having my ass handed to me over this department and how many things have gone to total shit in the past few days. I need to know exactly what the hell is going on, so anything you two can tell me will help." He stared at Carol. "Massey, did you hear me?"

"Yes sir," she half paid attention. "It's like Luther said, sir — he's mad about getting his ass kicked. He's looking to even the score, I guess, but sir, he really did want to kill us. And he's gonna try to kill Harris if you don't apprehend him."

"Yeah, what are we waiting on for that, Macon? What did Stengele say?" Captain Kelly asked.

"They can't find him, sir," Macon said. "I told Stengele to have them spread their search and look for another 30 minutes. I told him we may have to request another agency's assistance if they don't find him by then."

"God damnit. That's all we need. "Macon, take over here. I have to make some more calls." The Captain got up and went to his office. Carol heard him close the door, and all she could think about was retrieving her staff and scroll.

"Sergeant," she said as she stood up, "I have to go talk to the Captain—"

"Sit down, Massey."

"Sergeant—"

"I will restrain you if I have to, Massey, now sit the hell down."

"Carol, what are you doing? Take it easy, sit down." Jay said. Carol slowly sat back down, but she didn't know how much longer she would be able to sit there. She fidgeted in her chair while the Sergeant thought up useless questions to ask.

"So tell me how Bell knew you all were at Bear Island." Sergeant Macon asked.

"We told you, Sergeant, we have no idea." Jay said.

Stengele swung the door open without knocking. "Sir... where's the Captain?" He asked frantically.

"He's in his office, what is it?" Macon asked.

Stengele started to close the door while he left and shouted, "Harris escaped." He slammed the door and ran to the Captain. Sergeant Macon jumped up and ran to the door. Jay and Carol jumped up and followed. Macon slammed the door before they could get to it, and he locked it from the outside. It wasn't a holding cell, but it was the closest thing they had.

"What the hell, Sergeant?" Jay said, slamming his fist on the door. Carol watched out the window at the commotion surrounding the Captain's office.

"We have to get out of here. We have to get to him." Carol said.

"Yeah, well, I don't see that happening. Right now we're in deep shit, and our jobs appear to be on the line."

Carol grabbed the knob and jiggled it. She considered breaking the window and reaching out to unlock it, but that would surely draw some unwanted attention. In a moment of complete clarity, Carol stopped trying to break out and turned to Jay. "Jay, we need to find out what the spell means. I feel like all of our lives depend on it."

"Spell? What spell? Are you talking about the gibberish on that piece of paper? What makes you think it's a spell?"

"Trust me on this, it's a spell. I don't know how I know, but I know. We need to decipher it. Call your friend."

"Ok, well that's crazy, but so is everything else going on around here." Jay reached into his pocket. "Oh, yeah, I don't have my phone because Rich destroyed it. Give me yours." Carol handed her phone to Jay. He tried calling his friend and repeatedly got no answer.

Captain Kelly, Sergeant Macon, and Officer Stengele all left the Captain's office and headed for the door. They rounded up everyone in the station and left. Things just escalated. Carol and Jay watched from the window of the interview room.

"Forget your friend, open the email." She said. "Here, give me the phone." Carol opened the email, and they both read the words together.

"Souls through love forever bound
Eternal grip shall not release
Upon the solstice and on this ground
Unshaken spirits will not cease
Blood of the body forever ties
That which the soul is truly drawn
Unending passion hears the cries
Sealed forever by the dawn"

"Ok, so what the hell does any of that mean?" Jay said.

"It's a spell for... it's... it joins together two..."

"What are you talking about, Carol?"

"Jay, the staff — it's enchanted or something. It has some kind of hold—"

"Um, you have lost your mind—"

"Listen to me, Jay. Someone or something had a hold of me. I wasn't myself. I was her. She's a part of the staff or something. As soon as I touched it, I could feel her. I could feel her taking over. She is so powerful. You have to trust me, I can't explain it. You saw that Bell couldn't shoot, right? You saw that." Jay nodded reluctantly — staring at Carol as if he knew it was nuts, but he wanted to hear the rest. She was half remembering things from when Imala had taken over. "That wasn't me. That was her. She controlled the staff and made him freeze. I only know bits and pieces because I know some of what she knows and vice versa. That's why she said Billy. She thinks Rich is this Billy. I can feel her trying to take over again — even though I don't have the staff. She is so unbelievably powerful, Jay."

"Ok, as crazy as this all sounds... well, this is crazy, there is no denying that, but your skin changed, Carol. Your eyes changed. They changed. And you face still isn't quite back to normal. But what do you mean, her? Who is she?"

"Her, the... she's a... she's a witch, I think. That must be how I knew it was a spell. I can't explain this, but Rich is in danger, and I don't know how long I can stay myself. Let's figure this thing out. It must be how Rich isn't himself right now."

"Ok, ok," Jay said as he took carol's phone and set it on the coffee table. The two sat down and looked together at the words. "'Souls through love forever bound', I'm guessing that's what is joined together, right? Bound? Like their souls, Rich, and this Billy person?"

"Not quite. I think it was supposed to be two souls, but... it was only Billy, and... I don't know."

"What about the part about the solstice? That's a time of year. Happens twice, I think, winter and summer. Look that up, when is the summer one?" Carol picked up the phone and searched the internet for 'Summer Solstice,' and quickly received the result, 'June, 20, 2020'.

"June 20th." She said.

"Tomorrow. That's got to be part of it. So how can it be something that hasn't happened yet if this spell has already taken place? Or maybe it hasn't."

"It has, and it hasn't. It has, but it wasn't done right, I think. But look, this says the solstice is the longest day of the year. The end of the spell says something about the dawn."

"So does that mean something will happen tomorrow at dawn?"

"I don't know, but look at this," she said, "on this ground. I think it is something that was done in a certain place and has to be done there again."

"The cave? It's got to be the cave, right? That's where we found everything. That's where Rich found the treasure. We found the bodies, the staff, and the paper scroll. It has to be the cave."

"Yes, I think you're right, Jay. The solstice is tomorrow, the joining of two things — souls, I'm assuming, on this ground — meaning the cave, and dawn."

"Ok, so what the hell do we do with this information?"

"Jay, I think we need to save Rich, and I think it has something to do with all of this." She got up and walked back over to the window. "When we get out of here, you grab the staff. Something tells me that if I have it, the witch will be back, and then who knows how we're going to stop her."

"Two problems with that. Number one, we're stuck in here, and number two, the staff if in the Captain's office."

Carol picked up the chair closest to the door.

"Carol, wait. What the hell do you think you're—"

She twisted as a windup and launched the chair as hard as she could into the window — breaking it into a thousand shards of glass.

" — doing..." Luther said.

"Let's go," she said as she reached out and unlocked the door from the outside. Carol opened the door ad quickly ran to the Captain's office, which was closed and also locked. Carol picked up another chair.

"Wait!" Jay shouted. Carol paused and looked back at him. Jay opened the key box sitting at Officer Stengele's desk and retrieved the key labeled "Capt K". "Here," he said as he walked over and unlocked the Captain's office.

Jay and Carol each spotted the staff and scroll at the same time. As Jay reached over to pick it up, he heard a loud crash out back by the docks. Carol looked in that direction.

"You get the staff and get the hell out of here. Meet me at Rich's. I'll go see what that was," she said.

"You're out of your mind. Let me go check it out."

"No, you have to keep that staff away from me. Meet me at Rich's."

Jay grabbed the staff, felt no strange transformation, and felt silly for a minute at the thought that he may. He picked up the scroll and headed out the front of the station.

Carol ran towards the back of the station and saw nothing strange. She went out the back toward the boat dock and saw that a bunch of trashcans had been knocked over. She figured it was raccoons or something and turned around to run back inside. As soon as she faced the station, she saw a terrifying figure in the doorway. His face scarred from battle, skin weathered and tanned from the sun, hands callused and blistered from years of sailing and fighting. Captain Billy Thompson. For the first time, she didn't see Rich Harris. She instantly knew this was not her friend.

"Well hello girly," he growled. She looked around for something to use as a weapon. "Let's get this over with. I need you to come with me." He walked toward her. Carol pick up a trashcan lid and stood her ground. Billy was in the way of the door, and was the only thing between Carol and the door to the station. Behind her was only water, and jumping in would have made her more vulnerable, since there was nowhere to swim in order to escape. She would have to rely on her fighting ability and hope there was at least a little of the witch still in her to help out.

Billy got closer and closer. "Now listen here girly, You know you ain't no match fir me. You can try all ya want, but you will just make me angry. We don't want that now, do we?" Billy got within arm's reach of Carol.

Carol swung the lid as hard as she could at Billy's head. Billy threw up his arm to block, and the lid crashed into it. It hit Billy's forearm hard, but his strength was too much. It did nothing to phase him, but it hurt Carol's hands. So much for the witch helping out.

Billy reached out his right hand and snatched Carol up by the throat. His movements were so fast she couldn't even flinch before she found herself being choked by his vice grip like hand. She instinctively grabbed his hand with both of hers, but could do nothing more than just hang on for the ride. Billy pulled her in close until they were nose to nose.

"I warned you, girly. No, you made me angry." He snarled. Carol winced at the wretched smell of his breath. This was more of a creature — a monster — than it was a man. Billy looked over Carol's shoulder and saw Rich's boat — where his precious treasure was hidden. He held Carol higher — the tips of her toes dragging on the deck — and walked toward his boat. Carol struggled to breathe as Billy seemed to grip harder with every step. She now wished that she hadn't sent Jay away.

They reached the boat, and Billy tossed Carol into the boat like a rag doll. She banged her head on the side of the boat and instantly grabbed her head in pain. Billy jumped on board and put his foot down onto Carol, holding her down. He started the boat and pulled away from the dock.

Twenty-Six

Jay had no idea what had happened to Carol, nor could he call her since he no longer had a cell phone. He pulled up to Rich's house and sat in his car, waiting. As he sat waiting for Carol to arrive, the thought suddenly occurred to him that Rich was on the loose — or whoever Rich had turned into according to their recent discovery of magic spells, witches, and mystical staffs. What if that guy shows up here? Jay had no weapon and no way to communicate with anyone. He felt like a sitting duck. He decided he would get out of the car and go around back to look inside the house. Maybe he would see Rich, or his alter ego, hiding out.

As he exited his car and started headed around back, he realized the police would surely be scouting this house since Rich was at large. Jay got a quick peak into the back of the house and saw nothing. No lights were on in the house, and it looked just like it did when he and Carol were last there. He started to jog back to his car. He figured he would park up the street a little, so no one would see him. He jumped back in the passenger seat and started to back out of the driveway. Looking in the rearview mirror, he didn't even see the new threat that had joined him. Jay came to a complete stop, put the car in drive and then felt something wrap around his neck like a boa constrictor. Someone was in the back seat. Whatever was tied around Jay's throat was choking the life out of him. He considered slamming on the gas, and as soon as he was about to floor it, the pressure released enough for Jay to take a deep breath and survive this deadly encounter.

"Put it in park," the man in the back said. "Now, or I shove a knife into your throat."

Jay threw the car in park. The strangulating object was still around his throat. He didn't know what it was, but he had no power to remove it. Jay decided that Rich's alter ego must have seen him walking around back and had jumped in the back seat to surprise him when he returned.

"Please, Rich," he said — his voice was raspy from having been choked. "Please man, what do you want?"

"I'm not Rich, asshole." It was Danny Bell. How the hell had he made it off that island?

"Danny, Jesus man. You... you're ok. Thank God—"

"Don't give me that shit, Luther. You two left me for dead, and I intend to finish what I started. Where is Massey?"

"Danny, listen, we didn't mean to leave—"

"Where is Massey?" Danny pulled harder on the rope he was holding around Jay's throat. Jay choked again, desperately grasping for air. Danny let up a little slack.

Jay coughed. "Ok, ok, listen. We went back to the station and sent help to go get you. They had us locked up." He struggled to breathe while he talked. He was trying to think of a way out of this while he was being interrogated. "She and I split up." He considered telling Danny that Carol would be on her way to Rich's as they spoke, but decided not to.

"So where is she now?"

"I don't know, Danny—". The rope tightened and Jay struggled. He grabbed the rope, but couldn't get a hold of it. He couldn't breathe as his windpipe was completely cut off. The lights were fading out. He could feel his life slipping away. This was it.

Danny released the pressure, and Jay took a shallow breath in. He coughed as he tried to breathe. He was still alive, but didn't know how long that would last.

"Where is Harris?" Danny asked. Jay braced himself for the inevitable choke that would end his life — a choke that should surly follow his unsatisfactory answer to Danny's question.

"He escaped police custody. Everyone is looking for him. The Sheriff's department, our station, everyone." He braced again, and when he didn't get choked to death, he continued — maybe if he kept talking,

Danny would wait long enough and Carol would show up and save him. "We took him down, Danny — Massey and I. We fought him to the ground and took him down. The station boats showed up, and we were able to arrest him for what he did. He was taken in to custody and transported to the station." Still no choking. Danny must have been intrigued by this. Maybe he thought better of them now that he knew they arrested Rich. Jay wished that were the case. "Captain Kelly called the Sheriff's department to take him because of the assault on you, and also for Harris robbing and trying to kill two fishermen."

"What was that? He tried to kill someone?" Danny was puzzled by Rich's recent behavior, but this was a new low... or high for Rich. Danny would have to remember not to underestimate him when he got his next chance to kill Rich Harris. He had seen Harris hold Massey and Luther at gunpoint, but he didn't think Harris would actually have tried to kill someone. He had figured at the time they were just having a really bad argument that ended in a huge fight. Attempted murder was different.

"Yeah, he uh... he robbed a couple guys on their boat, then he set it on fire after he had beaten them up. They barely made it off the boat before burning up with it. Anyway, so when we were being questioned about... well, about leaving you at the island, Billy was taken by the Sheriff's deputies. I guess he escaped shortly after that because the whole station left when they got the call. That's how Massey and I got out. Listen, Bell, we want to find him too. We all want the same thing. We need to bring him to justice—"

"The same thing? No, no, Luther, we don't want the same thing. We want him to face justice, but you and I have a very different definition of justice in this case. Harris is gonna die for what he did. You're gonna help me find Massey and Harris, or I'm gonna choke the life out of you right here in your piece of shit car."

"Ok, take it easy, I... I can maybe call Carol if you let me use your phone. Harris broke mine."

"Boy, you all really had quite the falling out, didn't you?" Danny said. He didn't feel any remorse or any kind of connection with Jay because of this new information. Danny's life had been ruined, and he was on a warpath now. He would take down anyone and everyone he could. Danny began to take out his phone and paused for a second while he considered whether this was a trap. He handed the phone to Jay. "I'll tell you what, Luther. I have a knife right here on my side," He slid over in the seat to show Jay the very large knife while still holding Jay tight to his seat by the rope around his neck. "You try anything stupid, and it goes right into your back. You got me?"

Jay nodded. He typed in Carol's number and wondered how he would warn her without tipping off Danny. The phone rang a couple times.

*****

Billy looked down at Carol as she heard her phone ringing in her pocket. "Well, should I answer it?" She asked.

"What's that racket?" Billy asked.

"It's phone. Someone is calling to talk to me."

"You can talk to others if you're somewhere else?" My, what the future has brought.

"If you want me to answer it, I can answer it." She said.

"Bring it here." The phone stopped ringing as she got it out. She saw the call was from a local area code, so it must've been Jay using someone else's phone to call her. She took the phone up to Billy and showed it to him.

"Talk to someone," he said, not understanding how it worked at all.

"I can't. They stopped calling. If you want, I can call them back so you can see how this works—"

"Not right now, girly," Billy was very curious. He liked new types of gadgets. He remembered a man in one of the various towns he frequented once had what is now known as a tuning fork. The man tapped the fork onto something and it rang in a certain key. The many would then use that tone to tune various stringed instruments. Billy thought that was mildly amusing at the time.

The boat got closer to the Southside of Bear Island. Billy wanted to hide his treasure back there and summon Imala once he got Carol into the cave. That way Imala could finally give Billy the staff and he could become unstoppable.

"Where are you taking me, Billy?" Carol asked.

"Billy, huh? Why ain't you calling me Rich anymore? Finally, see that I ain't him, eh?"

"You're not him. You could never be him. He's more of a man than you'll ever—"

"Now watch your mouth, girl, or I'll cut out your tongue. If you think I need ya that much, you may need to think again. There's plenty of girls I could choose from." Carol had no idea what he was talking about, but she somehow had the feeling he was going to kill her if she didn't escape this situation.

"Where are you taking me?"

"May as well let you in on it since you and I are about to be partners again." This was confusing to Carol. Did he mean Rich and Carol, or Billy and the witch? That must be what the joining of souls was. He wanted her to be a part of it. "You see, I ain't Rich, I'm Billy. I come from... well, I come from here, but a long time ago. 300 years ago, to be precise. My lady came with me too, but she's sort of stuck at the moment."

"You mean the witch."

"I do mean the witch. How do you know of her?" Billy almost stopped the boat. She could not possibly know who Imala was.

"I know that she is trying to find you. I know that you need her to finish your spell."

Billy didn't know how to take this information. The only way she could possibly know that is if Imala had appeared to her, but that was impossible. Imala was not yet of this world. Billy was only here because he had Rich. Rich had touched something of Billy's or something. That had to be how he grabbed a hold of this time. Maybe Rich had touched Billy's body, and that's what joined them. Either way, Carol had nothing of Imala's to touch. Or did she?

"Where did you find it?" He said as if he was ready to kill her then and there.

"Find what?" Carol asked.

"Where's the staff, girly? You found it at the cave, didn't you? You went into the cave and found it? Is it still there? I will kill you if it's gone. Where is it?"

"It's... it's safe. And if anything happens to me, it will be destroyed." She said. The threat lingered in the air a moment while Billy tried to compose himself.

"You listen to me. You are gonna tell me where that staff is right now or I'll gut you. Then I'll go find your friend and gut him too. Then I'll find your family and I'll them all—each one — until there ain't none of them left." Billy pulled the boat up to the shore of Bear Island just as that last threat left his mouth. He walked over and bent down into Carol's face. He pulled out his knife and held it up to her cheek. Carol's tears slowly made their way down her cheek and stopped when they reached the edge of Billy's knife. "I know where it is. It's safe. I have to call Jay back. He's got the staff. He can bring it to you and then you can let me go."

Billy thought about this for a second and decided he would have Jay bring him the staff. "Call your friend. Get him to bring the staff to the cave." Billy stood and walked over to her as she dialed the phone.

*****

Jay had hung up when Carol didn't answer. "Should I try again?" He asked. Before Danny had a chance to answer, the phone rang. Jay almost dropped it as it startled him. He looked in the rearview at Danny's patched face. Danny nodded, and Jay answered the phone. "Hello, Carol?" No one said anything. He heard breathing. "Carol, is that you?"

"This ain't Carol," the raspy voice on the other line said. This was the man who used to be Rich. What did they keep calling him, Billy?

"Billy?"

"Well, look here, we got us a smart fella finally. You finally call me by my proper name. Now listen here, boy, I got Carol here with me. Gonna be taken her on a little hike." Jay listened and Danny tried to hear what was being said. He had no idea who 'Billy' was, so when Jay had said that name Danny had stuck his knife to Jay's throat, letting him know not to try anything. "You want her to die, then go right ahead and call your friends," Billy continued, "You want her to live, then do as I say. You bring me that staff. Bring it to the cave. You listening to me, boy?"

"Uh, yes... yes, I understand. The cave. I can bring it, but—" Danny tightened the rope as he heard Jay say 'but'. He didn't want Jay giving anyone any hints.

"Good, get here now, and if you don't have it boy, I'm gonna kill your little girlfriend."

"How do I know she's ok? Can I talk to her?"

"Say someone thing girly," Billy said, loud enough for Jay to still hear him.

"I'm ok, Jay," Carol said. She sounded distant because Billy didn't know to put the phone up to her ear. Billy hung up the phone.

"Who the hell is this Billy you guys keep referring to?" Danny asked.

"It's... it's not Billy... it's... Rich. He's had some kind of mental breakdown and he goes by Billy now. It's really weird, and I can't explain—"

"Boy, this just keeps getting better and better. Alter ego, huh? That's amazing. So you're telling me that Massey, Harris, and you are all gonna be in the same place. That makes it much easier than I had hoped."

"Ok, take it easy, Danny. You can still come back from this, man. Think about it. You help bring Rich in and you're a hero to the station. No one has to know about you trying to kill us, man."

"Oh, they're gonna know about it Luther. They're gonna know when they find your bodies. I ain't got nothing left in this world that I give one shit about. I had the job, that's it. That's all I needed. Now I don't have it, so I got nothing. Help the station," he said sarcastically, "why the hell would I ever help this worthless group of chicken shit fake cops? Drive the God damn car." Danny loosened up the rope, but kept the knife near Jays throat just in case he got any ideas. "Where is it he's having you meet him?"

"Bear Island. There's this cave."

"After all the shit I went through to get off that island and now we're going back. Fantastic."

Jay kept trying to find a plan to save their lives. He knew Danny would kill them all once they got to the cave. "What about money, Danny?" Jay asked.

"The hell you talking about?"

"What if I were able to give you a lot of money? More money than you've ever had in your life."

"Trying to save your hide, I see. Offering me something you ain't even got."

"Wait, listen," Jay thought about not telling him about the treasure, but it may have been his last Hail Mary. "We have millions of dollars, Danny. Rich found a chest full of gold and silver — a whole chest full — millions of dollars' worth. He's got it hidden, but I've seen it and so has Massey. That's why he's been acting so strange — he's got this new fortune, and no one else knows about it."

"Just what in the hell do you take me for, and idiot?" Danny asked. Jay thought it best not to answer that.

"Danny, I know it sounds crazy, and believe me, it is. But a lot of crazy shit has been happening lately. You have to believe me. I am telling you, you could be rich beyond your wildest imagination. Job? You wouldn't need a freaking job. You could buy anything you would ever want. If I'm lying, I'm gonna die, right? So what would I be accomplishing by lying about this?"

Could this be a real thing — millions of dollars; a new life? The offer did sound appealing to Danny. He might be ok with having millions of dollars, but he sure wanted Rich dead still. Even the thought of money didn't extinguish that fire. Maybe he could have both — the money and the revenge.

Twenty-Seven

Billy and Carol made their way toward the cave in darkness. The only light was the bright moonlight that kept the island pretty well lit. Billy didn't know that Carol had a device that could easily light the way, but he was used to traveling in the dark like this using only the light of the moon. Light would attract someone, and he didn't need that. They were almost to the cave. Billy was distraught after having to leave the treasure on the boat. The full chest weighed close to a thousand pounds, so not only would Carol not have been able to lift the one side, the chest wouldn't be able to withstand the weight, and would have surely broken apart as soon as they tried to lift it. Billy needed Imala and her magic to transport the treasure to the cave.

As they walked, Billy had a hold of Carol's wrist. He dragged her along, but she didn't struggle much. Carol knew it was no use struggling because this man was extremely strong and equally dangerous — and it was not Rich Harris. They reached the cave. Billy pulled Carol up to the hole and began to push her in.

"Ok, ok, I can do it," she said, not wanting to be shoved through the opening and fall to the ground.

"Get in," he said.

Carol did as she was told. She back in, feet first, and climbed down the beam. Billy followed behind her. For a split second, she thought about hitting him over the head with one of the sticks on the ground, but that thought quickly dissolved. She knew it would have been for nothing.

Get over there on the other side," Billy said. He pointed to the furthest point away from the cave opening. Billy grabbed a piece of the old tattered cloth that used to be a shirt off of one of the two skeletons nearest the entrance. The shirt ripped off of the skeleton easily as its bones all fell apart as soon as they were moved. "Sorry, Sammy," Billy said, as he removed any dignity the corpse had left. He threw the piece of clothing over at Carol. "Tie this around your wrist."

Carol was disgusted, but more afraid of dying than of touching a dead man's clothes. She wrapped the cloth around her right wrist.

"Now put it behind your back." Billy grabbed both of her wrists and tied them together behind her back with the cloth, hoping it would at least hold her until Imala arrived. He walked over to the other skeleton near the entrance and removed the handkerchief from its skull. He walked over and tied a gag around Carol's face. This made her gag consequently as she thought about the dead man's hair that was still tangled in it. "Hate to have to do this," Carol thought he was finally showing some hint of humanity, "My boys deserve more than to have their clothes ripped off of their bones just to keep you still." No, he wasn't being humane, he cared more about the bones on the ground than this living, innocent person. "Now listen here, girly. You're gonna sit here quietly. I'll be right outside the cave. If you so much as make one little peep, I'll grab your friend down here and slit his throat right in front of you." Carol nodded that she understood, and Billy climbed back out of the cave.

Carol looked around at the gruesome scene again. This time she had more time to take it all in. She wondered how these people died, but this time she felt as though she understood a little more of the story than before — probably because of the witch possessing her when she held the staff.

*****

"What's the stick for?" Danny asked from the back seat of Jay's car — he saw the staff laying in the passenger seat. It looked quite out of place.

"I don't know, it's something Rich wants. It's part of his whole fantasy about being Billy." Jay didn't want to give away too much, but he didn't have much of an idea of what the staff was for other than the possibility that it made an ancient witch possess Carol. As strange as that seemed, he remembered how she looked, and he believed it did hold power.

"Give it here," Danny demanded.

"Danny, don't mess with it man, it's just a stupid old stick," Jay had to make sure that Danny didn't destroy the staff, and with it condemns Carol to certain death by Billy's hand, "but Rich has to believe it's intact or we won't be getting his money."

"You want the knife in your throat, or do you want to give me the stick?" Danny put the point of the knife back on to Jay's throat. Jay reluctantly reached over and picked up the staff. He handed it to Danny.

"Please Danny, if you want your money, just... just be careful with it."

Danny grabbed it and looked it over. He didn't see anything special about it; it was just a stick. He hadn't noticed the scroll sitting on the front seat until he threw the staff back up to the front of the car. "What's that?"

Jay looked over at the scroll. "It's... it's a paper... it goes with the staff. Billy... Rich thinks it's a spell of some kind. Listen, Danny, we just need to take him this stuff and exchange them for Carol and for Rich's treasure." Jay needed to get Danny's mind off of the only value things that Billy cared about, and onto the prize, "you really have to see this treasure. It's the most amazing thing I've ever seen—"

"Lemme see it, give it here." Danny reached out his hand like the typical bully, wanting to destroy anything someone else held dear.

"Danny, did you hear me—" Danny pulled back on the rope, choking Jay so hard that he swerved the car.

"Give it hear, Luther." Jay reach over and picked up the scroll.

"Jesus man, you're going to get us killed." He handed it to Danny. "It's got to be intact if you want that treasure. He's psychotic. He will dump it in the ocean, he doesn't care."

"Shut the hell up, I'm just looking at the stupid thing." Danny opened the scroll and could not read the words or understand the symbols. "Holy shit man, this is old. Where did it come from?"

"I'm not sure. It was in the same place as the staff. It's part of the whole delusion Rich is having, though. He thinks it's a spell, and the witch can read it."

"Witch? What witch?" Danny asked. Jay had just realized that he was now speaking so freely that he had told Danny about the witch — someone he himself barely knew anything about. How would he get out of this mess? "Speak up, Luther, what's this about a freaking witch?"

"Uh... it's... it's... you know man, this is all bullshit. I can't explain it, it's all bullshit, so none of it makes any sense."

"Just when did he tell you all of this?" Danny was becoming more and more suspicious about the story he was being told. "I mean you say he turned on you or something after our little incident on the sandbar, right? Y'all had to team up and beat him up or something? So when exactly did you all sit down and discuss all of this?"

Jay thought for a second. No matter what he told Danny would be ludicrous. If he said Billy told him, that was a lie, and it would quickly be found out. On the other hand, if he told Danny how they had discovered everything, he would know that this was more real than any of them could imagine. He could try to figure the spell out, or use the staff to summon the witch, or do any number of things that ended in Carol's death.

"I... Carol and I... when we first started noticing he was acting strange, we kind of started to figure out there was something off about him. We found the treasure and then started to research it. Rich had found it, apparently, but we didn't know anything else. I didn't know any of the staff nonsense until the altercation with Rich when Carol and I confronted him." Jay decided the lie was the safer bet. "He started going on and on about it and told us he would get this witch to show up if he had the staff."

"That doesn't add up. Then why is he ok with parting with this treasure?" Danny was already skeptical about the whole thing. He didn't believe in any of it from a supernatural standpoint, and the crazier it sounded, the more he figured he should just kill Officer Luther, and go looking for Rich Harris and Carol Massey on his own after that.

"I don't know man, look I've got a rope around my neck and a knife keeps getting jabbed into my throat, it's hard to think straight. The treasure, that's what you need to worry about."

"You're leading me into a goddamn trap. This is all bullshit. You're making up some bullshit story to keep me off guard so you can walk me into a trap." Danny held the knife back to Jay's throat.

"No, I'm not, I swear to God."

"I'm such an idiot that I started believing there was some treasure. Bear Island, huh? I should've known. The department waiting out on Bear. Is that it? You got a trap set for me?"

"No, Danny, I swear to you, this is real. Listen, if you don't believe me, call Massey back and talk to Rich yourself. You'll see it's not him. You'll see he sounds completely different."

"What the hell does that prove, Luther? You could have another person talking. This is bullshit. Pull over, you're getting yours right now."

*****

Billy sat outside of the cave as the night went on, waiting for Jay to show up with the staff. He sat and waited for Imala to show up, as well, and help him. "Imala," he called out. Nothing. "Imala, I have the woman. Your staff is on the way, witch. Come now, and you can have your vessel." Nothing. Billy sat in silence as the time passed, waiting for Jay to approach in the darkness. He figured Jay would be dumb enough to use a light, and that thought made him wonder whether he should walk to the south side of the island to meet Jay and just take the staff from him there. Billy thought it best to just stay put though, so that Carol didn't somehow escape.

Carol sat silently in the cave, trying to devise an escape plan. Her hands were still tied behind her back and her mouth was gagged with a foul tasting cloth taken from a dead man's skull. She felt as though she had been in this cave before — even before she and Jay had first discovered it. She somehow remembered the first time she walked into it... centuries ago. She could see the two men digging as she and... Billy looked on. There was no cave, and these two men were digging it... a long, long time ago. She saw herself holding the staff, and she saw Billy by her side watching the men dig.

"*Put your back's in to it men,*" she heard him say, as if this were a dream, "*there's a reward for your work once the cave is dug.*" She remembered helping the men by simply pointing her staff and watching mounds of dirt fly out of the whole — much more dirt than two men could shovel. The staff worked with them, and the cave was formed. She and Billy walked forward and seemed to float down into the cave while the men set the two beams up at the newly dug hole of the cave. The beams looked like brand new lumber.

The cave was dug, and there were four of them inside the cave. Carol then thought about the four skeletons she now saw in the cave. Of course. This was them. These were the four bodies, she realized. That meant that the two closest to her were Billy and Imala. "What happened here?" She said out loud without meaning to speak.

She thought and daydreamed more. Somehow it wasn't a daydream, but a memory. She could see herself with the staff, talking to Billy. She heard him say, "*Now bring the treasure down.*" She pointed her staff to the hole above and watched as the thousand pound treasure came floating in as if it weighed nothing at all. She placed the treasure at Billy's feet as he had commanded. She would have done anything for Billy. She loved him more than anything else in this world.

"*Now, my love, we shall join our should and be forever joined. We shall rule this world for eternity,*" she said... centuries ago. She pulled the scroll out of her pocket and it looked different — not quite as old, but she could tell it was ancient even back then. She saw the words and could read them as if they were written in English.

Twenty-Eight

Danny held the knife to Jay's throat, ready to push hard and watch Jay bleed out. The only two things stopping him were the thought that there may actually be a treasure, and the fact that Harris was now on the run from police, and this may be his only opportunity to get to him first.

"Danny, I swear to God I'm being honest with you. Harris has lost his mind. He is going to kill Carol, and he's sitting in a cave on Bear Island waiting for me to bring him this stuff. He doesn't know about you though. He has no idea you're coming. You have the element of surprise. You can sneak in and take the treasure. Just don't kill anyone—"

"That simple, huh? Just show up, no gun, and take the treasure. No hostage, no leverage, just me and my trusty knife, and who knows what he has, and he's just gonna hand it over to me."

"We come up with a plan. I can distract him," Jay said, grasping for any answer that would keep him alive. He needed to save Carol. "I can go up ahead and you can follow behind and surprise him before he kills us. Obviously before he kills us."

"I could take the stick."

"What? No, he'll kill me on sight if I don't have that."

"That'll be my insurance policy. I take the stick, and you go on ahead in the cave with him. He won't kill you if you tell him you hid it or something. He would never find it if he kills you." That actually wasn't a bad plan, except Jay couldn't see how he and Carol get to stay alive after all of this.

He wanted Rich to stay alive too because that was his best friend, but he had no idea how that could happen with him this far gone. Jay finally believed Rich wasn't himself. He knew his friend couldn't have done the things he had recently done. "What about Rich and Carol? You have to give me your word you won't hurt them. You just take the money and disappear."

"Word? I don't have to give you shit, Luther. In case you hadn't noticed, I'm the one holding the knife. You're not exactly in a position to negotiate." Jay nodded in humble agreement.

"So that's what we'll do. You're gonna go on ahead and meet Harris at the cave. He'll bring you in and yell at you for not having his stick, but you're gonna tell him it's safe, and you hid it, so you could make sure Massey was safe. I'll be outside the cave and I'll take it from there. If you don't screw this up, I might just let you all live. But understand this, Luther, I will not hesitate to kill you each as slowly as possible if you so much as blink your eyes wrong."

Jay nodded again, thankful that he would live a little longer and possibly save his friends.

*****

Captain Kelly and his men walked around Rich's house searching for any clue they could find to let them know of his whereabouts. The warrant had been pretty easy to secure since multiple agencies were searching for Rich Harris. The first thing the Captain noticed was the broken window at the back of the house. He wondered who else had been there, but as crazy as these past few days had been, it couldn've been any number of people. One thing he was pretty sure of was that Officer Harris probably didn't break his own window.

"Sir, we found this in the garage," Officer Dayton said, holding up a coin. "Looks pretty old."

The Captain took the coin and looked it over. He walked out to the garage to see if there was anything that would help. He wondered what significance, if any, a coin would have in all of this. As he entered the garage he noticed some rope, a jack, a tarp, and a backpack — all items that would cause alarm for anyone that were missing. "You show me a coin, but you don't mention all of this?" The Captain said to Officer Dayton.

"Sorry sir, this is the garage, so I just figured—"

"This stuff was recently used. It's all laid out. If it wasn't recently used, it would be put away like all the other tools in here, Dayton." Captain Kelly noticed all the items had sand on them. "I wonder what the hell he used this stuff on. What ever it was, it was at a beach." He thought for a minute. "Stengele!"

"Yes, sir!" Stengele yelled from the living room while running in to see what the Captain needed.

"That day Harris broke down, that was Bear Island, right?"

"Yes, sir."

"And we picked him up at Bear Island when he was attacking Luther and Massey." He was thinking out loud rather than asking a question, but Stengele answered anyway.

"Yes, sir."

"What the hell is the deal with Bear Island?" This too was rhetorical.

"I don't know, sir—"

"He used this stuff recently. He used it at a beach, and I'm betting he used it at Bear Island. I don't know what the hell the coin means, it's probably unrelated." The Captain tossed the coin to Dayton, who barely caught it. "Bag it and tag it."

*****

Jay pulled the car into the nearest parking spot at the dock where Danny's boat was docked. The parking lot was empty since it was the middle of the night. "Remember Luther, you try anything, and I will kill you all and leave you in the cave. You want to try me? You go ahead and try me. I got nothing left to lose."

Jay nodded nervously and slowly got out of the car. Danny loosened the rope and Jay let it drop on the seat. Danny grabbed the staff from the back seat while Jay grabbed the scroll, which Danny hadn't noticed or cared about. The two walked to the boat and got in. Danny untied it from the dock and told Jay to drive. This way he could try anything during their little trip to Bear Island.

"Guess I'll be able to buy a better boat soon, eh Luther?" Danny chuckled.

"Yeah, I guess so." Jay wasn't in the joking mood. He still had no idea how he was going to get out of this. He had a murderous one-eyed captor seeking vengeance who was taking him to meet a murderous schizophrenic and possible possessed person, who used to be his best friend. There wasn't really a way this would end well.

Jay pulled the boat away from the docks and started heading toward Bear Island. He wished there was a way to call ahead and warn Carol that Danny was coming, but there was simply no way.

"So you remember the plan, right? You go up ahead, I'll follow behind. You get there and tell Harris you have the staff hidden or some shit—"

"Yeah, yeah, I got it. I tell him it's hidden and that he can have it when he lets Massey go. Once he does that, you get the treasure and we all part ways."

"Yeah something like that."

*****

"Imala, you have to come out now," Billy said as his frustration grew. Soon he wouldn't have to wait for her spirit to arrive any more. Soon she would be joined to the woman inside the cave, and she would be flesh and blood. No more waiting for her to come and go with no warning at all, and no way to summon her at will. "You have to come out, witch. The woman is here, the staff is almost here. Come out." Nothing.

Billy was irritated. He thought about roughing the woman in the cave up a bit to see if that would entice Imala to show up, but he decided against it. The other friend might show up while he's in the cave, and then he couldn't very well get the jump on him.

"Imala, come out. Now is the time to take the woman's place, Imala. Why are you not taking your so-called vessel? You wanted me to find a woman, and I found one. Here she is in the cave. Now show yourself Imala." Nothing. He sat and thought in silence. He thought about the past. He still couldn't remember everything, but he thought about the cave and the treasure. He remembered finding this very spot. It was in 1720 that he, Imala, and two of his men, Sammy and some other insignificant man he couldn't remember the name of. They had found this spot so Billy could hide his treasure. He remembered having the men dig a cave, and he remembered Imala helping to ease their labor by using the staff's magic to remove dirt as they worked. He remembered that day as if he were there again.

"Billy," a voice called out behind him. "I am here." It was Imala approaching from the darkness in her dreamlike state.

"The woman is in the cave," Billy said.

"Where is my staff, Billy?"

"It's on its way to us right now."

"I cannot take her form without the staff, my love. She must hold the staff in order for me to return. Only then will I be able to give you the power of the staff. Only then can we rule this world."

"I remember finding this spot. I remember the day we dug it. It seems like it was only days ago, but I can't remember everything."

"For us, it was only days ago. We were frozen in time. Do not worry, your memory will return. Just remember that we are each other's strength, and that together we will take what is ours."

"I remember going down into the cave—"

"Billy, do not worry so much about everything," Imala could sense that Billy was remembering almost everything, and he might just remember what happened at the end, "I am here now. I will help you with everything once I have my staff." She needed to keep his mind occupied. She needed him to need her.

"What's taking this bastard so long?" Billy said, annoyed that Jay hadn't arrived yet.

"We have little time, Billy. We must carry out the spell at dawn. It is quickly approaching. We must hurry. Where is the staff?"

"I told you, witch. It's on its way. The woman's friend is bringing it."

"Friend? Is he a danger to us? You must kill him, Billy. No one must know of this place, or of this spell."

"Don't tell me what I must do, woman. I know I need to kill him, and I will — just as soon as we get what we need."

Inside the cave, Carol could hear Billy talking to someone. She couldn't make out the words, but she thought she heard a woman's voice as well. "Mhmmm," she mumbled, trying to scream out, but the gag was too tight. She continued looking around the cave for anything that could help her escape. She may have found something useful after all.

The skeleton next to her, which she somehow knew was Billy's skeleton, had a knife on its belt. The knife was inside of a sheath, and the skeleton was about 5 feet from her. Carol began to scoot over toward Billy's remains. She struggled to scoot as her hands were tied behind her back. When she got to the body started to bump it, trying to get to the knife on its hip. She moved a piece of the skeleton's clothing and there on the ground was an old pistol. Carol couldn't believe her eyes. It was a pistol from long ago. She grabbed the knife and began cutting the cloth that tied her hands together. Struggling to coordinate the cutting, she frantically moved the knife back and forth against the cloth. It finally began to cut slightly — just enough for her to rip the old cloth apart and free her hands. She quickly grabbed the pistol on the ground and went back to her spot in the corner and sat with her hands behind her back. As she sat in the corner and watched the opening of the cave to see if Billy came back, she inspected the antique pistol to see how she would even operate it. Realizing that it was a single shotgun, she knew she couldn't fire it. She could see that it was the type of gun you had to put gunpowder into. It had the rod attached to it, but she didn't have gunpowder, nor did she have the type of bullets she would've needed to load. Carol had some experience with loading guns that way as she occasionally went hunting, with a muzzleloader, with Jay and Rich some seasons. She looked over at Billy's remains again and notices a sort of satchel, shaped like a horn, that had a cork in it. That had to be the gunpowder, though she had no idea how old it was or if it would work. Just then, Carol had an idea. She could always make Billy think the gun was loaded and fireable. She quickly ran back over to the Skelton and took the satchel of powder. She looked around for bullets, but didn't find any. No matter, as long as should could make it look like she had loaded the gun. She may just have some leverage now.

Twenty-Nine

Jay and Danny got off of the boat and anchored it at the south side of Bear. They had parked right next to Rich's boat, which, luckily for Jay, they had no idea had the treasure chest on board. Danny grabbed the staff and poked Jay in the back with it. "Lead the way, shithead." He said.

Jay started walking in the general direction of the cave. Danny had hi knife in his hand, ready to slash anyone who came near him. "I can hardly see anything, I need your phone," Jay said.

"Oh yeah, so you can call the police? I think not."

"Danny, I can't see where I'm going."

"Figure it the hell out. The moon is enough. I have to let you go up ahead a hundred yards or so in order to stay hidden. I'm not risking you calling for help, asshole. Boy, you all must think I'm pretty stupid."

"Fine." He walked on, stumbling here and there, tripping every couple of feet. "So how long are you gonna wait until you come to talk to Rich about the exchange?"

"That's not your concern. Besides, I haven't quite figured that out yet. This whole thing seems a little off to me, so I think I'll play it by ear. You'll go talk to him, convince him of the trade, and make sure he understands that if he doesn't give me the money, then his little stick gets broken right away, and all three of you die on this island."

"Ok, ok, I'll talk to him." Jay wasn't sure how this was going to go over with Billy. He had seen the rage in Billy. He had witnessed, first-hand, how erratic Billy could be.

"Good, now go on up ahead. I'll come in when I'm ready. Get him talking. I don't want to walk into a God damn trap. You get him talking, and I'll come in when I'm ready." Jay started to walk ahead. "And remember, Luther, you so much as alert him that I'm coming, and you all die."

Jay nodded and walked ahead, tripping every few steps. He began to wonder what happens if he were to show up without the staff, and Billy just up and kills him. Billy was capable of doing that. Jay would have to cross that bridge when he got to it. His friends were in danger, counting Rich, and he knew he needed to save his friends — he just didn't yet know how.

Billy heard movement approaching — sound travels a good distance on Bear Island, as there were no trees in that area to block it. He looked in the direction of the sound and couldn't yet see who was approaching. "Here comes the staff, Imala," he said as he turned to her. She wasn't there anymore, but Billy wasn't concerned. She would be reunited with him soon. He crouched a little in order to keep from being seen as Jay approached.

Jay walked and walked closer and closer — not seeing Billy in front of him, or the hole he would have fallen into if he had kept walking.

"That's far enough," Billy said. Jay stopped in his tracks and looked up, squinting to try to focus, and saw a large shadowy figure standing just feet in front of him.

"Rich... Billy, hey, it's me."

"I know who it is, boy. Come closer." Jay hesitated, but he slowly walked closer until he was within arm's distance of Billy.

Billy looked Jay up and down. As he noticed the staff wasn't with him, he became enraged. "Where is it?" He growled furiously.

"It's safe... I have it... I mean, don't worry, man. I want to make sure Carol is ok before I give it to you, and then you can have it."

"You're trying my patience, lad. Why should I let you live now?"

"Billy, if you want your staff, you will show me Carol. Otherwise, it stays hidden forever." A very bold statement from Jay. His cards were on the table. This was the moment of truth. Now he wondered just how quickly Billy would kill him.

"Well, well. Look who thinks he's in charge all of a sudden." Billy said. He grabbed Jay by the back of the neck. His extremely strong grip made Jay feel like a baby kitten. "You wanna see yir girlfriend? Fine, let's go see her." He walked Jay over and threw him into the cave. Jay fell hard on the ground, letting out a grunt as the wind was taken out of his lungs on impact with the ground.

"MMMhmm!" Carol yelled. She was trying to yell Jay's name, but the gag she wisely left in place didn't allow the words to be formed.

Jay coughed as he started to come to his feet. Billy jumped down the hole and landed on his feet. He grabbed Jay by the back of his shirt and lifted him straight off of the ground. He pushed Jay over into the corner where Carol was sitting. Jay fell down and let out another whiny grunt as he landed next to Carol.

"Carol... *cough*... are you ok?" He said as he tried to catch his breath. Carol opened her eyes wide, trying to signal Jay not to untie her hands. They were already untied, and if he did that, then Billy would be alerted.

Billy walked towards them. "Now you've seen her," He said, "where's the staff?"

"Billy, listen to me. You have to let us go and you can have it."

"Let you go? Now why would I go and do such a stupid thing as that? You're about to witness your girlfriend's last breath now, boy." He walked toward Carol. Carol quickly took out the pistol and pointed it at Billy. Billy stopped dead in his tracks. He was thrown off. How did this girl get the jump on him like that? How had she gotten her hands untied? Where did she get a pistol? Billy didn't realize at first that it was his pistol from 1720. He had no idea whether it could even fire. "Now you wait just a second there, girly," he said. "Think about this now, you don't want to be going and doing anything stupid." He looked on the ground and saw the canister of gunpowder and figured she had loaded the gun.

Carol reached up and untied her gag as Jay watched in anticipation. "Get out of the way, Billy," she said. Billy didn't move. He didn't scare easily, and he didn't become the fearsome Captain he was today by cowering at every gun that pointed at him.

"You're not leaving this cave just yet," he said. "Imala, come now." He tried to get her to take her form, but he didn't know she had to be holding the staff.

"Imala won't be coming anywhere near me, Billy. This isn't happening. Now you listen to me, we're walking out of this cave, the three of us. And we're getting our friend back."

"You may want to rethink that plan of yours. It ain't exactly going to go that way. You see, Imala will be here any second now, and you won't be here no longer. Your little friend here might be spared if he tells me where the God damned staff is hidden." He looked angrily at Jay. Jay flinched at the sight of Billy's murderous stare.

There was a noise at the entrance of the cave. Billy turned and looked behind him and saw a man sliding down one of the beams. The man wore a patch over one eye. He held a knife in one hand and a staff in the other. Danny hit the ground and looked at the three of them standing on the other side of the cave.

"Well, look here," he said. "This is just getting better and better." He looked around on the ground at the skeletons. He saw the spot where the chest had been. "You really did find a god damn treasure, didn't you, Harris?" He looked at Rich, but saw someone almost entirely different. "What the hell happened to your face? Jesus Christ you look strange."

"Looks like I didn't quite finish the job," Billy said as he pointed to Danny's eye patch, "but I have to say, I like the new look."

"Danny, what the hell are you doing here?" Carol said. "Keep the staff over there, do not come any closer." She kept the gun pointed at Billy.

"Danny, hold on man, you'll get what you came for," Jay said, "but just hang on man, don't come over here." Carol looked over at Jay, wondering what he meant by that—you'll get what you came for.

"Where is it?" Danny asked. "Where's the treasure?"

"Oh, is that what you're looking for?" Billy said. "You thought you'd follow this little man here and try to take my treasure? My treasure? Well listen here sonny," Billy said as he turned and started walking toward Danny.

"Billy NO!" Carol yelled.

"Wait right there Harris," Danny said as he held the staff up with both hands, showing Billy that he would snap it in half if he came any closer. "You come over here and I break this thing." Billy stopped and stared at Danny.

"I'd be real careful with that if I was you, boy." Billy said. "Imala—"

"Jay, I can't hold her back, I can feel it—" Carol said.

"Hold on, hold on, you can do it," Jay said.

"Someone want to tell me just what the hell is going on here?" Danny said. "Why is everyone crazy all of a sudden? Why are there God damned skeletons all over the place? Who the shit is Imala? And where is the God damned treasure? Someone start talking right God damn now."

"Give me that staff, boy." Billy said.

"Don't do it, Danny," Jay said. "He'll kill you if you do."

"You want to know what you got yourself in to, lad?" Billy said. "How's about we make a little deal. I tell you what's going on here, and then you hand me that staff. I might even be able to compensate you. Now how's about that?"

"I'm listening," Danny said.

"Well, you see, it all started in 1717 when I was a pirate on a ship that hit port somewhere around here, I can't remember exactly where—"

"What the hell are you talking about," Danny interrupted. His expression showed Billy that he didn't believe a word of what Billy was saying.

"Shut up, Danny," Carol said, "Billy, keep going." She needed to know the whole story. Jay listened intently.

"As I was saying, it was 1717, and we hit port. I walked into the town where there happened to be a slave auction. That's where I saw her for the first time — Imala. She was a beauty, and I could tell there was more to her than just her looks. She had a power she hadn't quite yet come in to. Well, I bargained with the owner who didn't exactly see eye to eye with me," he looked over and winked at Danny — a stab at his newly develop handicap, "so I decided to liberate the girl, and I killed the owner. My Captain at the time, Captain Charles Kent — known by most as 'The Butcher'…" Billy paused a moment and realized that he had remembered with complete clarity, "The Butcher. Yeah. Anyway, the Captain had ordered that no one kill anyone whiles ashore, and seeing as I disobeyed that order, he had me tossed in the brig."

Jay and Carol watched and listened in amazement. They knew from their recent experiences that what Billy was saying was true.

"So I'm sitting in the brig, and who shows up, but the very witch I had freed earlier in the day. She had that in her hand," He pointed at the staff Danny was holding. Danny looked down at it and had no idea what was happening. He still didn't know what Billy was getting at. "She pointed it at the lock of the cell door and opened it right up and freed me. She had stolen the staff from her people, you see. You know her tribe, or whatever you call them. Turns out she came from a long line of witches and they all used the staff for various magical works until my Imala snatched it for herself." Jay noticed Carol becoming uneasy. She was beginning to squirm, and looked as if she was going to interject. "So you see, we go up the stairs to the main deck, and wouldn't you know, there stands The Butcher, looking me eye to eye, out of his mind with anger that I escaped. He looked at me and said, '*What do you think you're doing Billy*', and I says back, '*I think I'm taking this here ship from you, Captain,*' and he seen red, boy he really seen red, and I says, '*and I'll be the new Captain, fellas.*' I looked around at the crew, they was shocked at what they was seeing. They just knew I was digging myself a grave, and that The Butcher would surely kill me. They just knew it. So Butcher says to me, '*that right?*' And before he could finish the words, Imala points the staff at him and pulls his soul right straight out of his body — a real good trick to watch if you ask me. The boys looked at the Captain losing his soul, watched it get sucked right out. They were scared to death that the devil hisself just walked onto the ship. They thought they was next, but I never had no problems with the crew, aside from a few bad apples. So, after Imala did her little trick on a couple of the boys, I asked the crew, '*So what do you say, boys, are you ready to follow your new Captain?*' And they all looked at me and nodded. They figured out real quick that they was safe and I took real good care of them." Carol wiggled some more, as if she was uncomfortable in her own skin. "From that day forward, I was Captain Billy Thompson, and the witch was by my side. We took all sorts of ships and treasures—"

"Like Blackbeard," Danny said as he rolled his eyes. He didn't believe the story one bit.

"What the hell did you just say?" Billy asked.

"I said, like Blackbeard. Like you think I'm gonna believe you were a pirate like Blackbeard, and you got some treasure—"

"Now you listen here, boy, Blackbeard," Billy spit on the ground at the name, "Old Edward Teach, the man who wasn't half the pirate I am, was no match for me. His was the best loot I ever got—"

"Wait a second, you're saying you knew Blackbeard?" Jay said in shock.

"Knew him?" Billy said. "I guess you could say that. But I find it hilarious that you all heard of him, but you ain't heard of me, don't you? Well, that there is because my witch used her magic on him, on everyone we robbed. You see, I met Mr. Teach sometime in 1718 when I boarded his ship and held him and his crew up. You think Blackbeard could ever do that to me? No, sir. So I held him up and he wasn't very happy at all, he says to me, "*You're gonna hang for this, boy, don't you know who I am?*" And I says, "*I heard of ya, but you ain't heard of me, and you ain't gonna remember it neither,*" you see I figured if I killed him, I would miss an opportunity. I wanted to keep him alive, so everyone would come after him, and not me. I left him as sort of a decoy. Boy, he sure was confused when he and the crew came to, and he was missing his precious treasure. He even killed some of his men, he suspected of taking it. After that he ended up retiring cause he was pardoned. It didn't make no difference to him cause he had no treasure left. All them years of stealing it, and he loses it, and has no idea where it's at—"

"They still don't," Jay said. Billy looked at him. "That's the most famous missing treasure there is. Everyone thinks Blackbeard hid it somewhere. You're telling me the treasure in that chest belonged to the actual Blackbeard? We actually saw the real treasure from the real Blackbeard?"

"Wait a second," Danny said, "Wait, there really is a treasure?" He was growing impatient with the story.

"So old Edward never did quite recover from losing his treasure," Billy continued, "he even came out of retirement to go try to rebuild it, or look for it or something. He ended up getting killed by some crew sent down from Virginia. He never was quite himself after meeting Captain Billy Thompson. So yeah, your hero pirate wasn't as great as you all think. I was the real hero. After a while, Imala and I figured we was tired of running, so we was gonna hide the treasure and take a break like old Mr. Teach did. We was gonna lie low for a while and come back to it later. So we take a couple of the boys and we take the treasure and we hide it here. Right here," he pointed at the spot where the treasure once laid," and we figure we'd leave it, and we'd clear the memories of the two crewmen that helped, and as we're finishing up, she tells me there's a way we never had to run again. She tells me we could become more powerful than ever. We could become immortal—"

"That's enough, Billy," Carol said.

"What, what are you talking about, what are you doing?" Jay asked. "Carol, let him finish, we need to know what happened," he whispered the next part, "we need to know how to beat him."

"Billy, my love," Carol said. Billy looked at her closely — he squinted.

"Imala," Billy said. "Is that you, witch?"

Thirty

Captain Kelly rounded up the men and headed toward the station. He called the sheriff's department to let them know that he and his men were going to search Bear Island because that had been the spot they initially picked up Officer Harris. It was almost morning. The search for Rich Harris had gone all night, and the crew that was searching were all day crew. Everyone was tired, out of sorts, restless, and ready to get this over with and get Harris in to custody. The sheriff's department said that they would be sending some deputies over to assist so that some of Captain Kelly's men could go off shift. He appreciated the offer, and would accept the help, but this was their officer, and his officers would want to be there when he was brought in.

As they reached the station, Captain Kelly walked with Officer Stengele into the building. "Stengele, I need you here for this. Need you on the radios—" Captain Kelly stopped as he looked up and saw the broken glass from the interview room window. "What in the hold hell is this?" He walked toward the glass and looked into the interview room. "Have they lost their God damned minds? What has gotten in to these officers? Listen up!" He yelled to everyone in the station. "Anyone sees Massey or Luther, arrest them on the spot. Right now, our priority is Harris, but if you see on of them you arrest them, and so help me, if anyone here knows where the hell they could be right now, you better speak up." He paused and looked around at his officers. "Fine. Get what you need, split into boat teams of two, and let's get to Bear Island."

The station was like a beehive with officers running around grabbing various things like life vests and flash lights. The sun would be up soon, but some had left the building unprepared earlier in the night. This wasn't their usual routine as wildlife officers.

"Stengele, if you hear from them, you tell them to get their asses back in here ASAP. You tell them that they're facing felony charges if they don't get the hell back here."

"Yes, sir."

The Captain headed out the back toward the boat docks along with the rest of the officers.

*****

"Carol, tell me you're still in there," Jay said.

"Imala, is that you?" Billy said.

"Who the hell is Imala? I'm having a hard time keeping up with all of this," Danny said.

"Billy, you do not need to relive the past with them. All that matters is that we finish the spell so we can be together forever. I can give you the power." Imala said. She turned to Jay, "I'm sorry, Jay, I'm trying to fight this, but she's too powerful. She doesn't want Billy to know what happened—"

Billy turned to Danny, "I'll be needing that staff now, boy."

"Now wait just a minute. Where the hell is this treasure I've been promised?" Danny said.

Jay couldn't think of how to get out of the situation. He needed to think.

"Billy, you have to give me the staff. I cannot move without it... I can't stay here... time is—" Carol fought as hard as she could, but Imala was overpowering her. The staff was close enough to Imala to give her some power, but she couldn't fully take hold with physically touching it.

"Billy," Jay said. "What happened next?"

Billy looked over at Jay, confused.

"Billy, do not listen to him," Imala said.

Billy was becoming annoyed. Why did everyone think they could control him all of a sudden.

"What happened when you got into the cave and Imala said she'd make you immortal?" Jay asked.

Imala could not move, but was desperate. "Billy, be quiet!" She yelled.

That was it. Billy looked at Imala fiercely, speaking with his eyes — telling the witch she had better remember her place.

"I'll tell you what happened next," he thought for a minute, and it all came back in perfect clarity, "next, Imala pulls out a scroll. It had the spell on it. That's how she'd keep us immortal. She wanted our souls joined for eternity—"

"*We* wanted that, Billy—" Imala said.

"Quiet now, witch. I'll tell the story. Don't you forget who I am."

Imala's anger was building as well. She was, after all, a very powerful witch. She was constantly underestimated, and undermined by this man — this man who was only powerful because... of her.

"Now where was I," Billy said. "Oh yes, the souls. But something happened..." he paused as he remembered. "Ahh, yes. It did indeed happen, didn't it, witch? That's it. That's why you didn't want me remembering."

"What?" Jay said. "What happened?" He was trying to stall Billy, but he really wanted to know what happened. Danny was also on pins and needles awaiting the explanation. He had grown interested in the story as it went on.

"The betrayal," Billy said. He looked at Imala, who was unable to move. She was powerless. All she could do was sit and listen while Billy figured it all out. She was so close to having her staff and ending it. "Yes, yes, the betrayal. You see, Imala wanted to join our should for all of eternity. On this ground, on a certain day, at a certain time," as Billy spoke, Jay pulled the scroll out of his pocket and looked at it. He couldn't read it, but he remembered a little of what it said, "and by the blood of this, that, or the other, our souls would be forever bound. Except that ain't exactly how I saw things going." He watched as Imala squirmed in Carol's body. She held a gun she couldn't control, and she couldn't get up and walk over to the staff. She was paralyzed. She was enraged. "The thing I loved the most wasn't you, Imala. I guess you had to find that out in a pretty hard way."

"So what happened?" Jay asked, trying to keep him talking.

"The thing I wanted was the treasure. Imala realized that when she finished her spell, and before she could take my blood, I pulled out my pistol and shot her." Billy gave a sinister grin, as if he was proud of getting one over on the great witch. "But you put up quite the fight, didn't you, witch? My men drew their daggers. They was there to help me. The plan was for them to finish you off when you focused on me. I knew the staff would keep you powerful, so I'd need them to help me. But you did your little trick, didn't you? Yes, you sucked their souls right out of their bodies and they dropped where they stood. But then you didn't die right away. I guess my aim wasn't as good as it once was. Should've gotten you quick, but you got yourself a good lucky thrust of the staff, didn't you? Because the last thing I remember was you, pushing that thing into my chest before I took my long sleep." Billy stared Imala down. Jay and Danny looked on in complete shock.

"Yes," Imala said. "Yes, that is what happened. You betrayed me. I gave you everything, Billy. I gave you a ship, and a crew, and a treasure. I gave you everything, and I was prepared to do it again, but it is clear that you do not love me. Your blood spilled upon the thing you loved the most, and your soul was joined to your precious treasure — the thing you love the most."

"Well, well. You know what that means, Imala," Billy said, "it means you and I ain't so different. Your blood spilled on the staff, and you was joined with the thing you love the most — power. Don't pretend to be high and mighty, better than me, and you just wanted power."

Imala hadn't realized it until now, but he was right. She thought about it, and she was right. It was the power she wanted. She didn't need Billy. She needed... her staff. With all the strength she could muster, Imala began to lift her hand and reach out to the staff.

"What's this?" Billy said. "Oh, so you can move, eh witch?"

"Carol, you have to fight," Jay said.

Danny felt a slight pull on the staff, like it was being taken from him. The staff raised in Danny's hands. "Stop that. What the hell?"

"Now you wait right there, witch," Billy said.

Imala concentrated on the staff, and she could feel it like a magnet pulling toward her. "Destroy... the..." Carol said as she fought to be able to speak. Jay looked at her. He could see that the witch controlled her arm, and that Carol was crying and struggling to speak.

"Carol, is that you?" Jay said. "Fight Carol, fight her."

"Destroy... the... spell." She said.

Jay looked down at the scroll he held.

"No!" Carol yelled — it was Imala trying to stop him. "Do not do that, or I will kill her."

Jay, holding the scroll with both hands, stopped.

"Ok, just what the hell is going on with you, Massey?" Danny said. Danny had lost his patience. He wanted his treasure. "Ok, listen here. Someone better tell me where the treasure is, or I'm gonna start stabbing each of you. Think I won't do it?" The pull on the staff didn't feel as strong as Imala was slightly distracted from the thought that Jay may destroy the scroll.

"Give the staff to me, boy." Billy said as he lifted his arm to reach for it. Danny swung the staff at Billy.

"No!" Danny said. "Not until I get my treasure."

"If she gets a hold of that staff, you ain't getting no treasure, and none of us is getting out of this cave alive." Billy said. Danny gripped harder on the staff. He didn't believe in any of this, but better safe than sorry.

Jay thought about the scroll. How would he stop her and keep Carol alive?

Imala raised her hand again and began to pull the staff harder. Danny's grip tightened as he felt the staff being pulled harder.

"Imala, you can't do the spell without me," Billy said. "It don't work without two souls, you know that."

Imala did realize that in order to do the spell and stay in this world, she would have to do join with another. She considered her options and knew that deep down, she still wanted it to be Billy. Maybe she could change him.

"Then, if you would like to continue to live," she said, "I would suggest you help me. Join me and we shall finish this. We can only stay if we work together."

Billy thought about that for a second. He realized she was right, but he knew the minute the spell was over, she would kill him. She'd probably suck his soul right out of his body. "You're right, witch." He said.

Jay looked up at Billy, now more worried that he was going to have to fight two crazy, immortal, murderous people and one crazy, murderous ex-cop who was currently blocking the only route for escape. The odds were better when Billy and Imala were against each other.

Billy turned to Danny. "Give me the staff, boy, I ain't asking again."

Danny rolled his eyes. He wasn't that worried about Billy, or Harris, or whoever this was. Danny had a knife, and the staff. Billy had nothing. Billy took a step closer to Danny. Danny raised the knife up to show that he was ready to kill anyone and everyone. Billy advance another step. Danny swung the staff as hard as he could at Billy. Billy reach up his hand and caught the swinging staff. Danny's look of anger turned to one of complete fear. He could feel Billy's overpowering grip on the staff. Danny let it go and fell to the ground.

Billy now held the powerful weapon. He turned around and looked at Imala. Billy knew that he was in a bind. He needed Imala for the spell if he was going to stay in this body. If they didn't complete the spell by dawn, they would go back... back to...

"What happens if we don't finish it?" Billy asked. "What happens to us?"

"We must finish it, Billy," Imala said. "We die if we don't finish it. Now you have the staff, but we also need the treasure. Where is it?"

"It's on my boat. You can bring it here and then do the spell. I will tell you this, witch, you better not get any ideas about killing me. You want to join me for eternity, then so be it. I want to live, so I'm on board, but so help me God, I'll haunt you forever if you cross me."

"Let's not forget who crossed who first... my love," she said. She looked up at him and winked.

Billy reached out the staff to hand it to Imala.

"No!" Jay yelled. "No, Billy, don't do it!"

Danny sat on the ground like a defeated child, upset that he had yet again been bested. He had to find a way to kill Rich Harris.

Imala reached up and grabbed the staff as Billy handed it to her. The ground shook, dust flew out from under her feet as she stood. Danny, Billy, and Jay each watched as a glow came around Imala. They saw her transform completely into Imala. All traces of Carol were gone. Imala and Billy stood face to face, staring tensely at each other as if either would turn on the other at any minute. Jay thought about that and felt as if that would be the only way this could end. His friends were gone. Rich was now Billy completely, and Carol was now Imala. How would he save them now?

"The treasure," Imala said, "concentrate on it."

Billy thought about his treasure. He focused on the boat and thought about where he had hidden it. Just then, Imala raised the staff and summoned the treasure.

Back at the boat, the entire chest started to move and shake, and the whole boat started moving. The tarp ripped open, and the chest bursted out and up into the sky. It floated toward the cave as the staff's magic held it steadily moving.

At that moment, Stengele heard a strange noise on a desk near his. He looked around the station. "Who's there?" He said. He looked over at the top of a nearby desk and saw papers moving around. Just then a plastic bag with a coin inside jumped off of the desk and into the air. It floated toward a window, and crashed through it, out of sight, and it flew into the night. "Ok, I have to get some sleep." Stengele said.

Back at the cave, the chest floated down into the hole. Danny couldn't believe his eyes. He thought he must have been dreaming.

There was a floating chest. That couldn't be real. Jay watched and wondered how he could save anyone. He began to feel that all hope was lost, and that he would die in that cave.

The chest landed, and Billy opened the lid. "My treasure." He said. Danny was in awe. He had never seen so much treasure before. It had occurred to him that this was all real. He had now seen it with his own eyes.

Everyone looked at the treasure for a moment, and as they looked at it, a plastic baggy came flying down into the cave and landed right on top of the treasure. Inside sat one of the coins — the one the Captain found in Rich's garage and had Officer Dayton bag and tag. It was all here now, and they could commence with the spell. Dawn was quickly approaching.

"There," Imala said. "We have all we need. We must hurry," she said as she looked around the cave. "You," she said, pointing at Jay, "give me the spell."

Jay looked down at the spell and knew that he could not give it to Imala. She pointed the staff slowly at Jay.

"Hand it over, boy," Billy said. "I ain't going back to an eternity of nothing." Billy clinched his fists, ready to pounce on Jay.

As Billy faced Jay, Danny so an opportunity, he quickly got up and wrapped his arm around Billy's neck, holding his knife in his right hand. "Ahh," Billy grunted. Danny was latched on, Billy couldn't do much.

Imala quickly turned her staff to Danny. "Release him!" She commanded.

"You want him?" Danny said, he reached the knife up to Billy's throat and with all of his strength he pushed it hard into Billy's neck. Billy had an instant look of terror come across his face. Jay was devastated and shocked.

"NOOO!" Jay yelled. He watched Billy slowly falling to his knees.

"What have you done?!" Imala yelled. "NOOO! Billy, my love!" She pointed the staff at Danny angrily and with a fierce pull she removed his entire soul. Jay watched it come out of Danny like a cloud of smoke floating over to the staff. He watched as Rich's face slowly returning to his body. He saw the light fading from his terrified eyes. He could see that Rich knew he had been lost, and had no idea where he had returned to as he took his final breath.

Outside, the sun was rising. Dawn had arrived and Billy was gone. Danny and Rich were dead. Imala had only one chance left, and she had to perform the spell within minutes. With tears of anger running down her face, and rage in her heart, ready to destroy everything around her, she pointed at Jay. "You will have to do," she said, "give me the spell."

Jay knew he would die in that cave with Rich and Danny, but he had to save Carol. A tear fell from his eye as he grabbed the scroll with both hands and tore it completely apart.

"NOOOOO!" Imala screamed. The scream was louder than any scream Jay had ever heard before. The walls and the surrounding ground shook. The dust spread from around Imala as she seemed to float above the ground. Light appeared to glow all around her, as if she was at the peak of a display of complete power. Jay, knowing his fate, continued to rip and tear as quickly as he could, completely destroying the scroll. It began to fall apart and crumble as if it were being held together by some sort of magic before this. The sun was up outside as Imala's glow started to fade. She settled back to the ground, crying. She pointed the staff at Jay. The sun had risen. Dawn had come and gone. She fell to one knee. "Now you will join your friends," she said — her voice fading as she spoke the words. She began to close her eyes and fall further down. Jay was braced and ready for his final fate, but it wasn't happening. Imala dropped the staff. She fell to all fours and couldn't speak. She fell all the way down — her eyes closed. Silence fell over the cave.

Jay was shaking. His life was surely over, yet he was still breathing — still looking around the cave. He didn't die. He looked at the ground, at the torn up scroll, which had completely disintegrated. He looked up and saw Rich lying dead next to Danny — also lying dead. He looked over at Imala. He saw that it was not Imala, but Carol, laying on the ground with her eyes closed, not moving. Carol was dead. No sooner than the thought leave his head, did he see her move?

"Carol!" He said as he ran over to her. He kicked the staff over to a corner of the cave just in case this was still Imala. He turned her over and saw that it was definitely Carol. "Carol, talk to me, are you ok?" He said, wiping the dirt from her hair and he held her in his arms.

Carol coughed. She was disoriented. "What happened?" She asked.

"Oh my God, thank God you're alive." They both looked over at Rich and Danny laying a few feet away. Carol began to sob as she saw her friend laying there. After all of this. After everything they had done, they couldn't save him. Jay was crying too. Rich did not deserve to die in a cave like that.

Thirty-One

Rich's funeral was nicely put together. Jay and Carol had worked together to make sure their friend was honored properly. Captain Kelly allowed Rich to be honored rather than be remembered for the bad things he had done in the end. After Captain Kelly had heard the entire story from both Jay and Carol, separately, he was convinced that Rich had been blackmailed those last couple weeks by Danny Bell, and that was the reason for his erratic behavior. Captain Kelly was under the impression that Danny Bell had planned on stealing Rich's newly found historic artifacts, and that he was making Rich do all the things he had done until Rich stood up for himself and his friends at the sandbar. They twisted the truth a little, but Danny Bell was actually a terrible person, and if it weren't for him, their friend would still be alive. There may be a witch and a pirate trying to kill, maim, and steal on their way to ruling the world, but that was beside the point. Danny had it in him to be a killer. He had always pushed Rich for no reason, and when Rich, or Billy rather, stood up to Danny it had been too much. He snapped and killed Rich.

Later that day, the department threw a little party at the station to celebrate the life of one of their officers. Officer Rich Harris died a hero, after all. According to Officers Massey and Luther, Officer Harris saved them both from being murdered by Bell. He sacrificed his own life to save theirs. They still both felt terrible about Rich's final days, how he must have been in hell being trapped inside of a lunatic with no way to speak or move. Carol knew the feeling because she was possessed by a much more powerful soul. She felt as if she were caught in a nightmare and was only able to see bits and pieces of what was happening. She had felt completely gone when Imala finally had gotten the staff, and then she remembered waking up.

"Here's to Officer Rich Harris," Captain Kelly said as he raised his beer, "a man of few words, a kind man, a gentleman," although everyone knew the Captain meant timid rather than gentle, "a man who would give you shirt off his back."

"To Officer Harris!" The department all said back in unison, holding their glasses out. Everyone drank their drinks and thought about Rich.

Jay and Carol sat on the couches by the TV, which happened to be on in the background. "Did we do the right thing?" Jay asked.

"You mean by making Rich a hero? Of course. He would've done anything for us."

"No, that's not what I mean. I mean—"

"In a shocking discovery by the North Carolina Wildlife Resource Commission, one of the most famous treasures ever known..." The TV overpowered their conversation, and they were both taking off guard and listening. They looked at the screen and saw a reporter standing in a museum next to the treasure. Billy's treasure.

"That," Jay pointed. "That's what I mean. Did we do the right thing?"

"Of course we did," Carol said. "You saw what that treasure did to Rich. He's dead because of it. It belongs in a museum, and that's where it'll stay."

The reporter continued, "thought to be the lost treasure of the most famous pirate ever to haunt the North Carolina coast, the famous Blackbeard. Until now, this treasure was lost, said to be hidden by Blackbeard, otherwise known as Edward Teach, for 300 years. There have been countless search parties, treasure hunting groups, and people looking to get rich overnight, who have searched up and down the east coast. It turns out Blackbeard hid it right here in our town. The wildlife officers found the treasure in a cave on Bear Island. Captain Kelly had this to say..." The scene switched to an interview inside the cave the day of the 'discovery'.

"Well, it looks like Blackbeard still gets the fame," Jay said with a smirk on his face.

"And no one will ever know who Captain Billy Thompson was." Carol said. They both watched the Captain being interviewed as if he had found the treasure himself. The scene cut back to the reporter at the museum. Jay and Carol both caught a glimpse of the staff in the background, sitting inside of a display case. "Good riddance."

The two sat in silence, sipping their drinks, thinking about it all. The treasure and staff would be safe without the scroll, but they figured it was safest in a museum.

Carols phone started vibrating. She took it out of her pocket and answered it. "Hello," she said.

"Hi, is this Jay's friend, Carol?" A voice on the other line asked.

"This is she," Carol replied.

"Hi Carol, this is Madison, I'm the person you emailed your spell to. I'm really sorry, I've been out of town, and I just got back." Carol looked up at Jay as the woman spoke. "Listen, I've never seen anything like this. I have been researching it, and I couldn't find anything at all, so I met with a Wiccan friend of mine who deals with stuff like this. She knows a ton about witchcraft and stuff. She'd like to meet. Would you guys be up for that?"

The End

CPSIA information can be obtained
at www.ICGtesting.com
Printed in the USA
LVHW021318290121
677810LV00001B/61